IT'S
ADDICTING

LAURA L. SMITH

Birch House Press
Est. 2015

It's Addicting

Copyright © 2014 by Laura L. Smith

Cover: photography - Kelci Alane Photography Design - Four S

Scripture quotations in this publication are taken from the following: the *English Standard Version*. Copyright 2001 by Crossway Bibles, a division of Good News Publishers. *The Message* by Eugene H. Peterson. Copyright 1993, 1994, 1995, 1996, 2000. Used by permission of NavPress Publishing Group. All rights reserved.

It's Addicting Status Updates Series (Book 3) / Laura L. Smith. – 2nd ed.

ISBN 9780996277013

First printing 2014

Printed in the United States of America

Birch House Press
Est. 2015

IT'S ADDICTING

For Maddie, Max, Mallory and Maguire.
There are bits and pieces of you scattered throughout this book and
throughout all of my stories, because the four of you are my story.
You fill the pages of my life with abundant love, laughter, joy and
grace.

1
PALMER

"DO WE DARE WRITE A feature on Shamrock Saturday for our next issue?" Summer, the features editor for the school magazine *QuadAngles*, finishes tapping something onto her tablet and looks up.

I stand near some stools by the kitchen counter in Summer's apartment, praying I don't look as awkward as I feel. Awkward is not my thing. I am the girl who always knows exactly where to sit. I am the girl everyone wants to sit next to…at least I was. The university magazine staff doesn't care about my past popularity, or my $2,000 orthodontist-perfected teeth, waxed eyebrows, and fresh manicure. It's not the sort of club you just sign up for. I've been on staff since last year, but have never had even one of my stories end up in the actual magazine. After a trial article I submitted was nixed, I was relegated to the dreary office on the third floor of the English building to work on edits, layouts, and selling ads. But somehow I landed an invite to attend the first editorial meeting of the semester tonight at Summer's. Does it mean they want me to write? Have I paid my dues? Was everyone invited? Or was my e-mail address accidentally on the list?

Uncertain, I called home for advice. Dad answered, which is usually a good thing. But not this time.

"If they don't want you one hundred percent, you don't want them," he bellowed. "I remember my first sales job. They wanted me to work only on commission, no investment in me. I told them to get lost. Within a week I'd found a job with full salary and benefits. Gotta go where we're wanted. All in. Maybe writing isn't your thing. You should go into sales like me. Lots of money in sales. You have the perfect personality for it, and heck, how could anyone *not* buy something from you?"

"Maybe," I'd said as tears he couldn't see slid down my face.

If they don't want me? I don't do "not being wanted." That's for someone else. And so is sales. I hated selling ads for the high school yearbook and pumpkin pies for the tennis team fund-raisers. I felt like a nerd calling my own aunts and uncles. I could never ask strangers to buy something useless. I have to write. It's who I am.

So here I am, scanning the room for a place to sit. The way I see it, I have three options, and none of them are perfect.

I'd normally sit next to Michael, the gorgeous senior who continues to flirt with me. But, one, he writes like a *New York Times* reporter and, two, rumor has it he flirts with everybody. And I don't want to be "that" girl.

Second choice is a guy I've seen once or twice at the church my roommates and I go to *when* we get our Sunday morning act together. He has black curly hair, razor stubble that's kind of sexy, and olive skin hinting at exotic ancestry. Usually it would be fun to chat things up with him. He seems interesting, but I don't know his story. And since stories are how you're judged in this room, it's too risky.

The third, and easiest, choice would be to plop on the couch with the other sophomore, April. She's tiny, has shoulder-length, straight brown hair, large eyes, and a load of attitude. We've logged countless hours in the office working on edits together, and she always makes me laugh. We were assigned as critique partners in my freshman comp class. Let's just say her writing didn't wow me. And I don't want anyone here to assume my writing is the same caliber as hers. Which makes me wonder, why is she here? Did they invite all the sophomores to move up?

Focus, I remind myself.

"It's a risk." Michael's voice commands the room. "But I'm all about risks." He glances around, assessing his audience. He rests his eyes on mine for longer than a natural moment. "Palmer, you don't have a glass."

"Oh." My voice sounds tinny. I smile, noticing almost everyone else is holding a glass of wine. We don't do that in the English building. "I'm fine, thanks." I slide my silver cross pendant on its chain back and forth with an unsteady hand. I inhale and stand straighter, feet planted, muscles engaged, shoulders rolled back. My yoga instructor would be proud.

Instead of crumpling under Michael's steady gaze, I draw power from it, like a dare or an invitation. I take his opening and inch my way into the room with words. "Wasn't there talk about changing the name from Shamrock Saturday to Green Day?"

"I love their music, but they're not exactly news," April adds in her raspy voice. She shifts a few inches to the left on the couch, as if making room for me. It would be so easy to slide next to her. But she would lower my clout. Here, people are not assessed by looks, or money, or who their friends are. Here, we are judged by our craft. That scares the crap out of me. It also sharpens every one of my nerve endings.

"Dude, not the band. It's, like, the biggest event on campus." Brennan, a guy who mostly writes about the music scene, takes a hit of whatever he's smoking, something thick and foggy smelling, his eyes half closed under his shaggy bangs.

"It is big, but the university hates Shamrock Saturday and everything it stands for: drinking at 5:00 a.m., hundreds of drunks walking the streets all day dressed in green, and, oh yeah, the arrests," Summer says. "I heard that too, Palmer."

I nod. She knows my name. Good sign.

"President Downing thought it would make a statement if Shamrock Saturdays were history. Which could be an interesting lead into our coverage—can you squelch tradition with a name change?" Summer raises her wine glass to me in a kind of salute. Her glossy scarlet bob shifts on her shoulders as a smile forms on my lips.

Take that, Dad.

She continues, "This staff meeting might run awhile. Red or white?"

She knows my name and she's offering me wine. Really? I rock onto my heels to steady everything wobbly inside of me. I know all of the usual excuses—the tricks my roommates and I learned freshman year to avoid drinking when everyone else is—the "Oh, I'm on cold medicine and they don't mix" excuse. "I'm drinking water. Need to rehydrate after that intense workout today." Or "Someone's getting me a drink, thanks." But none of these make sense right now. I don't have a drink. No one else is getting me one. And if I mention being sick, I could look weak. Plus, wine seems kind of fun, sophisticated. I slide my cross on my chain again.

"You should at least try the Moscato," Michael whispers over my shoulder. He must have snuck around the room during my short interchange with Summer. "It's easy on the palate. A great starter wine. Sit tight."

"Thanks," I say, but I don't mean it. First, I don't want him or Summer or anyone else here to think I'm so immature I need "starter wine," whatever that means. But the truth is, I'm really not into the whole drinking thing. This circular argument makes my brain flip.

Stop.

I will the negative thoughts out of my head. *Chill,* I tell myself. Inhale. Exhale. One thing at a time. The wine.

There's nothing immoral about a college woman drinking one glass of wine. If anything, it's a sign of maturity and style. Wine is not the same thing as the beer bongs they sell at The Brewery, and Michael is pouring. And it looks like he grew out a beard over Christmas break. Very grown-up.

Summer sits next to Brennan on the chic leather couch. "The president's office has threatened the local T-shirt printers they'll yank all university orders if they print any shirts with references to beer or drunk leprechauns."

My roommates, Hannah, Kat, Claire, and I, would kill for that leather couch. We are sharing a dorm room again this year. It's a cute suite in Tomarken Hall, but I would love to have an apartment with hardwood floors instead of 1970's linoleum. I crave an actual kitchen instead of our mini fridge and Keurig. I barely hear the rest of what Summer says, I'm so busy mentally redecorating.

"I say we do it," Michael says, back at my side with a glass of honey-colored wine. He hands the stem to me and lets his fingers linger around mine as I take it. His touch is warm and inviting. Is he trying to tell me something? I can't be imagining that, can I? The glass is smooth and has a solid weight in my hand. I feel sophisticated swirling my bowl-shaped glass and letting the wine dance around the edges like a magic elixir.

I take a sip. The wine is strong but sweet. I let the thick, syrupy flavor roll across my tongue. It coats my throat with warmth. I take another.

From where he leans comfortably on the counter near me, Michael continues. "We can treat it like *60 Minutes*. You know, show both sides—why Clarkston doesn't approve, why the students do. We can do an interview on the street thing. Ask random people on the corner their opinion, snap their pictures, and use that as a sidebar." Michael's face becomes more and more animated as he talks. He has some sort of inner magnet that pulls the entire room toward him and what he has to say. "Ahmed, would you follow me around with your camera?" he asks.

"Sure." The dark, mysterious guy from church nods. That's Ahmed? I've seen his photo credits all over the magazine. I should have sat next to him. Why didn't I sit next to him?

"Or I could." Van, another photographer, bats her eyelashes. Her photos frequent the fashion page and restaurant reviews.

Gag. Blatant flirting. Is that allowed?

I want to say something brilliant, but I'm not sure if Summer wants to hear anything else from this newbie who might have been accidentally invited. But there's no point in being here if I'm not going to talk. I take a quick drink, as if my glass holds speaking potion instead of wine.

"What has *QuadAngles* done in the past few years on the topic?" I ask.

"Good question, Palmer." Summer elbows Brennan to

keep him from nodding off, then continues, "Three years ago we tiptoed around Shamrock Saturday and wrote a St. Patrick's Day article that only mentioned Shamrock Saturday on a calendar listing of campus events. Two years ago we did nothing. Last year we did a story on all the positive events surrounding Shamrock Saturday—the Think Green recycling drive, the Green Mile race, and the green eggs and ham they serve at Murphy's. The president's office loved it."

"True. But all of those were sellouts." Michael steps forward and puts his hand on Summer's shoulder. She smiles. I stiffen. Michael and I have gone out to lunch twice to discuss some articles I was hoping to get in the magazine. Not that I'm counting. But he's never asked me *out* out.

"It's our job as journalists to explore the gritty, to go to the places no one else wants to go." He slides his arm off Summer's shoulder. I exhale. I notice she does too.

"Like the bathrooms of the Tipsy Toad?" Brennan laughs.

"Ew. Those are soooo gross. Definitely gritty." April scrunches her face and laughs. The only one who joins in is Brennan.

"Right." Summer stands and walks toward the stool where I'm perched. "Hey, that's not a bad idea." She paces back and forth clutching her iPad in one hand and her wine glass in the other. "You two"—she points to April and Brennan—"work on a one-pager on the ten best and ten worst restrooms on campus—include dorms, dining halls, book stores, bars, the works."

"Cool." April nods, her long beaded earrings swaying back and forth.

As Brennan and April argue over which downtown bar's bathrooms are the most disgusting, I flip through my journal.

"Please tell me you have some good ideas in there,"

Summer says, sighing and resting her chin on my shoulder.

"Well," I say. I turn my head to face her, hoping it diverts her eyes from my journal. My notes are poems, ideas, quotes, to-do lists, Bible verses, and ramblings, not content that would impress an editor. "I was thinking about a spring break guide. I know it's not original, but it could be if we highlighted some unique trips."

Stick a needle in my eye. How stupid can I sound? I should have sat next to April and gotten it over with.

"Spring break works." Summer glances at April and Brennan.

It does?

"Michael, why don't you take on the Shamrock Saturday article? Palmer, you'll work alongside him. Learn from him. Then show me what you've got with the spring break piece. A one-page spread with great images." Summer smiles, clinks my glass again, and says, "Welcome to the writing team."

"Thanks."

It's settled, then. I'm in.

"Cheers." Michael's glass nestles in the space between Summer's and mine so he can toast us simultaneously.

Death Cab for Cutie croons "I Will Follow You into the Dark" from the speakers, and the mood overtakes me. I would like to follow Michael, no doubt. I am surrounded by creative minds; writers and editors and photographers, bouncing ideas off each other, complimenting each other. I imagine this is what it was like for Hemingway and Fitzgerald in Paris in the 1920s.

I take another small sip. The wine is sweet and lingering, like Michael's touch.

Warmth spreads through me from the wine or the promotion, I am not sure which. My shoulders relax, and as

Michael holds out the bottle offering more, I extend my glass toward him, feeling like I belong here

2
HANNAH

THE HORN BLAST SIGNALS A time-out and the sound system blares "Forever Young." As if on cue, the entire crowd starts dancing.

"Do you really want to live forever, forever," I sing along. "This is way fun," I say to my roommates, bouncing on my toes, caught up in the electric energy.

"Way fun! Who knew? Thanks for putting it all together. Even the camping out in the hockey arena to get tickets." Claire rubs her arms.

"I told you it would be cold." I'm thankful for the hoodie under my puffer vest and my favorite grape-colored knit gloves. "And you're welcome. The camping out the night before at the rink is all part of the experience."

"My back still aches from sleeping on the floor." Palmer pops a couple of Advil in her mouth and washes them down with pink Vitamin Water. "I forgot, Claire. This is your first game ever. You were still in Cleveland with your mom when we went to the game after Christmas last year and then...what did you have in October?"

"Ballet performance," Claire says. "You all right?"

"Yeah. Just a headache," Palmer says.

"You sure?" I ask, touching Palmer's forehead. She does look a bit green.

She nods, but then winces as the horn signals the time-out's over.

We hold our breaths along with the entire crowd as skates scrape, sticks slap, and bodies bang against each other and the fiberglass backstops. Finally, the sirens wail and lights flash.

"And it's another goal for Clarkston!" the announcer roars.

"Doesn't he sound like my daddy?" Kat asks. "But with a Yankee accent."

"Ohmigosh, he totally does," I agree.

The band plays, the players perform, and the crowd is expected to act out its role. We stand and shout in unison a cheer every fan knows by heart. "One, two, three, we want morrrrrre goals! Sieve, Sieve, Sieve! It's all your fault. It's all your fault! It's all your fault!"

Claire watches me to follow my lead. I grin and shout at the top of my lungs. Maybe I shouldn't be calling Western Michigan's goalie a "sieve." I can't imagine having everyone yelling at me. But it's hard not to get caught up with the crowd.

When the buzzer signals the end of the game, the noise in the arena is deafening.

"I'll turn y'all into sports fans yet!" Kat yells as we work our way through the throngs of students.

"Hannah."

I turn and see Nate from my world studies class. Through the blur of faces and shoulders walking past, it's as if he and I are frozen in time and everyone else has fast-forwarded. Is that who called my name? I wasn't even sure he knew my name. My heart jumps as much as the hockey puck did in the third period.

Our prof sat us alphabetically, and since my last name is Trager, I ended up sitting next to Nate Tipton. His name even sounds like a movie star's. Since we have different majors, our paths might have never crossed, but everyone has a "global" requirement to fill. I'm certain it was fate. When I'm not taking notes, I'm studying Nate. He has neatly parted, dark blond hair, and I love how his brown eyes peek over his preppy tortoise-shell glasses. Seeing him here, out of class, he's even cuter.

"Nate." I chew my gum frantically, thinking of absolutely nothing charming to say, despite days of doodling his name on my to-do lists.

"Great game," Kat says.

"It rocked. So are you Hannah's bodyguards or her posse?" Nate snaps his fingers and points to my friends.

Finally a sound escapes my mouth, a laugh that frees my tongue to speak. "My besties." I look sideways at him. "My positively, splendid, awesome possum roommates."

"Well, Hannah's roommates, it's very nice to meet you." Nate bows dramatically.

"Nice to meet you." Palmer flashes her perfect teeth.

Claire smiles and nods.

"Hey," Kat answers, then gets our group moving toward the doors.

Nate walks out with us.

Is this really happening?

Where are his friends? He has friends, right? He's way too cute not to have friends, loads of them. So why is he walking out with us? With me? Maybe he has an instant crush on Palmer, like everyone else on planet Earth. It would not be the first time a guy got friendly with me only to get closer to Palmer.

"Have you considered the Germany trip they're offering over spring break?" he asks.

"Wh-what?"

My roommates clump toward the front, leaving me in a one-on-one conversation with Nate. I cover my stammer with more words. "I hadn't thought of it, really. I mean, I know Dr. Wheeler told us about that option. It would be amazing to travel, to see Germany and all. It just seemed really fast, like that's in a month and a half, and I'd have to book reservations, and get a passport, and I've never been out of the country before."

Do I sound completely immature?

"You can fast-track passports. And me either. But what an incredible chance to go. We'd only be gone a week." He winks. Like, at me. With one of his eyes.

"You make it sound easy."

"It is. That's the beauty of it. The university does everything. We write a paper at the end and get two credit hours. That totally helps free up a spot in my schedule next semester to fulfill all the requirements the business school piles on junior year."

"Clarkston does everything?" I can see my breath, but I don't feel the chill in the air. In fact, I feel very warm. Oddly warm. And I'm sure my cheeks are red. All I can think about is being on the other side of the world with Nate. Well, and if there's any chance my parents would consider paying for it.

"Sure, it's one of those cheap charter flights. We fly in and out of Berlin. They put us up in a dorm and arrange a bunch of guided tours. There's even a day trip on a train to Dresden."

"Wow. I had no idea it was so simple," my mouth says, but my brain repeats charter flight, dorms, guided tours. How much will this cost?

"So come to Germany. It'll be a blast."

"Germany?" is all I say, lowering my head so he won't see how deep I'm blushing.

This all seems so much like a scene out of a romantic comedy in which I should respond with something like, "All you had to do was ask." Somebody pinch me! And since I've answered yes to him in my mind, my gears begin creating the to-do list, starting with scouring Clarkston's website on the spring break in Germany program and ending with kissing Nate next to the Berlin Wall.

"Germany," he repeats, his cheeks turning pink from the January air. "I've wanted to go for a long time. I'm a World War II buff."

"Really?" Why do I keep asking stupid one-word questions? I'm usually too chatty.

Nate thrusts his phone toward me. "Plug your number in here. In case I need help with my homework." Another wink.

As I type in the numbers, too caught off guard to even offer my phone in exchange, he says, "Come on. It'll be great."

Undoubtedly great. "I'll look into it," I somehow manage to say.

3

KAT

MY BODY CLOCK, CONDITIONED FOR morning training sessions, wakes me at six—so not typical for a college girl. Why can't I sleep in on a Saturday? The Weather Channel app forecasted snow, so I peek out the window before I change out of my jams and into my Cold Gear Under Armour. Yes! Snow! After taping my ankle for extra support, I head out into the frosty wonderland.

After a nasty sprain during the soccer season, which benched me the last few games, which I can't stand to think about because there are few things I like less in life than crying, especially out of self-pity, I've made a pact with myself to be the most physically fit player on the squad. Come official team training in the spring I'll need to earn my way back up the ranks. I am going to be more than ready to blow Coach away. I already had to be separated from Alex. The very idea of being separated from soccer is too much to process. So even though we lift three days a week and work on agility and speed the other two, I train myself on the weekends. I run slowly at first, letting the kinks work their way out of my legs, then quicken the pace after circling the quad a couple of times.

The campus looks like a gingerbread house, its dark bricks the color of spice cake covered in a layer of thick, white sugary frosting. I sigh. Even though I've lived up north for two full years now, I still act like a five-year-old every time I see snow.

I run through the neighboring quad, around the academic buildings, and onward to the stadium. My legs pump up and down the steps to the soccer pitch once, twice, and three times for good luck before allowing myself onto the field. Technically it's off limits, except when our team is actually using it. But this early, there's no one to police it. Overtaken by the magic between the two goals, I hold my hands up in the air and charge down the field. I swing my leg, kicking an imaginary ball. I score an imaginary goal, then jump up to celebrate before running back toward the gate. It's a perfect moment.

Making my way back through campus, surrounded by the blinding brightness of snow, I hear Alex calling me in my mind. *"We've gotta go sledding."* He was as entranced with the snow as I was. We went sledding five or six times that first winter in Columbus. Somehow knowing he'd like this is reassuring. Not like the Ghost of Christmas Past in a *Christmas Carol*, but like a warm breeze or sunshine on my skin.

I run back toward our dorm, making a pit stop at the dining hall, which is now open for breakfast.

As I come back into our room, my arms full with a bag of cinnamon rolls and four cafeteria trays, I intentionally make a little noise, stomping the snow off my feet and clanking the trays.

Hannah walks out of our bedroom, coffee mug in hand. Predictable.

She raises her mug in a salute. "What's going on, Kat? Shouldn't you be running?"

Okay, maybe I'm the predictable one.

"Did already. But did you see the SNOW!" I shout, hoping to wake the others.

"For real?" Hannah runs to the window and squeals.

"For real."

"Everything okay?" Claire peeks through the crack of the

doorway leading to our beds so all I can see are her startled blue eyes and a mess of golden waves.

"Super fine. It's snowin'."

"Oh." Her face softens. "Going back to bed."

"Oh no you're not." I reach for her through the opening and pull her into a bear hug. "You can nap later. Pretty please, wake up and come sledding."

"Sledding?" Palmer stretches in her bed.

"Yeah, and we have to go now. It's supposed to get a couple degrees warmer, then it'll all turn to slush."

It takes forever and a year to drag my roommates out of bed, but the warm sweet rolls and strong aromatic coffee help.

"Has anyone seen my waterproof mascara?" Palmer walks out of the bathroom brushing her thick, dark hair.

"You don't need mascara!" I huff. "We're going sledding. As in, outside. In the snow."

"A girl should always look her best. You never know who you might bump into on the slopes." Palmer winks and wraps her hair into a low ponytail.

"She's right. Who knew I would see Nate at the hockey game? Well, I kind of hope I'll see him anyplace I go, but I didn't know I'd actually see him, let alone talk to him, and now we're going to Germany together!"

"No, you're not," Palmer calls.

"You worked that all out already?" Claire asks, pulling on a gray knit hat.

"Well, not completely." Hannah tries to blow her bangs out of her eyes, even though she's grown them out. "Oh my gosh, Claire. You need way more clothes than that. You'll freeze!" Hannah scurries around the room, opening drawers and pulling out coats. "This one or this one?"

Again, that strange sensation washes over me, but this time it pricks my skin. Goose bumps sprout under my sleeves. Alex held out two hats before our first sledding attempt. *This one or this one?* he'd asked.

A pain that is a real physical ache tears at my heart. Tears spring from nowhere. Alex died in a car crash a little over a year ago. Most days I'm fine. Well, that's not really true. Most parts of most days I'm fine, but when something triggers my memory, and I'm never sure what it will be, the emotion from missing him hits. Hard.

Before anyone can see my face, I drop to the floor. Lining myself up in a perfect plank position I push myself down, flat, until my chest touches the floor, then straighten my elbows and bend them again, over and over. *One, two, three,* I count in my head. Somehow filling my brain with numbers and making my body work helps pull me away from the hurt and back to reality.

"Are you sure?" Claire shrugs. "Whichever one you're not wearing."

"Both of them are extras. Here, this one will fit you better." Hannah hands her a lilac coat with a hood. It swallows Claire whole when she zips it up.

"Found it," Palmer says, waving her mascara. "And the Germany thing. You're not going. For spring break? Hello! What about my beach house in Florida? We're supposed to book our flights this weekend. Uh, Kat, why are you down there?"

"Push-ups." I lower my chest to the floor and push back up again, focusing on stabilizing my core.

"Why?" Palmer peeks her head down sideways toward me.

"Because"—I exhale, bending my elbows, tightly by my sides—"none of you were ready."

"I don't think I could do even one push-up," Claire says.

"But you could out pirouette me any day," I say, exhaling.

"About the flights. I don't know." Hannah sighs loudly. "I've set aside money for plane tickets to Florida, so I could use it toward Germany or go with you guys. And, Palm. I absolutely, positively love, love, love your beach house. And it is over-the-top sweet of your parents to let us stay there for spring break. But, I mean, what an incredible opportunity for me to go to Germany. Right? I've never left the U.S.! And for me to get school credit. It's like ice cream with cake and extra frosting. I got all the info at the International Studies office. I still have to convince my folks. But I think they're on board. Mostly. It's way cheaper than I thought. Apparently there's this German organization that's trying to encourage students from the United States to study there, so they're making it dirt cheap for us to go." Hannah paces back and forth across our tiny room. "We stay at Humboldt University—German dorms!"

"Careful, that's my head," I call.

"Oh, sorry. Stand up, would you? We're all ready now. Right?" Hannah's feet shuffle in a circle. "Hats, gloves, coats, boots?"

I can't see her face, but I know she's looking all of us up and down, making sure we have everything on her list. I touch my nose to the fuzzy rug one last time and let out a sharp breath.

"How many did you do?" asks Claire.

"Thirty-two."

"Wow."

"I try to do a hundred a day. I usually have to break it up." A rivulet of sweat trickles down my spine as I stand.

The walk to the sledding hill only takes seven or eight minutes. Our boots crunch in the newly fallen snow. The sunlight reflects along the pristine layer of white, sparkling like the glitter Mama used to sprinkle on my pillow on nights when I tucked a lost tooth underneath, in hopes of a surprise from the tooth fairy.

"It's so beautiful," Claire says.

"Sure is," I say.

Snowflakes cling to my eyelashes, making me feel parts of my eyelids I've never thought about before. The sensation makes me open my eyes wider. I feel like I can see more. Experience more. *Alex, you would have loved this.*

"Okay, so where again did you get those trays?" Hannah asks, pointing to the four plastic trays I carry under my left arm.

"Where do y'all think?" I laugh.

"Are you sure it's all right to take them from the dining hall? It just doesn't seem right or something," Hannah says, dropping her voice to a whisper.

"It's not like we're going to get busted for possession." Palmer pauses for effect, because with Palmer, everything's for effect. "Excuse me, ladies, you're under arrest for possession of cafeteria trays in the quad."

"We'll return them, right?" Claire looks at me.

"Of course." I pat her sleeve. "And here we are."

We duck through the trees behind the old women's dorm, from when the school was divided into men's and women's colleges about a century ago, to where the long expanse of white awaits us. A dozen or so other students fly down the hill, their shrieks of joy echoing through the crisp silence that snowfalls always bring.

"Awesome!" Hannah spins around in delight.

"So what do we do?" Claire asks.

"Here, take a tray." I hand each of them one of the cafeteria trays. "Sit on it like this." I plant my backside smack in the middle of my orange tray. "And away you go."

I push off and blast down the hill. Cold snow spatters my face, and in a rush of speed and chill and spinning, I'm at the bottom.

"Yes!" I pump my hand for my roommates to see from their perch at the top of the hill. I watch Palmer coax Claire onto a tray, gently push her, then climb onto her own aqua tray. Hannah takes off next to her, and they all tumble toward me in a *whoosh* of puffy nylon.

"I thought I was going to die!" Hannah yelps, brushing snow off her knees. "Seriously. If I would have hit that tree? Smack! Grand finale. Over. The end. Buy me a tombstone."

I swallow. Hard.

Grabbing my tray I sprint back up the slope. It's not that steep, but the incline and my snow boots give me the challenge I need. I zero in on getting up this hill faster. Faster.

"Kat, wait!" Hannah pleads. "I didn't mean it."

I know, I think. But it doesn't matter. I hear the smack of metal and squeal of tires louder than her apology. How did *die* get to be a word we take so lightly?

4
CLAIRE

SLIDING YOGA PANTS OVER MY tights, zipping
Hannah's coat over my leotard, and slipping my dance bag
over my shoulder, I give Ashley a quick hug. "You were great
today."

"Thanks." She beams. "I thought you would never stop
spinning. How many pirouettes did you do in a row?"

I laugh, wave, say, "See ya tomorrow," to a group of
dancers wrapping the ribbons around their pointe shoes and
tugging on sweatshirts, and walk as quickly as possible out of
the dance studio.

Ms. Kladinski, my ancient, fabulous, Russian ballet
teacher, does not allow running.

But outside, I can run. And I do. I dash through the fine
arts quad, skirting my way around giant iron sculptures and the
large, flat, triangular fountain that's been drained for winter.
I'm not overly punctual. But Hannah's mood seems to hinge
on our roommate dinners. They've replaced family dinners for
my roommates, and shown me what an at-home family meal

might look like, since I don't remember ever having one. I must have at some point, before Dad left. But I'm not sure. And that was so long ago. My mealtime memories are of me eating mac and cheese or Spaghetti-O's with Mom in our apartment's tiny kitchen.

I'm soaked in sweat from an hour and a half rehearsal, but the droplets of perspiration freeze into little hail balls against my skin in the February air. The wind whips my cheeks, and I'm grateful for the coat Hannah gave me, even if it is poofy and purple. It's way warmer than my favorite thrift-store denim jacket.

My legs are exhausted from *grande battements* and *jetés*, but I can make it across the next quad to the food court where we promised to meet.

Once inside the heavy door I stand to the side and sigh, allowing the heat from the nearby radiator to surround me and sink into all of the cold crevices of my skin. I remove my mittens and stuff them in my bag. My stomach growls so loudly I feel the vibrations.

Following the thick aroma of egg rolls frying and hoagie buns baking like a hound on the trail, I scan the tables for my friends. We usually sit near the windows, but those seats get taken up first.

I exhale when I don't see them yet, feeling my shoulders release some tension. Being the first one to lunch? That's a new one. I spy the Burrito Barn, which is the university's Chipotle knockoff and my personal favorite—relatively healthy and cheap—so I decide to get my food and then find my friends.

"Black beans, brown rice, cheese, and extra pico," I say to the older man wearing a hair net. Poor guy.

"Guacamole?" he asks.

"No thanks." I shake my head, knowing they charge an extra buck fifty for it.

I slide my student ID at the checkout and turn with my tray.

"It's jammed in here today. Do you know if there's something going on?" a thick boy with fluffy hair and sideburns asks.

I catch my breath and shake my head.

"Like, is one of the cafeterias closed? 'Cause there's nowhere to sit." He tilts his head, still looking at me.

"I…I don't know. I'm just supposed to meet my roommates. It is crowded, you're right." I add in my head, *They're here. I haven't found them yet.* I don't like letting strangers know I'm alone. I always say I'm meeting someone, whether I am or not. Since Paris. Since what Phillip did to me there.

"Well, if you don't find them, I'm snagging that two top." He points to a tiny square table. "You're welcome to join me."

"Thanks." I give a small smile. One that I hope says, I appreciate it, but I'm not flirting and don't really want to talk.

The boy eventually gets the hint and sits at the table he's scoped out.

I roam past the sushi bar, Palmer's favorite, and the pizza stand, our fallback, but don't see them in line or in any of the surrounding chairs. Feeling a little dizzy from hunger and the crowd, I find a small empty spot, set my tray down for a second, and take an extremely undainty bite of my multigrain wrap. So delish. I collapse into the chair and take another bite and another. Slightly more stabilized, I rummage through my bag for my phone to text Hannah, or more likely to read the text she probably already sent asking where the heck I am and telling me specifically where they're sitting. No texts from Hannah. I type out a message and hit Send but it says the message can't be delivered. I look at the bars to be sure I have service and there aren't any bars.

I try again. Nothing. I turn it off and on again. I bump it against the table three times like a magic wand. *Bibbity Bobbity Boo!* I say in my head. Nothing. My phone has zero service.

"Crap," I say out loud, a hot sinking feeling sliding down my throat, and not from the pico. My phone's fully charged. I'm not always good about that, but today I made sure it was because I knew I'd be going to the library for a group meeting after dinner and would need the charge. Plus, the screen works fine. Nope, the service is gone. And there's always service in this food court, free Wi-Fi too. There's only one other explanation for my phone not working. I know, because it's happened enough times I've had to start counting on the fingers of my second hand. Mom didn't pay our phone bill. And Mom not paying the bill means she's tipped too far to one side of her precariously balanced psyche. Again.

5
PALMER

FEBRUARY 13, I WRITE IN my journal. The date glares at me. I've gotten a dozen long-stemmed red roses the past four years from Keegan. Even last year, after we'd broken up, he sent roses to my dorm on Valentine's Day. It was all part of his weird mind games/"we're not sure what to do with each other" deal. But after hearing the stories that traveled home with him last summer from his freshman year at Polaris State, it was clear to me he'd moved on.

And that I should too.

"Palmer." Michael smiles, a glint in his eyes.

"Hi." I shut my journal and try to sound relaxed, natural, not like I was thinking of my ex-boyfriend or like I've been waiting for Michael, although I have checked the clock on my phone about four times since I got to Corner Cup.

Michael sets his laptop on the table and sits next to me on the shabby-chic crushed velvet couch. He looks so naturally suave in his charcoal half-zip sweater. I spy a crisp white tee peeking out from his collar and notice his well-worn jeans.

Even with tiny holes in the knees he appears so put together. "Did you order yet?"

"Nope." I shake my head and shift my weight to stand. "I was waiting until you got here."

"Very polite." He laughs lightly. "What can I get you?"

"I've got it." I wave my hands, dismissing his offer. "What's your poison?"

"Thanks." He nods. I like that he doesn't argue, doesn't make a fuss. He leans into the cushions, looking like a *GQ* model posing for a cover. "I'll take a grande medium roast, hmm, with a shot of hazelnut."

"Perfect." I turn and walk to the counter, my head high and my back straight. Mom always drills how important it is to look in control, not just like you belong but like you're in charge, wherever you are, in any situation. Mom drives me crazy, but she's spot-on with this advice. I always start my "in control" strategy with my outfit. Today it's dark jeans, my tan suede blazer, shine serum on my straightened hair, and the plum lipstick that looks best with my Italian coloring. It's easier for me to be confident in this setting, on my turf at Corner Cup, one on one with Michael, than in Summer's apartment with a crowd I haven't decoded how to impress yet.

Returning with our coffees I slide back onto the couch, Michael's knee so close to mine you couldn't fit an issue of *QuadAngles* between them. I flash a smile and hand him his cup, and take a sip of my dark mocha to distract me from how close our legs are. I try to concentrate on the warm richness of my coffee, but it doesn't work.

"So, I was thinking," Michael says, nodding toward the counter, "while you were in line."

"Yes?" I reopen my journal, ready to talk shop.

"I was thinking I should repay you for the coffee."

"Sure." I bat my lashes. "You can buy next time. I'm a mocha drinker." I hold up my cup and take another warm sip. I haven't flirted in a while, but apparently it's like riding a bike. It's coming back to me quickly and it's fun.

"Well, I was wondering about tomorrow night." He lets his knee fall against mine. How can one knee radiate so much heat?

Does he realize tomorrow is Valentine's Day? Because some boys have zero awareness on these issues.

"A bunch of us from *InkSpot* are meeting for happy hour at Little Italy. I could buy you a glass of wine." He strokes his beard, giving him an air of maturity Keegan never had. "Do you have plans?"

"You write for *InkSpot* too?" I say a bit too eagerly. After all, it *is* the exclusive literary magazine on campus. Its poetry and short stories make my head spin with their complexity. I square my shoulders, resetting myself, and continue, "And, actually, I do have plans."

His chocolate eyes probe mine, as if he's waiting for me to say more, which I won't because I've always believed in letting the boy do the pursuing. They enjoy it. I think it goes back to their primal hunting instincts. I put my mocha to my lips as a shield.

"I know it's Valentine's Day, but maybe you could stop by early, like around five, and still make it to…?" He tilts his head forward, signaling me to fill in his blank.

I don't.

"I could probably do that." I nod, trying to keep a contemplative, not too eager look on my face. He doesn't need to know my actual plans are a moviethon and browniefest with my roommates. Better to keep him guessing. "What do you write for *InkSpot*?"

"Come tomorrow night and I'll tell you all about it." He narrows his eyes. "Little Italy at 5:00 p.m. for appetizers, drinks, and literary talk, then you'll be free to head to your previous engagement."

"Great." I nod. "I haven't been there before, but I hear their food is fantastic."

"You've heard right. Now, about our article." Michael sets down his coffee. "I was thinking we could meet early on Shamrock Saturday morning." He raises his thick eyebrows.

I went on sabbatical from boys when Keegan and I had our grand finale, but this boy might be worth coming out of sabbatical for, just maybe.

6
HANNAH

"AND FOR YOUR NEXT CLASS, your assignment is to read *The Translator* by Daoud Hari." Dr. Wheeler touches the collar of his pinstriped oxford.

Nate turns to me. I know this, because I'm staring at him. Again. Busted.

"Do you have it yet?" he asks.

I nod, closing my notebook and sliding it into my floral tote. "I ordered it for my Kindle before classes started."

"I started reading it while I was waiting in line for those hockey tickets the other night," he says. "Pretty eye opening, and a fast read. It's hard to fathom in our day and age that something so gruesome could still be taking place."

I curl my lips recalling the chapter about violent rapes and murders in the villages. "I had to set it down sometimes. It would get to be more than I could stomach."

Nate sets his hand on my arm and nods. "I know. That's why we have to read it. To understand the evil that exists in our world. To be grateful for what we have and to take action where we can." His voice escalates with each statement as if he's giving a speech for candidacy. I'd vote for him. "I wish there were a trip planned to Darfur over spring break. That would be incredible." He slings his backpack over his black wool coat and pulls back, allowing me out of the row first.

He read ahead, is fascinated by third-world countries, and he's a gentleman? Sigh.

"And kind of scary." I widen my eyes.

Nate knits his eyebrows behind his frames. "That might be why they don't offer that one."

"Germany is way safer. At least all of their atrocities are over. Hitler's dead. Nazis are gone, and even the Wall's been knocked down." I wrap my scarf around my neck as we plod through the hallway.

"So you're going?" Nate's eyes spark. I swear they do, like I could almost catch the glint of light that just shot out from them.

"I hope so. I checked out the website, and you were right, everything is prearranged by the university. I'm working on my parents."

"Need any ammunition?"

"I think I have all the info. Thanks, though. It looks like we need permission from Dr. Wheeler first, then we register on the website and Clarkston takes the down payment out of our electronic payment system. Right?" We walk outside and the blast of winter hits my face and grabs my words for a moment.

"Sounds right. And Dr. Wheeler approves everyone because he wants it to be a big group. Which way you headed?" he asks, ducking his head against the cold.

"Back to my dorm. I have two hours before my next class. That way." I point.

"I have to go to the library. I have a finance exam tomorrow, but I can walk with you till we get to The Oak."

Despite the freezing temperatures, I feel warm inside. He's choosing to walk with me. Again.

"A finance exam sounds killer. I am so glad I don't have to take that class. I might keel over." I stick my tongue out.

"Not that bad. It all kind of clicks up here." He points to his forehead. "But I still need to study, make sure it's all sorted out."

"I don't think it would ever click up here." I touch my hair, sleek from the straightening iron I used before class.

"Maybe other things click for you, right?" Nate smiles. "What's something you can do that most people can't?"

I shake my head. "I don't know. I'm not that girl. I'm kind of good at a lot of things, but not spectacular at any one thing. That's why I'm elementary ed. I get to jump from one subject and activity to the next with the kids. I'm oddly good at making up little songs about how to remember the multiplication tables, and I love going on hikes looking for fossils. Don't have to linger on anything too long. A little art, a little history, some grammar. I'm decent at all of those things, but not an expert on any of them."

"I doubt that." We split to make way for a guy zooming past on his bike. "I bet there are lots of things you're great at."

We're at the giant oak tree now, the one that sits smack in the middle of the central academic quad. Legend says it was here before the university—that they chose this spot for the school because of the grand old oak. Legend also says that if you kiss under the branches, you'll get married. What would it be like to kiss Nate under this tree?

"Hannah?"

"Yeah." I startle a little, wondering how long I zoned out,

imagining him leaning forward and brushing his lips against mine with Adele singing "One and Only" in the background. I watch way too many Nicholas Sparks movies.

"I know it's last minute, but tomorrow is Valentine's Day, and I was wondering…" He looks down at his boots.

Okay, I've stopped breathing again.

He looks back up, his eyes so contemplative I wish I could see all of the thoughts behind them. "Would you like to see a movie with me?"

I nod like a bobblehead. Too fast. Too many times.

"Yes?" he asks.

"Yes."

7
KAT

"I'M IMPRESSED." I NOD AT Nicholas, who waits on the front steps of my dorm.

"I don't like the idea of you running around campus by yourself. And you know I'd use just about any excuse to see you."

I twitch my thumbs, used to being able to twirl the rings on them, but currently they're trapped inside my running gloves.

"I'd be fine," I tell him. There's more I want to say, like how my jaw unclenches when he protects me like that. When he's around, I feel I can do most anything, even deal with the ebbing and flowing pain of losing Alex. Nicholas was Alex's best friend, so he'd understand. If I told him.

"This way I know you'll be okay. I have to admit I'm looking forward to it getting a little warmer for these runs." Nicholas stands from the stretch he'd been holding and zips his fleece as far as it will go.

"Ready?" I ask.

He laughs and nods.

I take off toward the trail running through the untouched nature preserve.

"Hey, Speedy Gonzalez," Nicholas shouts. "Wait up!"

"Wimp." I slow my pace, just a little. "I've already lifted this morning."

"Geez! You may remember I used to be an athlete," Nicholas says, catching up to me. "But since I've thrown in the towel, I'm not quite as fit."

"Ha! You're plenty fit. You're just not awake yet."

"Oh, I'm wide-awake." He snorts. "My phone said it was eighteen degrees when I left my dorm. Eighteen!"

Our feet find a natural rhythm together. It's quiet out here. So quiet. That's one of the reasons I love running in the mornings. It's pristine and crisp, nothing to muddle my brain or cloud my thoughts. All I hear is the echo of our running shoes thudding on the frozen dirt.

"Which way?" Nicholas asks as we get to a fork in the path. "I always forget."

"Come on." I laugh, turning to the right, taking the path along the stream. "How many times have you run this with me?"

"Not enough." He laughs back, swatting my back.

The uncontaminated air fills my lungs. It feels like it's cleaning away all the cobwebs in my mind. We run on the path cut alongside a frozen creek, swinging into single file as the trail narrows a bit to accommodate a giant maple tree.

"It really is beautiful out here," Nicholas says between breaths.

"You say that every time you come running in the woods."

"Maybe I say it because you're out here."

"Hush."

I don't look at him, but feel my stomach muscles flutter. I love Nicholas in so many ways. He's always here for me. Always says the right things. He gives me all the space and time I need, and he's the only one who truly gets how I felt about Alex. Daddy tries, but he's also dealing with Mama. Mama's basically given up on everything—work, life, being my mom. My roommates are great, but Nicholas is steady. Calm. He doesn't try to fix anything; he just makes himself available when I need him. Which is a lot.

We run again in silence, processing the words, the morning, us. I pull a branch out of our way. It crackles at my touch, brittle from lack of rain and sun. I wait until Nicholas is through to release it. It snaps back into place, like a swinging gate, granting passage. To where?

"Happy Valentine's Day," Nicholas says.

I blush, then realize I didn't answer. "Hey, thanks. Right back at ya."

"You still having a movie night with your roommates?"

"Yeah, you know how Hannah is about holidays and planning. She lives for this stuff. It's guaranteed she'll pull out some kind of deliciousness shaped in a heart. Last year she found these Little Debbies with cream filling and heart sprinkles. We ended up eating the whole box."

"No chance Hannah would let a guy crash your party?"

I breathe out. Having Nicholas to lean against on the couch sounds perfect, but complicated. "Doubtful." I shake my head. "I'm not sure you would want to come anyway. Her Netflix queue starts with *Pride and Prejudice, New Moon*, and *The Sisterhood of the Traveling Pants*."

"Ay yi yi! No James Bond? Did you ever see *Skyfall?*"

"Uh, yeah, remember you made me watch it with you

about twelve times this summer."

"Oh yeah." He smirks and nudges me lightly with his elbow. "I forgot. Well, if you want to make it a lucky thirteen, I don't have major plans tonight. I could probably rearrange my schedule. You know, if you needed me to."

"Good to know."

"Watch out," Nick calls, just in time to save me from taking a bad step on a thick root lodged in the middle of our path.

"Thanks," I say when the shock of fear is replaced with the knowledge I'm safe. "That could have been bad. I could have re-sprained my ankle." I shudder, remembering my injury, which felt like a prison term, not being able to play. "Thanks for always looking out for me." I force myself to look at him. His green eyes glint like the layer of ice on top of the stream.

"I'll always look out for you, Kat. You know that." He reaches out his hand and places it on my shoulder.

For a few strides we're running through the woods together connected like that, and all I want in life is to keep running with him. Nicholas's hand feels solid and safe, and my legs and body feel free sprinting through branches and past rocks, like nothing bad could ever catch me again.

8
CLAIRE

"YOU SURE YOU DON'T MIND?" Kat's words always seem to come out so slowly, which I really like about her.

"Honest. I like Nicholas," I answer. "He's nice, and it feels oddly safe having him around. Plus, you guys never get all smoochy in front of me."

"Claire!" Kat's bright eyes bulge.

"I'm just saying I'm glad of that. I mean, whatever you do in private is up to you. I just get uncomfortable when people kiss in front of me. I mean, what am I supposed to do? Look away? Pretend I don't see, because I do."

"Right. Well, ya know I wouldn't have asked him if our whole roomie party hadn't dissolved. But he asked me to do something with him earlier, and I felt like a bit of a jerk saying no, so when Hannah canceled…"

"I know." I pick at the hole in my jeans.

"Who knew Hannah would be the one to break a roommate date? It's so unlike her. She's got it bad." Kat slides lip gloss over her lips. She tries to act casual, but it's hard to ignore she's wearing skinny jeans and a fitted sweater instead of her usual sweats. It makes me smile. She is incredibly beautiful—porcelain skin, eyes the color of green glass, dark sleek hair. She usually does nothing about her appearance. Doesn't need to. Not that I'm a fashionista, but it's nice to see her let her beauty shine.

"I'm really happy for her." I pull on the fuzzy pink slipper boots Mom got me for Christmas. "She's been on the prowl for a boyfriend since I met her at freshman orientation. She wants a guy so badly! And Nate seems nice enough." I pull my thickest hoodie on, getting cozy for our movie night.

Thunk. Thunk.

I jump and shriek at the unexpected racket at our window.

"It's all right." Kat touches my arm firmly and looks me in the eyes. "It's only Nicholas. I told him to knock on the window because it's easier than walking all the way around to the other side of our dorm to use the buzzer."

I nod shakily.

"I promise."

I nod again and breathe deeply, like my counselor always tells me to do—to remind my central nervous system not to panic. Kat walks out to let Nicholas in the side corridor. She and I have a secret, silent understanding. We both get weirded out by little things, things that make us remember what we're trying so hard to forget. For me, it's the night Phillip raped me. For her, it's the death of her brother, Alex. We both know that the other one has little triggers, triggers we don't even know about or expect, like someone unexpectedly rapping at our window. So we both try to look out for each other and remind each other it's okay.

"Pizza delivery," Nicholas chimes, entering with his arms

full of white cardboard boxes.

"Mmm. Ragazza! And I'm starved." All that inhaling and exhaling brought the tangy scent of tomato sauce and cheese to my nose like a tidal wave.

"How much do we owe ya?" Kat asks, taking the boxes and setting them on our coffee table.

My stomach sinks. Unless I won the lottery without buying a ticket, I'll have to borrow money from Kat.

"What kind of gentleman would I be if I didn't buy dinner for two of my favorite girls on Valentine's?"

I blush, wondering if Nicholas read my mind.

"Wow. Thanks," I say. "I totally benefit from the residual effects here."

Kat thumps one of her rings on the pizza box. "You are a sweetheart." She drags out the word.

"Remember that." Nicholas playfully glares at her. "You girls ready to put the movie in?"

"Should we wait for Palmer?" I ask. "She said she'd catch up with us soon."

"Let me check and see if she's texted. She thought she'd be back around now." Kat pulls her phone out of her pocket and scrolls down the screen with her thumb. "Nothing."

"My phone's still not working." I pull a small section of hair from where it parts, divide it into three smaller clumps, and start braiding.

"Still?"

"What happened?" Nicholas asks.

"My mom didn't pay the bill," I mumble.

"Should you remind her?" Nicholas asks. Kat elbows him. She didn't mean for me to see. But I did.

"I don't think she forgot."

"Is this how she punishes you?" Nicholas opens the lid of

a pizza box.

"No." I keep my eyes trained on my braid. "She has…" How do I say this? That my mom at various times in our life has been hooked on diet pills, stayed home sick for several weeks straight in a depressive kind of coma, become so distracted juggling multiple boyfriends that she pretty much ignores everything else in her life, including me, and gone on various spending and eating binges? I never know what will be next. But I'm always pretty sure there will be something. I exhale. "Issues."

"Have you tried to call anyone?" Kat asks, then hits herself in the forehead. "You know what I mean." She grabs a slice of pepperoni, the cheese stretching as she pulls it from the box.

I nod. "I e-mailed Mom. I used Hannah's phone the last two days and left messages. But if Mom didn't pay the bill, her phone's not working either. I keep looking for her on Skype, but she's never on. I've been meaning to call my aunt." I focus on wrapping a tiny rubber band around the end of my braid so I don't have to meet either of their gazes.

"Why don't you call her now? Here. Use my phone."

Kat hands me her phone in its neon orange case that reads "Life is Soccer, The Rest is Details." I let my fingers dangle over the screen. I haven't really forgotten to call Aunt Denise. I haven't wanted to. I haven't wanted to hear what she had to say. Although I want to know what's going on with Mom, I don't know if I can stand to learn what she's fallen into this time.

"Don't you know her number?" Kat asks.

"Um, I had it programmed into my phone. I'll have to find it." I stand and walk into our room where I crawl into my bed. I fluff my covers around me. What am I going to do?

Kat and Nicholas are laughing in the next room. They won't notice if I'm gone for a while. I slide my hand under my pillow. My fingers find my Bible. I know there's something in the book of John, something about nothing being too big to handle, something I read yesterday, or maybe the day before. I flip through the worn vellum pages, scanning the parts I've underlined. Here:

For God is greater than our worried hearts and knows more about us than we do ourselves. 1 John 3:20

All right, God. My heart's pretty worried. I rub my index finger over the passage. Here goes.

I actually do know Aunt Denise's number. I mean, I lived in her house all summer since Mom moved into a one-bedroom apartment closer to the high school where she teaches and didn't really have room for me. I didn't mean to lie to Kat. I just couldn't make the call in front of her and Nicholas. Plus, I wasn't ready. Now I am. Kind of.

I feel that crazy, spazzy feeling my body gets when my inner radar senses danger, like when Phillip had the lights turned out in his room or when Mom had boxes piled by the door of our old apartment. Or even just a minute ago, when Nicholas knocked on the window. It's like my heart is shaking between my ribs so hard, if I acknowledge it, it might bounce out of place, so I focus on pushing my intuition away and press my cousin Megan's phone number digit by digit. She'll be easier to get information from than Aunt Denise, with her high drama tactics. I listen to the ring on the other end. Once, twice, three times.

"Yeah?" Megan answers.

"Hey, Meg, it's Claire."

"This isn't your number."

My cousin does not score high on the manners scale. She's rich and pretty in a copycat kind of way, but she's actually nice to me. Megan and I are different, but we sort of balanced each other out over the summer. She wouldn't let me count teaching little girls ballet as a social life. And when we were at the pool parties and barbeques she declared worthy, I drove her home before she got too out of control. I helped her with the class she took for summer school. And her subtle way of thanking me was handing me a giant shopping bag full of beautiful clothes she never wears at the end of summer under the guise of cleaning out her closet.

"No. My phone's dead. This is my roommate's."

"Oh. What's up?"

"Well, the thing about my phone not having service, sort of."

"What happened?"

"Mom didn't pay the bill."

"You're sure?"

"Pretty sure."

"Are things that tight? Give me your account number. I can activate it with Mom's credit card," Megan says.

"We can afford it." *Maybe*, I think to myself. "Mom just gets, well, she isn't the most responsible person in the world." I exhale loudly.

"Duh."

"I was just wondering if you guys have heard from her. If you've heard your mom talking to her, or about her, or anything."

"No, but I usually tune out what Mom's saying. You want me to ask?"

I nod.

"Claire?"

Guess she didn't see my nod. "Uh, yeah, if you don't mind. But don't make a big deal about it."

"Let me text her real fast and I'll text you right back. K?"

"Yeah. To this number."

The phone goes black and I sit. I clutch my Bible to my chest like a teddy bear.

Kat's phone vibrates in my hand.

"Hello?"

"Claire?"

"Yeah."

"I decided it was easier to call her. Mom said Libby, I mean, your mom, has been calling a lot, super chatty actually, kind of crazy upbeat."

"So that's good, right?"

"Yeah, I would have said the same thing. She's kind of a bummer sometimes. No offense."

"None taken."

"But then Mom said, 'Now that you mention it, Libby did ask me for money last week. Something about supplies for her latest venture.'" Megan does a pretty spot on imitation of Aunt Denise.

I hold my breath. For Mom, a venture could mean anything from a new exercise regime to a new boyfriend to her newest DIY project. "How much?"

"She wouldn't tell me at first. You know how my mom likes to act like it's a big secret, but then totally blabs?"

"Yeah."

"Two thousand bucks."

I drop Kat's phone.

9
HANNAH

I LEAN AGAINST THE DOOR, humming, tucking away each moment of my date before even a shred of it can escape my memory. It was all too much for me to absorb while it was happening. I wouldn't allow myself to soak in the wonderfulness. I was afraid if I did, it might disappear, like the rainbow shining on the exterior of a bubble when it pops. I take two steps away from the door, sneak toward the darkened side of the window, and watch Nate disappear between the brick buildings and winding sidewalks. Sigh.

Now, back down the corridor, against the door to our suite, I allow myself the happy dance I've bottled up inside for hours. I clench my fists, stomp my feet, and squeeze my eyes shut in pure celebration. My stomach is still bouncing around like it's full of Pop Rocks, and I don't want the feeling to stop. Ever. I open the door and four faces turn toward me.

"Well," Palmer says, adjusting her weight on the futon, "let's hear it."

"Itwasthebestnightofmyentirelife," I say in one breath. I

do my stamping party again, because the first one felt so good, and hang my purse on the hook by the door. "He is so adorable. Look." I hold up the single pink rose Nate presented me with at the beginning of the evening, its head sagging slightly from being clutched all night.

"So sweet," Palmer says. "Maybe I should have paid more attention to him at that hockey game."

Heat pokes like little needles down my neck. I open my mouth, but before I can formulate a single word, Palmer flashes that smile of hers, tilts her head, and says, "JK."

"I brought pizza," Nicholas says, standing from his spot on the futon while I resume breathing. "That counts for something, right?"

"It was delicious. Thanks, Nicholas." Claire brushes crumbs from her lap onto the carpet.

I shrug off my coat to keep myself from rushing toward her with a vacuum. I will not allow the urge to clean steal this moment from me. I'll get them later, after Nicholas is gone, after I've told my story.

"It was perfect." Kat gives him a sideways squeeze.

"Yeah, really great. Love Ragazza." Palmer winks.

"You ate Ragazza! Without me?" I put my hands on my hips.

"Next time we'll share." Nicholas laughs lightly and grabs his wallet from our coffee table. "I better leave while I'm on a roll."

Kat walks him to the door while I try to keep all of my thoughts and stories inside for one more minute. But I feel like I'm going to explode. Palmer, Claire, and I try not to stare as they say good-bye, but we can hear them whispering.

"Come sit," Palmer says a little too loudly to cover the awkwardness and pats the seat Nicolas just vacated.

"I thought you'd never ask," I answer noisily, shuffling and rearranging myself on the futon.

"Bye, ladies," Nicholas calls from the door.

Kat sits back down on my other side and leans in to smell my rose.

"Mmm."

"Well?" Palmer asks her.

Kat shrugs.

"I love the soft pink." Claire turns to me and fingers one of the petals on my rose so lightly, I'm not sure if she actually touches it.

"Me too." I smell the delicate flower for the hundredth time, grateful Kat's not chatty and I can share about my date. I have to or I'll bust. "Do you think it means something? Like yellow means friend and red means true love. What if he had brought me red?"

"C'mon," Kat says, elbowing me gently, "let's hear every last detail. We've been waitin' for ya."

"Really? Ohmigosh, it was amazing! Okay." I blow the remnants of my mostly grown-out bangs out of my face. "So you were all here when Nate picked me up. Except you, Palm."

She nods.

"He buzzed me down, and when I got to the door he handed me this rose and said, 'Happy Valentine's Day.' For the record, unlike the rest of you, I have never had a boy give me flowers on Valentine's Day before, so it was a *really big deal.*" I tap my feet against the floor for emphasis. "And he was wearing khakis and a button-down, and get this, penny loafers."

"Down girl." Kat pats my knee.

"I know, but it was so perfect. He got completely dressed up for me. And the rest of the night was like that. He already had tickets for the movie, like he'd planned it, like he really wanted to do this." My heart thumps loudly in my chest just remembering the events.

"What did you see?" Claire tilts her head upward.

"The new Leonardo DiCaprio movie! What boy picks a movie set in the 1800s complete with gowns and carriages? I mean, that's what I would have picked."

"Was it any good?" Kat twirls one of her funky, silver rings.

"I have no idea." I lay my head all the way back and close my eyes.

"What?!" Palmer slides her hand under my head and pulls it back up. "Miss Write a Movie Review and make us compare notes of every film we've ever seen since *The Little Mermaid* doesn't know if she liked the latest epic with period costumes she's been talking about since summer?"

"I know!" I shake my head and lean forward to unzip my boots. "The costumes were stunning and, Leo is, well, gorgeous, but I couldn't concentrate. Somewhere near the beginning of the movie, Nate reached out and held my hand, and not in a grabby kind of way. It was sweet, but also like we both had these magnets inside of us that needed to touch. And I was hoping he wouldn't let go, because my fingers felt like icicles after the walk to the theatre, and then it was kind of uncomfortable how we were arranged with those armrest thingys, but I didn't want to let go." I stand and tote my boots to my closet. "It was like he knew it didn't feel quite right, so he settled our hands on his thigh, and well, how could I concentrate then?" I plop back on my spot between my dark-haired roommates, remembering how warm his thigh had been.

"Sounds like you really, really like this guy." Palmer's so

close I can smell her thick perfume and garlic and something else sweet lingering on her.

"Um-hmm." I nod too many times. "When we're together it's like an awesome song you hear on Pandora, and you're afraid when you get home you won't remember what it was called or what band sings it, but now, telling you all about it, it seems real, like I'll never forget." My voice catches in my throat.

Palmer swings the silver cross back and forth on her chain, like she always does when she's contemplating something. Is she going to quiz me about his character?

I watch her for a second. "Oh, Palm. I completely forgot to ask about your night. I'm sorry. And, Kat? Did Nicholas give you a Valentine's kiss? Were you a good chaperone, Claire? I am completely carried away." I rub Palmer's arm. "Have you been out hobnobbing with high society, my dear?" I ask in my best uppity voice.

"Something like that." Palmer nods. "You know the typical literary magazine happy hour. Appetizers. Wine. Impressive vocabularies." She pauses.

"Sounds fancy," Claire says.

"It reminded me of one of my parents' parties. A pianist played show tunes on a baby grand in the corner. It was extremely sophisticated. Everyone was over-the-top smart." Palmer licks her lips. "You all would have been proud of me. I got at least three interesting spring break trips for my article. I learned that taking sips of wine keeps me from nibbling on fatty snacks. And, despite how gorgeous Michael looked in his black sweater and sideburns, I bowed out way before anyone else. I don't want him to think I'm too accessible." She raises her eyebrows. "I just wanted to make a grand appearance."

"You always make a grand appearance." I rub her

shoulder. "Always."

"Should we be at all worried about the wine part or the Michael part?" Kat asks.

"Please!" Palmer waves her hands in the air.

Claire sighs. "I could watch *The Notebook* over and over again. Nicholas was a good sport to watch it. Don't you think he's trying to tell you something?" Claire tugs on the leg of Kat's jeans.

"Get out." She reaches across me and swats Claire's hand.

"Now, girls." I laugh. I do want to hear their stories. I do. But I can barely concentrate. Nate's voice fills my head. I interlace my fingers, trying to remember the weight of his hand in mine.

"Nicholas is so into you." Claire climbs up and squeezes onto the couch with us. "Why is that a bad thing, Kat?"

Kat drums her thumbs on her thighs. "It's not. Nick's great. I just...I'm not...I don't know if I can be what he wants me to be."

"Just be you." Claire smiles.

"Right." Kat laughs her loud, hearty laugh, then turns to me. "So, did Nate kiss you?"

I nod and feel warmth pour down my face and spine and all the way down to my toes.

"He kissed you!" Palmer screams.

"And...?" Kat nudges.

"And..." I shake my head, still not believing how perfect it was. "He held my hand all the way home. When we got to the dorm, he raised our hands to his lips and kissed the tips of my fingers." I rub the spots on my hand. "Then we chatted a little about the movie, about the frozen yogurt we got afterward—strawberry milkshake and birthday cake swirled—it was soooo good! And about Germany—the whole time with my fingers still by his lips. My brain was strategizing how I was going to convince my parents to let me go to Germany with this beautiful boy when he leaned forward and kissed me softly, gently." I raise my fingers to my lips and exhale. "Just as I realized what was happening, he gave me two more quick, light kisses, and the last thing he said was the same as his first words of the night, 'Happy Valentine's Day.'"

"Ain't that sweet." Kat bats her eyelashes.

"Earth to Hannah," Palmer says.

There's a pleasant tightness in my throat as I stand and bolt our door, gather a few stray cups from our coffee table, and sing to myself the Carolina Liar song I've had on my romance playlist for years, "Save me, I'm lost. Oh, Lord, I've been waiting for you."

10
CLAIRE

"CAN I USE YOUR PHONE?"

I am so sick of having to ask people that, but the entire walk back from dance class I've known that's what I'd have to ask. I promised myself I'd borrow from the first roommate I saw, no matter what they were doing. My conversation with Megan three nights ago has been poke-poke-poking somewhere in the back of my brain. I knew when I hung up with her I'd eventually have to call Mom. I half hoped Aunt Denise would call Mom and let her know I was on her trail. But even if she did, that doesn't mean Mom would follow up.

I can only imagine what Mom's doing. And at first, that was good enough, safer actually, to just imagine. But my brain's been going crazytown thinking of all the possibilities, and none of them are good. I'm just going to have to break down and call her.

But I don't want to.

Please say you're expecting a call from Nate.

"Of course. I'm going to have to let my nails sit for a

good twenty minutes anyway." Hannah waves her fingers, teal with purple polka dots and purple with teal stripes.

"Okay, those are so fun," I say, stepping next to where she sits on our couch. "How did you even know how to do that? How long did it take?"

"Not very long. See?" She holds up her latest issue of *Marie Claire* to a page filled with different nail art. Pink and teal zigzags are in the lower right hand corner, glossy and perfect. "Zigzags looked way too Mount Everest, but dots are just"— she holds her thumb and index finger together like she's holding an imaginary nail polish brush and dabs up and down—"just dots."

"They're awesome." I turn my head so I can see them from different angles.

"I can do yours too," Hannah chirps. "Please, pretty please with polka dots on top."

I glance down the page. "I like these." I point to a pastel pink frosty polish with a thin gold line running down the middle of the nail.

"Oooo. Me too. I think Palmer has gold, and I for sure have a pink close to that one in my crate. When you get off the phone?"

"Maybe. And what are those?" I ask, noticing three colorful rubber band bracelets under the edge of her magazine.

Huge exhale from Hannah. "They're from Sammie. She made them for me, which was really sweet, and this." She nods to the magazine. "Look under it."

I lift the glossy pages for Hannah so she doesn't smear her manicure. PRETTY PLEASE WITH A CUPCAKE ON TOP COME HOME FOR SPRING BREAK! I MISS YOU! XOXOXOXOXOXOXO YOUR ONE AND ONLY SISTER is written in alternating colors of glitter markers.

"That'll pull at your heart strings."

"No kidding." Hannah puffs air. "I love her and I do miss her and it's incredibly sweet that she wants me to come home." She leans back in her chair.

"But Palmer wants you to come to the beach," I say, setting the magazine back in place.

"And there's the whole Germany thing." Hannah shakes her head back and forth. "It might just be easier to go to Germany. Then I won't hurt anybody's feelings. It'll be a school thing, not a personal thing. How would I ever pick between Sammie and Palmer? It's painful."

"You're in such high demand. They both love you, Han, and that's awesome."

Hannah scrunches up her face. "But still hard. Oh, sorry, you were trying to use the phone and I've totally distracted you. Go ahead, but I still want to paint your nails."

"Deal. When yours are dry. And if I don't need to run to therapy." I move my hair over my left shoulder. "I'm calling my mom. Sure you aren't expecting a spectacular text from Nate?"

"He's in class for exactly one hour and thirty-two more minutes." Hannah looks at the clock. "And you are? Good for you. I don't know what to say." Hannah cracks her gum.

"I don't either." I shrug. "A little prayer for strength would be appreciated."

"You got it."

"Thanks."

"My phone is in my purse, which is hanging from my chair. And would you mind changing the channel to Netflix? If I'm going to have to sit still for twenty minutes I might as well catch an extra episode of *Gilmore Girls*."

"Might as well." I click the remote a couple of times.

"Matter which episode?"

"I've seen them all a hundred times. Surprise me."

"There you go." I slide her phone, all purple and flowers, out of her purse. "I'll just be in here." I point to our bedroom.

"Good luck," Hannah says. "Praying!" She holds her hands palms pressed together like a little kid praying.

Here goes nothing. I close the door behind me, curl into the corner of my bottom bunk, and dial.

"Hello. May I please speak to Libby Lassiter? This is a parent of one of her students." My lie seems justified given the circumstances.

"I'm sorry, ma'am, but Ms. Lassiter is in class right now." The receptionist's voice is nasally.

"I understand. It will only take a moment, and I can hold. It's actually urgent. And too private to e-mail her about." I try to sound desperate.

"I'll put you on hold."

I lean back and close my eyes. I could be here awhile.

"Hello, this is Libby Lassiter." Mom's voice startles me.

"Hi, Mom."

"Claire, sweetheart." Her voice gets really loud. "This is a surprise. They said it was a parent...never mind. I haven't heard from you in forever. Everything okay?"

Mom loves to act like nothing's wrong. In her mind, maybe that way it won't be.

In the beat that I'm processing her feigned innocence, she continues, "I've been so busy around here. On top of my teaching, I quit yoga and took up spinning." She pauses and giggles. Giggles?

I remember to ask, "You have?"

"Uh-huh. Isn't it great? It's super intense and really gets me pumped up and I feel like I ride that stationary bike to the moon and back. And there's a very handsome man who comes on Wednesday evenings. His name is Craig. We've gone out for coffee. Twice."

Surprise, surprise.

"I'll text you a picture of him after class." She sounds too perky.

"Mom, my phone isn't working."

"I do have to go in just a second. Shouldn't leave my students for too long."

I've lost her. Like I lost her to Arnot, when she ditched me and all her summer tutoring clients to spend quality time with a guy who ended up being married. Like when she decided to open her own preschool and bought a zillion desks and picture books at garage sales and crammed them into our tiny apartment, and screamed about the conspiracy against single moms when she found out she had to be certified and have insurance.

"Mom, my phone isn't working. You didn't pay the phone bill."

"Of course I did, silly. We're talking on phones right now. Anyway, I really have to go. I have to get back to my class and swing by the doctor right after school."

"The doctor? Everything okay?"

"Oh, did I say doctor? Silly me, just the pharmacy. Just need to pick up a little prescription is all. Nothing to worry about."

"Hey, Mom?"

"Yeah?" Her voice sounds vulnerable for one second, like she stopped her rehearsed speech long enough for me to sneak through.

"Are you okay?" But the gap's closed. She's back on her manic spin.

"Of course." She laughs again, but it sounds forced. I can picture her shaking her head, dismissing such a silly question. "But, oh my goodness, I have got to go."

And she hangs up.

On me. On her financial responsibilities. On life. Again.

11
KAT

TODAY IS ALEX'S BIRTHDAY.

I tug my running gloves over my fingers and zip up my outerwear as I leave the weight room. I turn backward on the step and alternate lowering my heels, stretching my tight calves. I should call home. But I can't.

I have to move.

Turning my iTunes to Lady Antebellum, I bolt from the step along the paved sidewalks through the quad.

For a normal girl with a normal family, her brother's birthday would be an excuse to connect, probably got out to dinner, eat some cake, and enjoy the warm family glow that comes not just from candles but from being together. Old stories are brought out of the closet and tried on for size. Familiar jokes are retold again and again. But I don't have a normal family, not anymore.

On a mission, I trot toward the Rec Center. Once there, I run up the concrete steps, Rocky Balboa style. At the doors, I turn around, not losing my nerve, just not ready, not yet. And just like in Rocky, I run down the steps and back up again over and over. Feeling the ache on the tops of my thighs as I mount the hefty flight of stairs for the fourth time, I open the door, flash my student ID, and duck to the right. I open the heavy glass door leading to the Olympic-sized pool and breathe deeply the familiar scent of chlorine. It's so strong it makes my eyes water. I sit on the edge of the bleachers, like I did for chunks of my childhood. When I wasn't at soccer tournaments, I was at swim meets.

The splash of a swimmer diving into the pool, the arc of his arm as he pulls it above the water, stroke after stroke, is like a nursery rhyme to me. I know the pattern, could clap it out with my hands. I know what happens next, and what happens after that. My mind moves with the swimmer as he gets to the end of the lane and plants his feet against the wall, pushing off, propelling himself back the other way.

The sides of my eyes feel so heavy they melt into my cheeks, which tug toward the floor. I feel like I've been kicked in the throat. I can't swallow, and the chlorine stings, and my eyebrows pull forcefully downward, and I can't breathe or form a thought. As the swimmer climbs out of the water, I turn and dash out the door, unable to look at his face, unable to process that he is not and never will be Alex. I retrace my steps out the door, down the steps, along the walkway and step forward.

I run through the main campus, dodging students rushing to morning classes, past the football stadium, and toward the Clarkston trails. The fresh air rushes into my lungs and replaces the chlorine. Already I feel my face tightening back to its normal shape. My legs reach out in front of me, one after the other, refueling me.

Alex's green eyes sparkle in my memories. His laugh

echoes in my head. My calves are still tight. I started at too quick of a pace. I should stop and stretch, but I don't slow down. The ache is good, reminds me I'm working. I'm moving. I'm living.

You would be twenty today. Wow. That sounds so adult. So grown-up. I laugh, knowing that's what Alex would do if I called him grown-up. I talk to his memory a lot. It helps me sort through my thoughts, thinking what Alex would say and do, how he would react.

There's a split in the trail. I could turn left to circle back to my quad or right to stay in the woods and end up by the track. I veer right, maintaining my pace, but lengthening my stride, finding my full rhythm.

What would you have done to celebrate?

Everyday was a celebration for Alex. He would've ordered pizza and invited the guys he swims with, including Nicholas, over. Nicholas would be the first to arrive. They would laugh and eat and guzzle Gatorade and include me in all of their guy conversations and jokes, even though they wouldn't have to, then devour the red velvet cake Mama makes every year for all of our birthdays. My stomach growls just thinking about the rich cocoa cake and creamy frosting. Mama uses an entire bottle of red food coloring. That can't be good for us!

Around bends, over bridges, along the creek, my feet pound the earth. I'm coming up on the clearing, and the trees part and all of the brick and ivy comes back into view. My feet adjust as they transition from the give of the dirt to the solid concrete. And just like that, my thoughts revert back to birthday celebrations.

After all the guys left, Nicholas would've stayed to help Alex and me clean up, but mainly to go over the night together—the who said what, the funniest joke, the lamest story.

Nicholas. What am I going to do about that guy?

I enter the public track, not the one the Clarkston track team uses, but the one built a couple years back for everyone. I chase myself lap after lap, ignoring the other students working out today. Winding the memories of Alex around and around my heart so I don't lose them. I should run one for every year of Alex's life, they're only a quarter mile long. The average professional soccer player runs about six miles per game. Any extra now will only be a plus for my stamina.

My heart beats all the way up into my throat as I dig deep inside to find a final burst of energy to speed up to a strong gait for the last leg of my run. My ribs ache, or maybe it's my lungs. Finally, gasping, I grab my thighs and lower my head. I take a few large gulps of air, and although I'd like to stay here, I walk, shaking out my arms, stretching my neck from side to side, regaining a breathing pattern. I'm filled with the euphoria that comes from a good workout—heart thumping, blood flowing, lungs expanding, muscles flexing.

"Happy Birthday, Alex," I say out loud as the mammoth bell tower bongs ten distinct peels for all of campus to hear.

I find "Birthday" by the Sugarcubes on my phone and play it, singing along to the mournful melody as I walk back toward my dorm. My body's warm from the run and doesn't even notice the cold anymore. A handful of students meander around campus bundled in coats. The scent of sausage sizzling leaks from the dining hall, and my stomach growls again, louder this time. I could sure use my morning oatmeal. About four helpings. The granola bar I ate on the way to practice was burned off long ago.

Claire's probably still asleep, but I bet Hannah's already back from her first class chomping at the bit to organize dinner plans or a study session. Palmer should be at class now. My steps slow. None of them know it's Alex's birthday. I haven't told them. Should I tell them?

My phone buzzes in my hand. I squeeze it, afraid to look. I'm sure it's Mama and Daddy. It's like they have some sixth sense and know I'm stalling calling them.

HOW WAS LIFTING?

A text from Nicholas.

GOOD. YOU MISSED THE RUN POST LIFT.

I DON'T REMEMBER BEING INVITED. WHERE ARE YOU?

I look around, realizing I've somehow meandered left of my quad to West quad. I feel strange typing my answer.

OUTSIDE YOUR DORM.

I'LL BE RIGHT OUT.

I sit on the stone steps by the side entrance, the one closest to Nicholas's room. It's relaxing to ease my body down. To give it a break after its performance.

I can sense Nicholas's smile before I see it. The door creaks, and I know it's him, and I know he's pleased. He always acts like seeing me is a treat. I love and hate him for that. I turn and his grin is there, right between his freckles and just below his smallish nose and his Crayola green eyes.

I can't contain the sigh escaping my lips. It's a relief he's here. That his smile is where it should be. That he texted me just as I was walking past. Like it was all supposed to be like this. That's how it always feels with Nicholas.

He holds out a small white box and sits down next to me.

"Schneiders?" I ask in disbelief. "Did you get them to deliver?"

"Nah. I got it last night. But I did get them to make a red velvet." He opens the lid of the bakery box, revealing a giant maroon cupcake with white cream cheese frosting, and hands me a fork. "How far did you run?"

I can't answer as tears leak from my eyes.

With shaking fingers I take the plastic fork and box holding the cake.

"How did you...?" I get out.

"I miss him too, Kat."

I nod.

12
PALMER

I CAN'T BELIEVE IT'S FOUR in the morning and I'm putting on lipstick. But it is March 1, a.k.a. Shamrock Saturday, and I'm reporting on it with Michael. I tug my moss-colored cashmere over my head, smooth it over my hips, and pick out delicate silver earrings with jade beads. That's as green as I get.

Grudgingly, I grab my coat. It's a shame to cover up my ensemble, but Michael did have the compelling idea of sitting on the giant graffiti rock marking the segue from university property to downtown and interviewing people as they either set off for the Shamrock Saturday festivities or stumble home from them. Although it's pure genius from a reporting perspective, it looks to be a long, cold morning.

"G'luck," Hannah mumbles from under her comforter.

"Thanks," I whisper and kiss one of her auburn waves.

"*Bitte*," Hannah mumbles. She's been listening to too many German podcasts. Makes me want to strangle her. She is so not going to Germany.

I tiptoe out of the room before I disturb Kat or Claire

and catch the shuttle bus from our quad to Graffiti Granite. The knots in my stomach tie themselves tighter and tighter with each stop sign. I can tell Michael likes the way I look, but I want him to like the way I write.

The cold hits my face as I leave the heated bus, but I smile when I see Michael waiting there for me with drinks from Corner Cup in each hand.

"I can only hope one of those is for me," I say, taking in how much the wool scarf hanging around his neck reminds me of Ryan O'Neal in *Love Story*.

He hands me one of the cups. "I tried to buy you another glass of wine at Little Italy the other night, but you disappeared before I got a chance. I'm making up for it with coffee. I had them add an extra shot, considering the hour. Mocha, right?"

I nod, welcoming the warm, sweet caffeine. But it's a bit too warm going down and the taste is stronger than my usual, even with the extra shot of espresso. "What kind of shot did you have them add?" I ask, waving my left hand in the air.

"The kind that'll keep you warmer on this crazy assignment." He laughs, sliding his free arm behind my back. "Come on. You ready to interview some crazies?"

I start to suggest we walk the few blocks back to the coffee shop and get one that hasn't been spiked, but a group of nine or ten guys all wearing giant floppy leprechaun hats ambles toward us, climbs atop the rock, and attempts an Irish jig.

I break out laughing. "This is going to be a blast."

But Michael's not happy. "Where's Ahmed? We need this shot," he growls. "He's never late."

"You're right, he's not. But Van begged Summer so much for this assignment, Summer finally caved. Didn't she tell you?"

"Let's just say Summer isn't my biggest fan right now." Michael's voice vibrates.

Does she like him and he doesn't like her? Did he ask her out and she felt it unprofessional? Did she take his flirting seriously, but he didn't mean it? Or was it his writing? It couldn't be his writing. Did he miss an assignment?

To shoo away my speculations, I pull my phone out and snap a dozen or so pictures of the guys on the rock. "No worries, I've got it." I zoom in and out, and turn my phone sideways. The would-be leprechauns prance away, and I thumb through my results with Michael leaning into my side to see. "Not quite quality pics, but I can play around with them a bit, maybe give them a green tint so you won't even realize I took them with my phone."

I feel Michael's hair graze my cheek as he looks up. "Incoming," he says while striding toward five students wearing running clothes with green numbers safety-pinned to their chests.

"Running the 5K this morning?" he asks, clicking the recording app on his phone and holding it in the middle of the group so the microphone will catch all of their voices.

"This is my fourth and final Green Mile," a tall, skinny guy with a hat pulled over his ears answers.

"It's actually more than a mile," a girl with a braid and calves made out of steel says. "It's 3.2. Which is nothing. Just a fun run. I might sprint." Her sentences are all as short and strong as she is.

"Did you know the race is actually named after the film and novel by Stephen King, *The Green Mile*?" I ask, stepping toward the group. Before they can answer, I continue, "The book begins with a man recalling the time he was a prison guard with his fellow residents at a nursing home. When you're in a nursing home one day, what will you tell your fellow residents about running the Green Mile?"

There's a pause filled only with a sharp wind and a whoop from some rowdies a few blocks off. I square my shoulders. I know this question is good. Is it too good for my classmates this early? *C'mon, guys*, I will them. *You're Clarkston students. You live for this stuff.* And then in a flash, they're all vying for the mic.

"I'll tell them how it wasn't about the distance or even getting up early, but about the tradition, that practically the whole school lined the streets of downtown to cheer on the runners at the finish," the guy running for his fourth time says.

Bingo.

"I'll rally up the other members of the nursing home to put together our own 5K, even if it has to be with walkers and wheelchairs. I'll tell them that if a bunch of college kids could run five at five, then they can hobble and roll around for 5K at midday." Muscle girl's voice deepens with her own challenge.

"I'll just be honest," a guy in the back adds. "The run is great, but the party afterward is what it's all about."

The whole group high-fives one another and in their excitement seems to forget about the interview as they move in a pack toward the starting line.

"You did some prep work." Michael pushes the red circle to stop the recording. "That was brilliant."

"Thanks." I swallow more hi-wired mocha, allowing myself an inner celebration. Brilliant. Uh-huh.

"Hi, guys. How fun is this?" Van appears. Is she really wearing that ubertight sparkly shamrock shirt and no coat. Her chest must be freezing!

"You better get set up. You already missed a couple photo ops." Michael nods toward the rock.

"Oh, like, sorry. It's crazy early, ya know? Could you help

me?" Van bats her eyelashes, which she's coated in Kelly green mascara, then proceeds to bend at the waist so her cleavage is almost directly in Michael's face as she sets down her camera. For real?

I take another sip of mocha. There can't be that much rum in there, can there? Or is it whiskey? Vodka? What *does* someone spike coffee with? At any rate, it's warm. And I have to laugh out loud as a group of girls who apparently got their shirts at the same shop Van did trot past the rock.

"Happy Shamrock Saturday!" They all wave.

"Hey, Van, why don't you get in this one? I'll take it," Michael goads her.

"Really?" Van blushes, as if this is a compliment. "Hey, girls, cute shirts." She wiggles her way into the middle of the picture and throws her arms around the unsuspecting girls.

"Okay, this is for *QuadAngles*. Say 'green.'" Michael holds up Van's Nikon.

"Green!" they all cheer on cue, apparently very well practiced in posing for pictures.

I feel a bit of the green-eyed monster crawling up my sleeve as I watch Michael ogle the human Barbie dolls striding off toward the bars. I take another sip, the chocolate and warmth soothing me a bit.

"Here you go." Michael hands the camera back to Van.

"Thanks." She blushes. "I bet you're a great photographer."

Have I ever mentioned *I* prefer to be the center of attention? But I will not lower myself to tramp mode to get there.

"I'll let you take the pictures from now on." Michael smiles. "I believe that's your specialty." And just as I feel the heat rising from my chest to my cheeks, thinking that should be my smile, Michael turns and winks at me.

I'll take a wink.

The warmth from my throat flows to my lips. I wink back. The heat spreads to my cheeks.

While Van clatters and fiddles with her tripod, probably all flustered by Michael's smile—I know I am—Michael comes up right beside me and whispers, "I don't know why some girls think shoving everything in your face is going to get a guy's attention. I prefer a girl who can think."

Did I mention it's getting warm out here? And just when I think it's safe to breathe again, he slips his hand under my hair and moves it away from my neck. His mouth touches that sensitive skin where my hairline starts, then moves back to my ear.

"Did I ever tell you how intrigued I am by you, Palmer Ruscilli?" His lips tickle my ear lobe.

A rush of heat and cold floods my body, prickling where his lips touched my neck, warming from the inside out. We are out in the open. Very public, and this feels so intimate. I could tilt my head toward him, and I swear he'd kiss me, but that seems more like a noir film than what I'd planned for this morning. I ache for that kiss. He is beautiful and smart, but not here. Not in front of Van. I lift my cup to my lips, to keep them from doing something they shouldn't. I sip my coffee so I don't have to say anything. But he's still right here, in my personal space, a part of it now, which makes my breathing too slow. I take another sip to stall one more moment, to give him a chance to back up. But when I raise my eyes, he's right there, waiting for me to answer.

"You are?" I ask.

As if to prove it, Michael leans forward, like he is going to kiss me right here on the sidewalk at four thirty in the morning.

But instead, he lets his nose touch mine. It's warm against my chilled face. His dark eyes look right into me, into the place where I've always struggled, that place between being Pretty Palmer enjoying the attention I get, to Pensive Palmer longing to be appreciated by more than just my English teachers for my writing. Michael is the first who seems to understand this longing I have in my gut to assemble words together to make people think or cry or laugh or reflect.

His nose on mine, him looking at me like this, feels more intimate than a kiss.

I feel courageous, so I hold his stare. "That intrigue goes both ways."

13

CLAIRE

I TYPE OUT THE CONCLUSION to my paper on the French Revolution as fast as I can. All the while the soundtrack to *Les Mis* floats through my brain. I'd play it on my laptop, if I still had it.

"Hi, hi, hi." Palmer opens the door. "I may or may not be in love." She raises her shoulders and turns her head.

"Just a sec." I hammer at the keys, click Save, and e-mail myself a version. I exhale, feeling like I've just done a dozen *grande jetés* or robbed a bank. "With who?"

"A certain intellectual editor I spent the morning with." She twirls around and lands on a beanbag on the floor.

"Did someone switch out your morning coffee for love potion?" I laugh, trying to close her laptop and slide it out of view before she notices. A dull ache spreads across my face and lands in my stomach. Maybe she's caught up enough in Michael she won't notice.

"He practically kissed me in broad daylight. I thought Van was going to pass out." Palmer laughs. "Is that mine?" She tilts her head toward the Mac I've slipped under Kat's desk chair.

"Uh…" I feel the burn in my cheeks. "Yeah. Is that okay?"

"Sure. You can borrow it whenever you want. *Mi casa es su*

casa, and all my other stuff too."

"Thanks."

"Your battery die?"

"I don't know."

"Can't you find it? Want me to help you look?" Palmer stands, wobbles a little, and scans the room. She picks up a throw pillow off the futon, looks under it, and puts it back in place.

"It's not lost."

"Okay." Palmer slides next to me where I sit crisscross, leaning against the legs of Kat's desk. "What happened?"

How does she always know something's happened? My mom never knew. Still doesn't. But Palmer...she sees through me like I'm cellophane. "I sold it." I stare at her knees.

"Why?" Palmer strokes my hair, which is wadded in a sloppy bun.

"I needed to pay a fee for next semester at the registrar's office."

"What about your scholarship?" Palmer's cool fingers slide slowly from my scalp to where my hair is knotted, then start at my scalp again.

"It's good." I bite my lip. "The scholarship pays for classes, room, and books." I lift my head a little. "But there are all these crazy charges the scholarship doesn't cover, like registering for class and my student ID, my locker at ballet, which I would skip if it were up to me. I don't mind toting things around, but every dancer's required to have one, so that's another forty-five dollars."

"It adds up." Palmer tilts her head.

I nod. I think of all the other things that add up, pizza and coffees and things my roommates don't ever pause about before sliding their debit cards, only my balance is nonexistent.

"Won't your mom help you with all that?"

I take in a sharp breath.

"I'm not trying to push, Claire. Or sound obnoxious. I know I totally take for granted what I have. I'm not trying to be nosy either. Just trying to understand. I clearly have no idea how your scholarship works or how much your mom's helping. What can I do?"

"Nothing." I swallow, looking up to catch the tears forming in the corners of my eyes. But it doesn't work. One spills down my right cheek. I feel its heat as it bounces down my face. "I started on that paper as soon as Hannah left to meet Nate. I wrote as fast as I could. I didn't mean to..." But none of what I say matters. "I'm sorry."

"For what?" Palmer snuggles in closer. She smells like the cold morning air and peppermint.

"I didn't even ask you." I nod toward the MacBook.

"You can use it whenever you want." Palmer waves her hand in the air. "But let's figure out your expenses. Did you get enough for your computer to pay them?"

I nod, but there's a ripping sensation in my sides as I consider trying to pay for anything else that comes up and how I'll get through the rest of college without a computer.

"Okay." Palmer shifts her weight. "Do you have any more fees, or is that all of them?"

"Mostly it." *Except my counselor fees*, I think to myself. But those aren't a necessity, although it makes me shaky thinking I can't go to a session. I could really use a long talk with Amy.

"You look like there's something else." Palmer narrows her eyes.

I hug my knees to my chest.

"What is it?'

I won't tell her about Amy, but there is more. I look back at her. "Might as well get it all out. I've been meaning to tell you, but didn't know how. I can't go on spring break with you. I'm really sorry." I pull one bobby pin out, then another and another, letting my hair tumble along my shoulders like my problems.

"Of course you can." She shakes her head.

"I..." I yank a stubborn pin from the left side of my head. "I paid what I owe, but I don't have anything left."

"Spring break is covered, silly." Palmer waves her hand again, dismissing the thought. "We're staying in my parents' condo. They'll take care of all the food and drinks, and we already booked our plane tickets."

"Right." I reach up and lay the bobbies side by side on the top of Kat's desk. "My mom said she booked mine, but she didn't. I talked to her again today. I got her new cell number from Aunt Denise. Apparently instead of paying what she owed on our old phones, Mom got a new phone for herself on some promo, but nothing for me. Thanks, Mom." I shrug. "Anyway, I called her from Hannah's phone, and she actually picked up. I think I caught her early enough she was off guard. After I sold my laptop, I realized I didn't have the confirmation or anything for the flight because she was supposed to message me, so I called her to get it. And she acted like it was some big mix up that she'll straighten out, but she won't." There it is. Out in the open. All Palmer has to do is connect the dots.

"Did she at least apologize? What the heck! Here." She holds out her phone. "Call her back and get her to book now."

I look down.

Voices of dormmates echo down the corridor.

"She's not going to pay?"

I nod.

"She's not going to pay for anything for you?"

I nod again, my stomach in a tangled coil. This is too much to throw at Palmer. I was trying to solve this on my own.

"Okay," Palmer whispers. Then louder, she says, "Okay. No problem. I'll book your plane ticket right now. And we'll need to get you a new laptop too. I think they have some used ones at the bookstore."

"You can't." I look up. "I don't want to be your charity case." My voice sounds as gritty as I feel, scratching its way up my throat. "You cannot buy me a laptop. It would make me feel sick."

"You are my roommate, and I love you." Palmer slides her Visa Gold from her purse. She puts her hands on my shoulders and stares directly into my eyes. "I'm not trying to sound stuck-up, but this isn't anything to me or to my parents.

Okay?" She pats my shoulders twice. "I don't want to brag, but Dad has plenty. To share. Really. So much he's not even sure what to do with it. And he knows how much I love you. He'd be happy to help. I know he would. But, Claire, what happened to your mom?"

"I d-don't know." I look to the ceiling. "She does this sometimes. She gets sick of how things are."

"And just stops being a mom? Just stops paying for anything or doing anything for you?"

"It's so weird to explain. She just takes on crazy projects or obsessions." I wind my hair around my finger, not sure how to word this.

"Hannah always has some crazy project." Palmer laughs.

I smile. "She does, doesn't she? But Mom's not like that. Hannah's cute. Mom's neurotic or something. This sounds silly."

Palmer shakes her head. "Go on."

"She gets an idea and sinks all of our money into her fantasy and kind of goes off by herself. This time, to be honest, she sounded high as a kite."

"Oh." Palmer's lips linger on the word. "Got it. So she does this a lot?"

"She goes inside her head somewhere, maybe with meds, she said something about a prescription that makes me way nervous. She's done that before. Or sometimes it's about men. She's always searching for her new soul mate, for someone to fill in all the gaps in her life, all of her emptiness." The words are pouring out faster than I'd intended them to. "It's not always guys. It might be late-night parties, dance clubs, or outrageous spending sprees. Every once in a while it's an actual great idea. Like one time she was going to make jewelry. She's actually good at it, but she spent a load of cash on beads and clasps and then gave up on it before she sold five necklaces. Mom lets these obsessions consume her. I know this makes no sense." I feel my ribcage expand with my breath.

"She's a teacher, for crying out loud. What does she do about work?"

"Yeah." I rock back and forth, still holding my knees close. "She's kind of got a system. She saves up her sick days. She gets over ten a year. On good years she doesn't use any of them and banks them, like saving for a rainy day." I roll my eyes. "When she crashes, she has people who cover for her. There's one teacher at her school who's been asking her out since I was twelve. I think Mr. Baze thinks she'll say yes if he covers for her. She switched schools when I was nine. I've always suspected she left because they were starting to figure her out. And her best friend is kind of neurotic too. They feed on each other."

Palmer's eyes are as wide as the bagels they serve at Bagels R Us.

"TMI?"

"Wow," is all Palmer says.

"Pretty much."

Palmer slides her laptop out from where I've stashed it, clicks through some screens, smacks it with the heel of her hand when the Delta Airlines site makes her reenter all of our travel info again, and finally announces, "Your flight is booked. We're halfway there. Should we head to the bookstore?"

"No, just promise to let me borrow your laptop when I need one?" I loop my arm in Palmer's. "Thanks for everything. I mean it."

"You are so welcome. Really. Having my Claire Bear with me on spring break is a very worthy cause. Dad would be disappointed if you weren't there for me. But your mom? Should you go home and check on her?"

"I thought about it." I look down, the familiar feeling of guilt creeping over me. "I did. But it's ten hours round trip, I have two mid-terms next week and the bus fare is more than I have. And honestly? I don't know if I can deal with it, with her. I feel stuck. Like I can't move, Palm." The tears I'd chased away earlier come back. "What am I going to do?"

14
PALMER

"SUN AND SURF, HERE WE come!" I call, rolling my suitcase out of our bedroom and setting it by the door. "I have been crazy stressed between all of the papers for class and getting my spring break article submitted for *QuadAngles*. It's time to unwind. I can hear the waves calling my name." I close my eyes, picturing the view outside our condo.

"Palmer," Kat whispers in a misty voice. "Palm-er."

"Huh?" I open my eyes, hating to leave the peaceful image but knowing I'll see the ocean in person later today. "You all set? We should head to the airport in a couple of minutes."

"I'm set. I just need to grab Chester." Kat shrugs. "He goes everywhere with me. Hey, Claire. Need any help with anything?"

"I think I'm good." Claire emerges with an oversized hobo bag strung across her back.

"Swimsuit?" I ask.

She nods.

"Flip-flops, jean shorts, at least one sundress?"

She keeps nodding, but her eyes seem to be quizzing herself.

"Just about anything else we have at the beach house, like

towels and sunscreen and toothpaste and stuff. How about underwear?"

"Oops!" Claire's laugh is light and airy, like her small, feather-like body.

Kat snorts, and I laugh too.

"What did I miss?" Hannah comes in the door. "Oh, Kat, Chester is so adorbs!"

"Thanks." Kat clutches her bear to her chest. "I love this guy."

"I almost forgot to pack undies!" Claire giggles from our room.

"That would be bad." Hannah snorts. "I'm totally freaked that I'll do something like that. And in Germany I won't be able to just run to the store and get some. What kind of underwear do they even wear in Berlin? And how in the world would I ask for it?"

"Leather studded, I think." Kat raises an eyebrow.

Hannah's face flushes pink and her eyes widen.

"Kidding." Kat nudges her.

I inhale. I've been trying so hard not to say it, to be happy for her, but I can't hold it any longer. "I wish you were coming to the beach."

"Thanks." Hannah gives me a quick squeeze. "But I am sooo excited about Germany. With Nate. Can you believe I'm really getting a chance to go to Europe? I've always wanted this. I actually have Euros in my purse! And, yes, I dreamed it would be on a gondola in Venice, but Germany's hip, right? Isn't it supposed to be funky and cool?"

"It's all that." Kat nods.

Funky and *cool* are not words to describe Hannah. And she has obviously forgotten that we were supposed to go to Europe together, the two of us.

"And to spend an entire week hand in hand with Nate, without the distractions of all our other classes or his roommate," she clucks.

But the unsaid sinks in my heart. "Or your roommates." I fill in the space.

There's a moment of silence that feels like an hour. She doesn't correct me fast enough. Doesn't deny it.

"I don't mean that, silly," Hannah finally says, shaking her head. "I'll miss you all like crazy."

"Doesn't really sound like it." My voice is sharp and I turn to enter the bathroom.

"That is so not fair!" Hannah says. "I finally have a boyfriend. Finally, after how long? Oh yeah, I remember, always. And now you're jealous. I held your hand through every spat with Keegan."

I freeze and pivot back to face her.

"I forgave you every time you canceled a tennis match or a coffee date with me so you could be with him, waited 'two secs' every time you took a call from him while we were talking, and now a really smart, totally together guy likes me, *me*! And you're jealous? So not fair, Palm."

Footsteps thud softly on the ceiling from the room above us. Hannah stands immobile. I don't even think she's blinking.

"You're right. You did all that for me." I swallow. "But that's now what I'm talking about, Han, and you know it." I wave my hands in the air, unable to connect them with anything concrete. My entire body feels like it might pop to pieces like a balloon that's been overblown with air. I hate fighting with Hannah. Hate it. But I can't believe she's not coming. Or how she just dug at my wounds. This trip to the beach was supposed to be a special time for the four of us. Surely she understands how disappointed I am.

Kat does a wall sit watching the timer on her phone. Claire fishtails her hair. But they don't say a word.

"Then what is are you so upset about?" Hannah puts her hands on her hips. Her voice quavers. "None of you guys are happy for me!"

"Nate seems great," Kat grunts.

"I'm happy for you," Claire says, weaving more strands over and under each other, but doesn't look up.

"I am too!" I shout. "I'm glad you met Nate. I really, really am. I know how badly you wanted a boyfriend, but…" My voice sounds horrible and thin. "This is spring break, Hannah. A whole week where we could all be together. Roomie time. I thought you loved that. No tests. No papers. No meetings. Just us. Kat could have gone with the soccer girls or home and hung out with Nicholas. It wasn't easy for Claire to go either. But *we* all made it work. And…" I feel a pull on my vocal chords, like they are harp strings being plucked. "And"—I force out the syllables—"I want you to be there."

"Don't turn this on me." Hannah stamps her foot. "Just because perfect Palmer didn't get her way, don't turn it on me." She's beet red and her freckles look like they're about to attack me. Her words already have.

"Forget it." I turn again and slam the bathroom door behind me before she can see my tears.

15
HANNAH

MY BODY FEELS TINGLY, A bit off balance, like when my foot falls asleep. It's like I want to eat something or say something, maybe do jumping jacks, but all I can do is stand here, trying to focus on what our group leader is saying. We've been in Germany for approximately three hours, which were spent going through customs at the airport, taking the train into the city, getting checked into our hotel, and assembling here with our group. The whole thing is a sleep-deprived blur of lines and luggage, but now Nate stands beside me and gives me a private smile as he lifts his head.

I smile back, even though I have no idea what he found funny or ironic or interesting. He's clearly grinning at something our guide said. If only my current attention span was longer than a millisecond. If only I could cut through this screen that seems to be separating me from the rest of reality. But his dimples get me every time. He has this totally smart, serious accountant look and then flashes those dimples. Sigh.

I strain to understand how the subway works and what our lights-out policy is, but I'm certain I read all of this in the brochure before I ever boarded the plane.

"Everyone understand?" the round woman with a floral

knit dress, dark tights, sensible shoes, and an ill-fitted coat asks.

Our crowd of twenty or so Clarkston students nods and murmurs.

"Hungry?" Nate asks.

"I think so." I laugh.

Nate takes my hand in his, like we've always been together, like this is how it is. I've been waiting for a boyfriend my whole life. I've imagined every scenario possible. It's easy for me to slide into my role.

"I'm starved. Let's rush to that bakery she talked about before everyone else is in line." He leads me down the street

I wish I knew what bakery he's talking about, but I'm grateful we're going together. I shut my eyes tight and take two steps with them closed, then force them open again. "I had no idea what people meant by jet lag. I don't even know if I feel sleepy. It's more like completely zoned out."

"Yeah, that three or four hours of on again/off again sleep didn't really cut it." He laughs. "That's why God invented coffee."

"Thank You, God." I look upward. The sky is thick with gray clouds, but I know somewhere up there God is watching. And Nate believes in Him? Another plus, as if he needed any more.

Nate guides me to a crosswalk.

"Oh my goodness." I laugh. "Look at the crosswalk guy!" I point to the profile of a green man wearing a fedora where I'd see a stick figure or the word WALK in America. "I love that guy. Totally love him! Did you know he was going to be on the crosswalk sign?"

"No." Nate shakes his head and laughs lightly.

Even once we're across the street, I strain my neck to keep an eye on the guy until he turns to red.

The bakery is a welcome rush of light and warmth from the gray chill of the Berlin air. Three students got here before us. I'd never seen them before last night at the airport. They must be from a different section of Dr. Wheeler's class. I gaze into the case at all of the decadent choices. My flip-floppy stomach begs me to be gentle.

I point. "Look at those pretzels. They're perfect. What could be more German than a giant pretzel?"

"Sounds good," Nate says.

The girl behind the counter looks to be about my age, but she has short, spiky black hair with white tips and tattoos running up and down both arms. She says something in sharp consonants to me.

"Two pretzels please," I say, pointing to the case. "Oh, and do you have anything like a Frappuccino here?" Before she answers I turn to Nate. "What kind of coffee do you like?"

Do I really not know what coffee he orders?

My body doesn't feel like it's attached to itself. A strange tugging at the back of my ears and an odd swirling in my stomach seem unrelated yet both seem pressing. Nate nudges me. "Huh?" I turn to see the girl looking at me as if I've said nothing.

"Frappuccino?" I repeat, louder this time.

More sharp sounding words and she shakes her head.

"I'm sorry." I look down at my Sperry's. "Okay. I'm really, really sorry, but I don't speak any German. I wish I did. I just don't. I took Spanish. And I tried to listen to a German podcast thingy, but I only did it two or three times, because I ran out of time with all the other planning for this trip." My words spill from my mouth in a tumble. The line is growing behind us. Nate takes my arm, gently.

"*Zwei Bretzeln bitte.*" Nate holds up two fingers, then points to the pretzels in the case. "*Zwei Kaffee bitte.*" He holds up two fingers again, then points to the espresso machine behind the counter.

She grunts and nods, stuffing pretzels in a paper bag and presenting us quickly with coffees that took no time to make. I have no idea how much she says I owe. My body is tense as I fumble for my purse.

Nate takes the bag, says, "*Danke,*" and hands her a twenty Euro note. He gathers his change and me, and ushers me to the side.

"Okay, that was so embarrassing. I am totally unprepared for this." Tears of frustration sting my eyes. "I can't speak German. I can't even order a coffee. How much do I owe you? I thought they'd speak English in Berlin. Everything I read said we didn't *need* to know German." I exhale, trying to catch my breath. "This is an epic fail. Why did I think I could do this?"

"We're on the other side of the world. It's going to be different." Nate's voice is soft and reassuring. "It's no big deal, Hannah." He slides out a chair for me. "Eat something and you'll feel better."

I nod and sit, feeling like I'm four years old at McDonald's, waiting for my parents to put my straw in my cup and open my bag of apple slices for me. I take a bite of pretzel and another and another.

"I told you we were starving. Didn't know how much until right now. If the line slows down, we'll grab another one to go. We have"—Nate looks at his watch—"about fifteen minutes before we have to meet back."

"When did you learn German?" I ask, holding my Styrofoam cup with shaking hands. I raise my cup to my mouth and— "Blech." My tongue curls at the bitterness. "Definitely not a Frappuccino," I snarl.

"Nope." Nate laughs at me. "But it's warm and it's caffeine. Chock it up to an adventure." He swallows some of his. "Very bad. And I don't speak German. Not really. I just downloaded some e-lessons from the university library and have been listening to them in my earbuds while I walk to classes. I learned enough to count to five and say thank you."

"Sounded like you knew more than that." I lean into him.

A tall, lanky guy shuffles with the chair at the table next to us. I look up. I'm pretty sure he's with our group. The chair won't seem to move right for him, and his body doesn't seem to want to fold itself properly in the seat, but the guy has a smile on his angular face and he seems to sway a little back and forth.

"Are you from Clarkston?" I ask.

"Yes." He smiles and nods.

"I'm Nate." Nate stands and puts out his hand.

"I'm George," the boy says, smiling and nodding some more.

"I'm Hannah." I smile and shake his hand. His grip is cold and bony, but friendly. "I don't recommend the coffee."

"I don't drink coffee," he says without excuses.

"Lucky you. I don't think it's going to be very good on this trip. Let's just say I miss Corner Cup, a lot, and we just got here."

"I like this trip. I like Germany. I like World War II. Very interesting." From anyone else his staccato responses would seem curt, but George's face is pleasant, not strained in the least.

"We're in Germany." I laugh. "How crazy is that?"

16
KAT

"YOU BROUGHT A SOCCER BALL to the beach?"
Palmer's question is more of an accusation. She tightens the
elastic in her hair and stares at my ball.

"I bring it everywhere." I shake my head. She doesn't get
it. Clearly. "Not to mention, the day we get back, official
practice starts."

"You workout with the team every single day. This is
vacation. We're supposed to relax." She finishes off her
ponytail, flipping the end out of the elastic where it hangs
perfectly.

"Right." I nod. "But all the girls from the team who went
to Courtney's mountain house for break will be playing every
day. Don't get me wrong. I'd much rather be here. Couldn't
stand the pressure there anyway, but I need to keep up, ya
know? Plus, I bet you brought your journal."

"Touché." Palmer snorts and turns back to her beach bag,
unrolling a towel. "But that's relaxing for me."

"And this"—I hold up my ball—"is soothin' for my

soul."

"Fair enough."

"It's so pretty!" Claire squeals. "I've never been to a real beach before. It's amazing. Like you see on TV, and you think it looks unbelievable, but TV does not do it justice. There's something in the air. It actually feels different and smells different. I had no idea you could hear it like this." Claire closes her eyes and spins in a circle with her arms outstretched.

"You've never been to the beach?" Palmer asks. "Ever?"

"I mean, we have 'beaches'"—Claire makes quotation marks with her fingers—"in Cleveland, but that's Lake Eerie, and, well, that's like saying you've eaten bread before when you've had a slice of Wonder Bread and then you eat a baguette baked fresh in a Paris *boulangerie*. So not the same thing!"

"There are beaches on Lake Eerie?" Palmer peers over her shades.

"You've never been to Kelleys Island?" Claire asks without taking her gaze from the ocean.

"Uh, no." Palmer shrugs.

"I have to admit, I had no idea there were beaches on lakes, let alone in Ohio. We always drove over to Hilton Head growing up," I say.

"How long have your parents owned this place?" Claire asks, flopping herself on a wooden lounge chair.

"Forever." Palmer straightens the strap on her bikini. "It's a bit dated. I keep telling them stainless-steel appliances would look gorgeous in the kitchen and a flat screen would be killer mounted on the wall in the great room, but they're perfectly content with that dinosaur of a TV in there."

"Who watches TV at the beach?"

"That's what my dad always says." Palmer shakes her

head at me. "But it would be great for movies."

"I think everything about this place is already great."
Claire fingers the wooden planks on her chair. "And who
needs movies? I could stare at the ocean forever."

"I'm with Claire." I drop my ball, catch it on the top of
my foot, and repeatedly hit it in the air. "This beach is
awesome, Palm. And your house looks like it came from a
reality show."

"Exactly!" Claire chimes in.

"Thanks." Palmer's teeth sparkle as she smiles. "I am a
total beach girl." She sighs and looks around. "It such a
beautiful place, almost separate from the rest of reality. It
almost makes me forget about everything else, like classes and
papers and deadlines. Do I sound dorky?"

"No." Claire turns her gaze to the horizon where Palmer
is focused and gets a dreamy look in her already dreamy light
blue eyes. "You sound poetic."

"I might have gone with dorky, but okay."

"Hey," Palmer calls.

I laugh and turn from my roomies to the object of their
distraction.

The scene hits me hard. The insane beauty of it. I guess
we've been going nonstop since we left our dorm this
morning—from the dorm to the airport, from the airport to
the car rental, from the car rental to Palmer's parents' house.
Even when we got here it was a flurry of activity: the grand
tour of the mansion, picking out rooms, stocking the fridge,
getting slightly settled. But now we're out here on the beach.
And it is spectacular. Sand stretches in both directions creating
endless pathways to kick and juggle the ball. But beyond that is
ocean that goes on forever.

Maybe I should say something. Comment on the view.

Ask about our plan for the rest of the day. But I'd rather soak this in. So I stand while the sunlight prickles my arms and shoulders, giving me goose bumps despite the radiating warmth.

I'm not good at standing still for very long. After a moment I say to no one or anyone, "It feels so darn good to be outside, with all this space. Pass with me?" My words seem to disappear into the breeze.

Claire shakes her head. "It does feel great. I've been freezing for as long as I can remember." She leans back in her chair and pulls her sunglasses over her eyes. "I need to just sit and soak the warmth. This feels heavenly."

"Me too. How would it help you to pass with us anyway, Kat? You know neither of us are any match for you."

"I don't need you to be a match. Every time I get a touch on the ball, my skills improve. What do you say?" She holds up her ball.

"Maybe later. I need to veg. But, yay! It's so perfect with you guys here," Palmer says, but her eyes look distant. I'm pretty sure she's still mad at Hannah, or actually wounded by her, but I so don't want to get in the middle of one of their spats. Claire tried to get Palmer to walk down to Hannah's gate at the airport, but it was in a separate international terminal. Later, I nudged her to just text a quick, "I'm sorry," to Hannah. But Palmer wouldn't have any part in it. Sometimes those two act like an old married couple.

Palmer pulls out a magazine, then sets it down and looks out at the water. "It looks like you could swim and swim and swim forever in there and never get to the end."

"Maybe that's what Alex is doing." The words pop out before I have a chance to filter them. I imagine Alex's muscled shoulders pulling out over the waves again and again doing the butterfly stroke. "He would love that. That would be his version of heaven." I don't give Palmer or Claire a chance to respond; instead, I let my ball fall to the sand and weave in and out with it, finding a rhythm, testing my agility, my ability to control it in the dense sand. I lose myself in concentration with my ball. It's just the leather sphere, speckled with stars, and me on a quest to disconnect and reconnect over and over again.

The ball rolls more slowly on the soft sand. When it hits a patch flattened by waves, it flies. I dodge a sand castle under construction, avoiding the brightly colored shovels and buckets of twin toddler girls wearing matching pink butterfly swimsuits. I splash through the shallowest of water as the ball threatens to go for a dip. The ocean is cold, sending a zing up my legs. I feel the thrill of beating the ball and knocking it back to the dry zone before it ventures too far. I zigzag around a couple of guys tossing a Frisbee.

"Hey," one of them shouts, snapping me out of the zone.

Did I get too close? Upset their game? I trap my ball under my bare foot.

"Sorry."

"For what?" the guy with sideburns holding the Frisbee says.

"For..." I search their faces, still absorbed enough in my personal game that I'm not sure if I bumped someone or not. "For however I messed y'all up."

"You didn't mess us up a bit," the blonde in a neon yellow swimsuit with two black stripes on one leg offers in a drawl that sounds like home.

"All right." I lean into my ball, still not sure why they called out to me. Not even sure which one of them hollered "hey."

The one with the sideburns speaks again. "You're good."

He looks down at my foot. "Excellent ball control."

"Thanks." I smile.

"Wanna toss with us?" The third guy, the one with dark brown skin wearing a backward baseball cap and a white and gray plaid suit, smiles at me.

"Well," I start. "I can tell y'all are from someplace spectacular by the way y'all talk, so you've got that goin' for ya."

Sideburns guy laughs.

"But I don't use my hands to toss. Just my feet." I kick the ball up in the air, right to the guy in plaid.

He catches it with both hands before it hits his chest.

"Handball!" I call.

17
CLAIRE

"COME ON, LET'S GET IN." Palmer nudges me. I must have dozed a little in the sun.

"Okay." I slide off my tank top, cut-off shorts, and flip-flops, piling them onto the lounge chair.

"You look sick in a bikini." Palmer stares at me.

"What?" I look down at myself, conscious of how pale my skin is. "Oh gosh. I know I'm white as a ghost. My skin has not seen sun in forever."

"Not that, but now that mention it, you better use some sunscreen. I mean, you have an amazing body, Claire. It's so unfair. My mom is all over me to lose weight. She's constantly giving me these little not-so-subtle hints, like the care package she sent me of Slim-Fast bars. But even if I watch what I eat I'll never look like you." She shakes her head.

I laugh. "Maybe you should join my therapy group. Are you serious? Why would you need to lose any weight? You are the prettiest girl on our entire campus. About twenty guys have had to pick up their jaws off the sand since we got here, what, fifteen minutes ago."

"Which guys?" Palmer looks around. "Seriously, what size are you?"

"Hello." I put my hand on my chest. "Girls' sizes. I don't even need a bra, I just wear one so you can't see through my shirts. You are the envy of every girl at Clarkston. You're perfect just how you are."

Palmer sighs loudly and leans toward me. "Girls? As in, before juniors? You are perfect, Claire Bear." She kisses the top of my head. "In every way. But you are going to fry."

"Can I borrow your lotion?" I ask. "Pretty sure I didn't bring any."

"Here." She hands me a tube of delicious-smelling cream for my body, which I take time rubbing on everywhere I can reach. Palmer gets my shoulders and back for me like my mom used to do when I was little. The thought of my mom makes me want to scream and cry simultaneously.

Where is she now? Maybe popping pills and bouncing around like a firecracker. Or maybe curled up in her bed, though it's hard for me to picture her bedroom. Even though I spent a few days over the summer and Christmas break at her new place, I spent most of summer at my aunt's in Detroit. Mom's apartment is just a beige and cream smudge in my mind. I wish I could hold her small hand in mine or give her a hug of reassurance. Although I'm experienced enough to know it probably wouldn't help. In the past she's been despondent for days, sometimes weeks, until she isn't. And then one day I wake up and she's already up and dressed and drinking a Monster or a Rockstar like it never happened. How many days has it been since I've heard from her? How many more will it be?

Palmer gives me another, smaller tube. "This one's for

your face. It has moisturizer and an SPF of 50 and won't cause breakouts."

"Do you need me to lotion you?" I ask.

"Nope. I did it before we came out. I don't like putting it on in front of people. Makes me self-conscious. Here, you just need a little dab, like this." Palmer squirts a drop onto her fingertip and starts rubbing my cheeks.

"Thanks," I say as her fingertip and the cool cream tickles my face.

"There." Palmer looks at me approvingly. A look like that from Palmer makes me forget I've never been to the beach before or that my skin is bleached white. I can't believe she has any self-doubts. She makes most of mine disappear.

"You ready?" She steps forward, and we walk toward the waves.

The closer we get, the louder they sound, the bigger they seem. A wave rushes toward us and grabs hold of my toes. "Oh!" I squeal, jumping at the chill and the tug.

"A little chilly." Palmer laughs. She skips in up to her calves, giggling the whole time. "We should grab the boogie boards later."

I smile, not sure what she's talking about, and take another cautious step, twitching as another wave collides with my feet. "There aren't any waves on Lake Eerie," I say, having to raise my voice so Palmer can hear me against the sea.

The waves whistle a mysterious soundtrack accentuated by an occasional shout from one friend to another or a squawk from a seagull.

"Makes sense." Palmer sighs, closes her eyes, and dunks under. She's gone for a second, then two, then three. *Please come out please come out.*

Pop!

She emerges, laughing and wiping her face. "It feels *so* good. Come on, your turn."

I look down at my feet. Somehow I've inched up to where the water hits my knees. Another wave shoots toward me, and something bumpy and rough brushes my leg along with the water. I step quickly to the side. "Something just touched me. What was that?"

"You all right?" Palmer asks, rolling her neck.

"I don't know." I look down, trying to figure out what touched me. "A jellyfish? A shark? Are there sharks here? I should have never watched *Soul Surfer*."

Palmer laughs and smoothes her hair out of her face. "Probably seaweed. No sharks. I mean, I guess it could happen. But I've only seen one or two ever."

"You've seen sharks here!" I step backward, my eyes glued to the water. "I can't believe you didn't tell me." I'm breathing too fast and only exhaling. *Inhale,* I remind myself. I grab a giant breath of air, but my pulse is still bump-bumping. I feel so childish, but I can't control my panic. Big girls can swim in the ocean. I can do this, but I feel so small, so unable to stop the swirling that encircles me.

"It's okay, Claire. Only two, and they were baby sharks. Dead ones, washed up from a storm. It's been years, I promise. It's safe, okay?" Palmer holds out her hand to me just as another crest of foam looms behind her.

I grab her hand for support, and maybe not just from the ocean, as the wave careens into us, making my legs feel wobbly.

"Wheeee!" Palmer shouts.

18
HANNAH

"NOT TO BE YOUR MOM, but, Hannah, I really think you should be getting up."

Umm, but you do sound like my mom, I think. *And if you're not, who are you?* I open my eyes from a dark, hard, deep sleep and it feels like a whole other world is pulling me back into its tunnels.

Rachel, the large girl with navy eyeliner around her pretty gray eyes, tilts her head at me. She and two other girls named Laney and Allie are the roommates I was assigned for the week. I was so exhausted from the all-night flight and the all-day tour yesterday that when we got back to our room after dinner, I crashed. Apparently hard.

"What time is it?" I search the room desperately for a clock.

"Seven thirty-eight. Laney and I are going to breakfast. Thought you'd want to know. I tried to wake up Allie, but it's no use."

"Seven thirty-eight?" I fling my covers back, feeling like

I'm on a reality show, where I wake up in a foreign country and someone has swapped out my roommates. My hand slides under my pillow for my phone, craving a connection with Palmer, Kat, and Claire.

"Umm. Like, we're going to breakfast now." Laney, tall and pale, with an angular face and a severe bun, scowls.

"Sorry." I jump up, phone in hand, and climb quickly down the ladder from the top bunk. "I can't believe how tired I was from traveling. What time is it back home? Like, two thirty in the morning! Yikes! I've never seen this side of two thirty before. I'm usually an early riser. Really. Give me five minutes and I'll be ready for breakfast." I don't know these girls. They needed a fourth, and, well, I needed a first, second, and third.

"Fine." Rachel sighs as she looks at Laney, who rolls her eyes.

Allie snores in the other top bunk.

I grab a pair of jeans and a long sweater and, feeling self-conscious, turn my back to the girls as I tug my clothes on as quickly as my half-asleep limbs will allow me. I'm used to changing in front of roommates. Roommates I know, trust, and love. I can walk around in my bra and underwear in front of them, and often do as we scurry to get ready, but here I feel awkward and obvious. Was it this weird last year, when we first moved in together? Couldn't have been.

Barely a minute later, fully dressed and frizzy hair pulled into a tight, low, hopefully cute bun, I nudge Allie, because apparently Laney and Rachel are content to leave her here. I thought they were all friends. "Wake up, girl. Germany awaits. We have to report to group in thirty minutes, but who can tour without food? We're going to grab breakfast first." She doesn't even bat a thick silver eyelash. "Come on."

"Catcha later," she mumbles and rolls toward the wall.

"Let's go," Laney says, turning the handle of the door.

"Almost. Really, I'll be fast. I haven't used my five minutes yet." I grab my makeup bag. "I just need to brush my teeth and swipe on mascara. It'll take a millisecond. Truly."

Rachel smiles tightly. Sheesh! She took time to put on makeup. I race down the hall to the community bathroom. Is this how Claire feels every morning as I wait for her at the door?

I scrub my face and teeth in a flurry. Give myself a quick brush of blush and—*ouch!*—gouge my eye with the mascara wand. *Ay yi yi!* I desperately try to blot my eye with a rough paper towel from the dispenser.

"For cryin' out loud!" I yell at the mirror. "I so do not have time for this."

Smudges removed, Great Lash reapplied, and lip gloss and gum in my pocket, I rush out of the bathroom to our room, toss my makeup bag on top of my suitcase, and jog down the hall to the top of the stairs where Rachel and Laney reluctantly wait for me. Beads of sweat spring along my hairline. Laney stares at her thick, bulky, military-style watch.

"Sorry, guys, really. I'm feeling way out of sorts here. I'm usually the one who wakes up my roommates. Aren't you wiped from the travel?" I ask as we head down the stairs.

"Not as bad as last year's trip to Prague. We had a five-hour layover in Paris that wasn't long enough to sleep, but so long, I thought I'd die," Laney says in a slow, low voice, drawing out the words *Prague* and *Paris* to make sure I know where she's been.

"Actually, it was almost six hours. And when we finally arrived, there was that huge mix-up with the charter bus. Remember?" Rachel laughs.

"What was it? Another two hours before they actually got that straightened out and we could leave the airport?" We enter the cafeteria, and Laney grabs a tray and loads it with a bowl, spoon, coffee cup, and napkin. I follow suit.

"You two went to Prague?" I chirp.

They both nod.

"I've heard it's beautiful," I try again.

"It's gorgeous." Laney emphasizes the "gor."

"Berlin is way better, though." Rachel grabs a box of muesli and pours it into her bowl.

"It is?" I ask, trying to keep up with the conversation and the cafeteria line.

"Please." Laney laughs, setting down her tray.

"This is my first time out of the U.S.," I confess. "I want the scoop. Details please. How is Germany better?"

"For one thing, the muesli." Rachel holds up her spoon.

The cereal is tasty. I'll have to tell my real roommates about it. Although I'm sure it doesn't match the crepes Claire ate in France or the churros Kat ate in Barcelona. It still makes a good story. I snap a picture of my bowl.

"Did you just post your breakfast?" Laney asks.

"I will, when I return to the modern world of the Internet." I smile.

"You turned off too?" Rachel says, reaching back and pushing on her bun as if to make sure it's still tight.

I nod.

"What did you say your major was again?" she asks.

"Elementary ed."

"Really?" Rachel looks astonished.

"Really."

Laney stares at me, actually looks down at me from her lofty view, and slugs her coffee, which I noticed she drinks black, which is just gross.

"How about you?" I'm trying here.

"International studies," they say in unison. Duh.

"How about Allie? I don't know her very well, but she's in my section of world studies. She sits in the back, so we've never really chatted. What section are you two in?"

"Allie's international studies too." Laney purses her lips. "She was in Prague last year, but she says she's only international because she's sick of the guys at Clarkston and wants to meet foreign guys."

"We're in the two o'clock class." Rachel takes another bite of muesli.

"We have about three minutes," Laney announces after looking at her watch. Again. "Apparently she's off to a good start too. I think she came in around four."

"Who? Allie?"

"You crashed early. Missed it all."

"Is that why she had on silver mascara and boots?"

"Yup. Apparently they were for that guy, Lars, who works in the snack shop," Laney says, then glances in the direction of the snack shop, even though it hasn't opened yet for the day.

"Get out!"

"She did it in Prague too." Rachel shrugs. "To each their own."

"Should we try to wake her up again when we're finished eating?" I ask.

"Not necessary. She always finds the group." Laney twists her mouth in an odd half smile. "I don't know how, but she shows up every day, just when you think she won't. She's actually really smart."

Rachel nods. It's almost like they're Siamese twins, picking up the conversation where one leaves off. "I've got to ask, Hannah, if you're elementary ed, why did you come on this trip?"

I'm beginning to ask myself the same thing. I scan the cafeteria for Nate, but don't see him anywhere. He is here, right? "I've always wanted to travel. The trip seemed fascinating, and the timing felt right." I leave out the "I'm obsessed with Nate and he invited me" part. Where is he?

"Good for you." Laney actually smiles. So she *can* smile. "Not enough other majors venture out of their little pods, you know? Everyone should travel."

"You're going to love it. We'll show you around." Laney puts her hand on my shoulder as she stands, signaling it's time to go. And somehow I've gone from being in their bad graces for sleeping in to being in their good graces because I decided to see the world. And I'm oddly relieved, because otherwise it would be a really long week. But part of me is wishing I was at Palmer's beach house, and the other part of me is wondering where the heck Nate is. What in the world was I thinking, flying to Germany for spring break in hopes of spending time with him?

But there he is, sliding on his jacket by the door. I want to scream his name so he'll see me. Did he look for me this morning? What are his roommates like? He might know all of them. I never asked. They could be his best friends and then he wouldn't spend time with me here at all. Why didn't I ask? That must be one of them, the dark-haired guy with a beard. And next to him stands George from the coffee shop.

Laney strategizes how to get in the front of the tour group so we can hear all of the important details the guide has to offer, but I barely hear her buzzing as we dump our trash and stack our trays.

And then Nate looks up and sees me. At least I thought

he did. My heart stops. So does my breathing. And everything else. The cafeteria and the muesli and the thought of Allie staying up with Lars, me missing my roommates, and figuring out how to keep up with Laney and Rachel. I thought we locked eyes. But he zips his jacket and walks out with bearded dude and George. Right out the door.

"You all right?" Rachel asks since I'm blocking her movement out of the cafeteria.

I should tell her I saw somebody, tell them I'm here with Nate. Call out his name. But instead I nod. "Yeah. Fine."

19
PALMER

"YOU COMING?" KAT ASKS, TOSSING her string bag over her shoulder.

"A string bag to the beach?" I ask. "This isn't soccer practice."

"It could be." Kat grins.

I laugh. "No, not yet. Go ahead without me. I need to finish painting my nails."

"Before ya go to the beach?"

"What color?" Claire pads over in striped sleeping boxers and a baby blue lacy tank.

"Coral Reef." I smile, giving my baby toe the tiniest dab of color.

"Pretty." She reaches out, as if she'll touch my wet toes, which makes me hold my breath. But she just kind of wiggles her delicate fingers over them. "Bright. Beachy." She yawns, her blond waves drifting around her face.

"I have tons of colors in the bottom right drawer of the bathroom. Help yourself."

"Thanks," Claire says.

"Your beach house is stocked," Kat says.

"We've been coming here for so long, we've figured out

what's nice to have around." I move to my other foot and start with wide, easy strokes on my big toe, enjoying the bright orangey splash the brush leaves. "And with my mom, Tia, and me, nail polish definitely makes the list."

"Maybe I'll look for polish later." Claire looks from Kat to the bathroom to me. "I really need to sleep more."

"I thought it was awfully early for you." Kat nudges Claire.

"I needed the bathroom. Going back to sleep now." Claire waves, her feet barely making a noise as she retreats to her bedroom.

"Now are you ready?" Kat laughs. "You can do your nails later. We all will. We'll do a mani party. But the ocean's calling us." She pulls gently on my elbow.

I stiffen, not sure why I'm not ready to go out to the beach. Part of it is I'm half done with my nails, and half done doesn't work for me. But there's something more. I feel unsettled and antsy. "I really want to finish them before I go out." I hold up my stark fingernails.

"C'mon." Kat twirls her silver thumb ring against her index finger.

"Easy for you to say. Your nails look great."

"Thanks." She flashes her short neon purple lacquered nails, which look gorgeous against her lightly tanned skin. "But I'd go out even if they didn't."

"I can't." I shake my head. "I'm a little OCD about my nails."

"A little?" Kat laughs.

I exhale, wishing I could be as laid-back as Kat. She slept in her swimsuit for all I know and looks great. I have to work at it.

I square my shoulders. "I'm almost done. I'll meet you out there in a few. I'll be out before you're even completely lotioned up." I over-smile and wave her out the door.

"All right, then." Kat beats her rings together like drumsticks. "If you're gonna be awhile, I might could go for a quick run."

"Run for me?" I ask.

"Will do." She pulls a dirty T-shirt and a pair of shorts she wore yesterday out of the laundry basket, tugs them on over her suit, and waves. "See ya."

I finish my fingernails and listen to the eclectic mix playing from the speakers, ranging from upbeat, finger-snapping tunes to drowsy melodies of bands I'd never even heard of before I met Kat and Claire. They're so different from me. But different can be good.

I sit with my eyes closed while my nails finish drying and then Hannah's favorite song bebops through the air. I wonder how Germany's going. We've heard zero from her. I grab my phone and scroll through my feed. She's posted nada. Not one picture of her grand adventure. So not like her. She hasn't checked out our beach photos either. Not a single like, let alone a comment.

It's like she's fallen off the face of the earth. Did she forget us all together? If she were here, she'd sit with me while I finished my nails. She'd understand why I need to paint them. She'd probably know why I'm off kilter too. Plus, Hannah knows where everything is here. And she's the best partner in the world for flipping through magazines at the beach. Claire brought a stack of French magazines, which are virtually worthless to me, although some of the photos are gorgeous, and if Kat brought anything it's *Sports Illustrated.*

I could kill you, Hannah!

I slam my hands down on my armrests, careful to keep my nails flat and upright. I don't mean it, of course. But why did she abandon me, us, on this trip? Germany? *That was so not the plan, Han. And you, of all people, should know how important plans are. You and me, we were supposed to go to Italy between our junior and senior years. That was always the plan. Since we decided to room at Clarkston together.*

I glance at the clock. It's ten. I touch my left index finger ever so lightly with my right. When it doesn't dent or mush, I press a little firmer. Good. I switch fingers. Nice. I hold out my hands in front of me, surveying my work. The glossy coral gives me a strange sense of satisfaction, like now everything is in its place, like now I *can* go outside. I can still hang out with them if they have a mani party later. I roll my neck, loosening my muscles.

A few minutes later I stroll out to our chairs. Kat's towel is still folded in a square, as if she dropped it and ran, which knowing Kat, she did.

I spread out my towel, situate my bag, and scan the beach. Kat is nowhere in sight. Probably still running. Man, she's been through a lot. I'm glad Kat's found a coping mechanism. Claire seems to be holding it together too.

What about me? I haven't been assaulted or had anyone I love die, but sometimes I feel alone, inadequate, like a dress that doesn't fit quite right. In high school I was always the perfect size. Everything just clicked. After breaking up with Keegan, I got some of the independence, my own identity, what I thought I craved. But the truth is, I'm not always sure what to do with it. Not sure who I'm supposed to be. I think my head will explode, or maybe my heart, if I don't get some of this on paper.

I slide my fingers into my bright pink and green beach bag and finger my pink leather journal I bought to match my bag. I packed it telling myself it would be for beach moments and memories. I pull a pen out of the narrow inside pouch and glance at the waves splashing against the sand, then let my thoughts splash onto the page.

The problem with me disappearing on the crisp, clean pages of this journal is that this defines me as a writer, and a bookworm, and an intellect, which some days I long to be. A writer. I do love the sound of that. I guess I've always longed to be one. And college has been my chance, especially now with the magazine. But it's so much harder than I thought!!! And I don't really fit in there. Not really. And not fitting in gives me a flip-floppy feeling in my stomach that makes me feel like I'm going to throw up. So some days, like this day at the beach, I miss the simplicity of being the old Palmer. Is that okay to actually write down? The Palmer of perfume and lip gloss. The flirty, smiley, popular girl who was liked, well, just because.

"Well, well, well, it is my lucky day." A blond with curls

peeking out on all sides from his baseball cap and eyes that have a mischievous twinkle that I swear I've seen before plops down in Kat's chair. "It's been a long time, Palmer Ruscilli."

He rests his elbow on the armrest and rests his chin on his hand. I remember summers and spring breaks in junior high when a scrawny blond did that same thing, making him look much more serious than his boyish expression let on.

"Tristan?" I ask.

"I hear you're going to Clarkston. Right? I'm at I.U. What are the chances our spring breaks would collide?"

I sit up straighter and grin. Tristan and I have raced bikes, dived off the pier, and even kissed during a game of spin the bottle at a bonfire the summer between eighth and ninth grade. He probably doesn't remember, but I do. I remember, because we'd been buddies forever, and I'd never thought of him, well, like that.

The next morning we left for home, and although I've seen him since then, I've always been dating Keegan, so I've been a bit distant, unavailable. And last summer I never saw him. Our weeks were off. I look at his lips now, peeking behind his fingers. Are they still that soft?

"Yes, I'm at Clarkston." I close my journal and slide it back into my bag along with my pen. "Journalism major. Everyone I know at I.U. loves it. Tristan Herring. Who'd have thought?"

He laughs, a warm laugh like the sunshine. "I.U. is pretty cool. I'm here with some of my fraternity brothers. We're all staying at my parents' place."

I glance down the beach, knowing full well his parents' place is just two doors down. "Two of my roommates are with me. Claire's still asleep. And Kat went for a run."

"And you're sunbathing?" Tristan strokes his chin now.

I smile, taking him in. The sideburns he's let grow in. The I.U. shorts that hit just above his knees, which are coated with blond fuzz. These things are new, but the chin, the eyes, and that little dimple on the back of his right shoulder, as if God made a thumbprint there, are all the same. He's definitely older, but he hasn't lost that sweet charm that would make him the perfect candidate for a slot in a boys' band. If Michael is all dark shadows and serious maturity, Tristan is light, golden, and breezy.

"Where's Hannah? You're rooming with her too, right?"

"Of course." I inhale deeply, trying to suppress the anger I wish I didn't have, the jealousy that makes me feel like I'm nine, all because she picked Nate over me. "She's in Germany, some international class credit thing."

"Cool."

"I guess."

"You wanna join us?" He motions down the beach to a group of guys lounging on towels and drinking beer. Their laughter floats toward us.

Laugher seems good. So does someone who chooses to be with me.

"I don't know." I scan the shoreline for Kat, but don't see any sign of her.

"C'mon." Tristan grabs my hand, just like the night in the bonfire circle, not like he's the boss of me, or like he owns me, which is what Keegan did, but like, "I'd like you to join me."

We half walk, half jog over to his friends.

"Hey, guys. I just found an old friend." He motions toward the guys. "Palmer, these are my brothers, and, guys, this is Palmer." He bows as if presenting a princess. His cap falls to the sand, and he scoops it up in one smooth motion and fits it on top of my head.

I like the way it feels there. Freeing, playful, like it doesn't even matter what my hair looks like, although I happen to know it is perfectly straight and probably looks pretty good topped with a cap, like all those magazine spreads of girls playing at the beach who look like they didn't try, but you know makeup artists and hair stylists spent hours on them.

"Man, Tristan, *my* old friends carry fishing poles and dip," a short, round guy says.

An unsettled feeling hits me, just like at Summer's apartment. Again, I don't know who to be. It's been, what? Three, four years? I'm not sure who Tristan is now. A fraternity boy? And I'm not sure who to be around him.

"Have any more old friends?" asks a tall guy with a thick New York accent.

"Here you go, old friend." Tristan hands me a beer and grabs one for himself.

Old friend? Is that how he sees me? If so, how long it will take me to change his mind?

The can is icy cold in my hand and feels like a treat in the already hot morning sun. I'm pretty certain I don't like beer, but I pop the top anyway. It tastes terrible, but it's cold, and Tristan is telling stories about us racing our bikes on the beach and how he always had a crush on me.

"You did not!" I swat him teasingly and bat my lashes, taking another cold, bitter sip, just because it's in my hand, or maybe because I feel like a ball of nerves and I know from my recent dabbles with wine that the alcohol will help me unwind. And I could use a little unwinding.

"Right," he says. "Every guy on the beach was crushing on you, Palmer. But especially me. Why do you think I was always waiting for you?" He takes a long slug of his beer, crushes the can, and tosses it in a nearby recycling bin.

So maybe it won't take too long to erase that "old friend" label.

"I never thought about it." I tilt my head toward him. "I mean, Tia and I, or Hannah and I, or the three of us, would just bop around and sometimes, well, I guess we'd run into you a lot." Thirsty and a little distracted, I take another longer sip of the beer. Not liking, but not despising the taste. I'm surprised by how little is left.

Tristan cracks another. "You ready?" he asks handing me one.

"I'm good. It's awfully early to be drinking." I smile.

"Just early enough that we can squeeze in a nap before lunch." The guy with glasses laughs at his own joke.

"Hard to argue with that." I laugh and crack the top of my new can, the hiss filling my ear.

Tristan's friends pull out a deck of cards, and we play a few hands of Euchre. With the sun hot on my shoulders, my melancholy washes away, replaced by a silly, light feeling.

I could get used to this happy place, no worries, just laughter. My biggest concern is who has the Jack of Diamonds.

Tristan, who's my partner, lays the Jack down on the pile, slaps the card with his tanned fingers, and says tauntingly to the guys we're playing against, "Euchre!"

So I don't even have to worry about that.

20
HANNAH

GRATEFUL FOR WI-FI AT THE café, I post as many pictures to my profile as I can while Nate's in line. Agreeing to turn off calls and texts while in Germany to avoid roaming fees seemed like an easy compromise with Mom and Dad when I was begging to come here. But now I'm seriously regretting that negotiation point. It's killing me not being in touch with my roommates. There's no Wi-Fi in our dorms, and when we're out it seems like I never get a chance to connect. Roaming, schmoaming, I miss my girls.

"You would look great with bangs like that." Nate sets down our tray and points in one smooth motion to a girl with jet black, poker-straight hair and severe bangs sitting on a stool in the corner. We're at Salomon Bagels, one of the few non-chain places we could find to grab dinner at Potsdamer Platz after our long day of touring. Turns out Nate never saw me at breakfast. Why do I get so worked up about imaginary problems? He came alongside me as soon as our tour started this morning, and we've been side by side ever since. Only we haven't had much chance to talk because our tour guide keeps shushing people.

The girl is wearing an extremely short black skirt, black

tights with white zigzag designs, a Hello Kitty T-shirt under her military jacket, and clunky, lace-up combat boots. Plus a silver hoop lip ring. But she doesn't look thuggish or harsh. She's breathtaking. She oozes Euro chic, a coolness factor I've never even attempted to achieve. The uber opposite of the pulled-together preppy fashion that permeates Clarkston's campus.

"I would?" My eyes are still on the German girl, soaking in her style. I spent all of freshman year growing my bangs *out*. Now they're officially long enough to tuck behind my right ear and virtually blend into the rest of my hair. Nate never saw those bangs.

"Sure. You have such a pretty face." He brushes my hair away gently and slowly from my forehead. Bumps crawl up my arms. He thinks I have a pretty face! I've been called cute and adorable, but not pretty, unless you count by my parents.

I glance down at my bagel, needing a break from the intensity of his gaze, then look back up. "Thanks." I picture myself in her outfit and laugh. "But I would never be able to pull off that outfit. Not to mention the lip piercing makes me wince. Man, that must have hurt." But the bangs...why did I ever let mine grow out?

Nate leans back and takes a sip of his Coke. "I'm guessing a lot. Please don't get your lip pierced. Too extreme."

"Right." I take a drink of sweet soda and change the subject. "What was your favorite thing you saw this morning?"

"Everything," Nate answers. "How powerful is it that this whole area was basically obliterated by the Nazis and has been completely rebuilt into a modern mecca?"

"Wild, right? I'd imagined things to be different, I guess."

"How do you mean?"

I'm self-conscious now. Nate is a complete and total history buff. He knows more about World War II than Kat knows about soccer. I've found myself nodding. A lot. It seems a better strategy than saying something stupid. I take a bite of bagel to give me a second to formulate my sentence, trying to retrieve any knowledge I have about Germany from our textbook, my Rick Steves's guide, and some things Laney and Rachel have droned about.

"I knew about all of the old stuff. And the Brandenburg gate was exactly how I pictured it—huge, ancient, impressive, symbolic. I knew Germany was bombed and rebuilt, but there's *so* much history here. I guess I still envisioned everything old, seeped in the stories of the past. I was thinking *Schindler's List*. It's almost like the history is only in the air: you can barely see it. Like dust particles I need to reach out and grab. I actually pictured the entire city to be black and white." I lean against the hard chair back and laugh at myself. "Okay, that sounds ridiculous when I say it out loud. How could a real place be black and white." I'm starting to sound like an idiot. I've got to change gears while he's still looking at me. I put my hands down on the smooth tabletop. "Maybe it's just because I am so insanely tired. I honestly could not believe it was morning this morning, because it wasn't really. It was really the middle of the night back home. Not to mention I was sleep deprived from our lovely plane ride awake-athon. I wish I could have slept better on that flight."

Nate smiles and lays both his hands on top of mine. "They say the second day of international travel is the hardest."

"Now you tell me?"

He laughs. "Go on. I love listening to you talk." He curls his fingers around mine.

You do? My cheeks get warm. I look down at our hands and smile. If the boy likes to hear me talk, by all means, give the boy what he wants.

"Don't you think it's strange to walk down these famous streets and see Technicolor glass and steel skyscrapers instead of black and white? Not that they shouldn't have rebuilt. It just seems…" I search for a good word here. "Unbalanced. The Sony Center looks like someone pulled it out of Times Square and dropped it in Berlin."

"I think that's why it's so great." Nate gives my hands a light squeeze. I have to force myself to hear his words because it would be so easy to stay completely immersed in the warmth and pressure of his hands. "That's the symbolism. The people survived, were resilient, rebuilt. You'd think having your country divided in two by an actual physical wall would destroy you. But, no way. Not the Germans. They rebuilt with a vengeance, with a 'you can't touch this' mantra."

"Resilient," I repeat as another wave of exhaustion seems to actually crest behind me and then crash over my body, leaving me soaked in sleepiness.

"You done?" Nate asks.

With what? I wonder. With holding his hand? Never. With listening to him? He's so smart, I feel like I'm taking an entire extra class just by hanging out with him. But he's looking at our crumbs and wrappers.

"Oh, right, the bagels, yeah. All done." I gather my trash and pick someone else's wadded-up paper napkin off the floor. I take one of our clean napkins and do a little wipe down so the next customer doesn't find a glob of cream cheese or a shred of lettuce on their table. We pitch our trash in the sleek cylinder by the exit and step out into nighttime Berlin.

The cold air opens my eyes and senses. It smells like metal and cigarette smoke and exhaust fumes. I shiver, instinctively rubbing my arms and tightening the scarf I bought yesterday after realizing I was the only girl in Germany who didn't own a black patterned scarf.

"It feels great out here." Nate's face lights up like the skyscrapers.

"Yeah, it wakes you up in a hurry. I was afraid I was going to nod off in the bagel shop. No offense, just groggy. But it's a little chilly for spring break," I babble.

"That, my dear"—Nate hooks his arm in mine—"is the beauty of it. Half of Clarkston is getting loaded on some packed beach, but you and I, we're seeing the world."

The beach. I could have been there. I picture Palmer, Claire, and Kat lounged out on towels, soaking in the sun, laughing with each other. For a heartbeat I wish I could hear what they're saying, be surrounded by their laughter. Is Palmer still mad at me? Sigh. I miss them.

The hee-haw sound of German police sirens interrupts my daydream.

"The curved architecture is extremely impressive," Nate says, pointing to the endless glass of the Sony Center, but as he looks up I'm struck by the flashes of a thousand lights, like a swarm of fireflies just across the street.

"Ohmigosh!" I squeal. "It's the paparazzi. Something is going on over there. Something big. Huge, maybe." I tug Nate's arm, and sure enough a real live red carpet has been rolled out and stanchioned toward an entrance of the Sony Center.

"What do you think it is?" Nate asks.

"I don't know. A movie premiere?" I peek through the mob of dark coats, trying to see who all of the photographers are getting snaps of.

"Ohmigoshohmigoshohmigosh!" I scream now, as we've somehow gotten within view of the stanchions. "I swear it's… Dang it. Who is that?"

"Who is what?" Nate might not get why I am so excited, but he's darn good at maneuvering a crowd.

"You know her, right?" I bite the inside of my cheeks, thinking. "I've seen her in a couple of foreign films. Makes sense. We're in Germany. But she's a big deal. Why can't I remember her name?" I look away from the hype to Nate for assistance.

"I have never read a *People* magazine in my life." He holds up three fingers in a salute. "Scout's honor."

"Never? You're under oath." I slap his arm. Is it possible I might actually know more about *something* than he does? Sudden shrieks from the crowd drown my words.

The screams are for the actress, whose name I still can't remember, as she walks onto the red carpet. She pauses in front of us. I mean, in front of the throng of photographers and reporters, but we're just behind them. I stand on my tippy toes and see her in a black, sleeveless (man, she must be freezing) velvet dress. She's beautiful, in a normal way, less Hollywood than most of Hollywood, more attainable and certainly just what a girl like me needs to see. Her dress isn't glittery and the V-neck isn't so low I can see her belly button. She has on makeup, clearly, dark lips and accented brows, but she still looks like someone I might know, like someone I'd be friends with, or who would be friends with me. She looks at us, straight on, although I realize she's actually smiling for the press, and I notice her bangs. Yes, bangs.

Nate mushes his lips against my ear. "All those guys should do a one-eighty. You're way prettier than she is."

I tear my eyes from my first-ever red carpet event.

"Yeah, you should definitely do bangs." Nate brushes my hair off my face for the second time this evening and kisses me. Right here with all the paparazzi to see. I feel like a movie star. His lips are warm on my cold mouth, and his breath tastes sweet and bubbly from his soda. And I swear I hear Matt Nathanson singing in my head, "You make my heart beat faster." There's more cheering and the click of cameras and pops of flashes, and it feels like it is all for us.

21

CLAIRE

I JERK UPRIGHT AND LOOK around. Only it's hard to look around, because my hair has wrapped itself around my face. I divide it down the center with both hands and pull my curls back like curtains. A gray darkness hovers over the room, but it's not my room. Not my dorm room. Not my spacious, catalog-worthy room at my cousin's house. Not the cramped, bland room I share with Mom in her new apartment when I'm there.

My ankles are tangled in a knot of sheets. Beautiful linen sheets with light gray stripes that match the color of the dimness in the room. My sleep fog melts into the stripes.

Palmer's beach house. Since I've come to college, I've learned that neutral colors somehow equate to money. Who knew the upper class preferred beige and stone and ecru? Just adds to their mystique, I guess. Between Palmer and Megan I've learned rich people still yell at each other, get stressed, cry, worry, put pressure on themselves, have hopes and dreams and screw ups and successes, just like Mom and me. They just have nicer things to package it all up in.

And Palmer's beach house is a *pretty* nice package.

I wonder how Mom's doing in her little box? Is she tangled

in her sheets too?

"Palmer?" I call, walking into the main room.

The chair where she was painting her nails is empty.

Everything is still. A bit too still. I look over my shoulder.

"Palm? You here? Kat?" I walk barefoot through the house, peeking in Kat's and Palmer's bedrooms, strolling through the kitchen and out onto the deck. Empty. Everywhere empty. Palmer must have finished with her nails and joined Kat on the beach.

Back in my room I collapse onto the bed and pull the covers all around me and up to my neck, uneasy about being alone. I can't stay here. I'm too anxious. I wonder how long I slept.

I walk back out to the kitchen. The clock reads 11:19 a.m. Not that late. Grabbing Palmer's landline, I dial my cousin. Desperate times.

"Hello. Who's this?" Megan sounds ticked that anyone would call her.

"Hey, it's Claire."

"How many phone numbers do you have?"

"Hmm, let me count. Okay, I'm done, exactly zero. My phone still doesn't work, but I'm a good borrower."

"Still no phone! How are you surviving?"

"Dunno. I'm usually with someone who has one."

"Right."

Megan is not in a chatty mood, so I get straight to the point. "You don't have any updates on my mom, do you? I texted her last night from Kat's phone and called her from Palmer's, thinking maybe she was ignoring one of the numbers and might answer the other. Nothing."

"Yeah, she's definitely been squirrelly. She doesn't want to chat."

"I'm pretty sure she's on prescription uppers. She's done it before," I blurt, then pause. Considering Megan's interest in marijuana, I'm not sure how this is going to fly. And I don't even know if she and Aunt Denise knew about Mom's previous addictions.

"Okay, *that* totally makes sense." I can picture Megan nodding, her straight blond hair moving with her head. "What makes you think so this time?"

"She mentioned picking up a prescription. Not so sly. Plus the cash issue."

"Right."

"I think Mom's not answering me because she's probably too nervous I'm onto her. Or maybe she was out, flying high on happy pills. Or maybe she crashed when the pills wore off or ran out. I'm just worried, 'cause I'm way too far away to get to her and I can't get ahold of her."

"Where are you?" Megan's voice perks up.

"Florida. Spring break at my roommate's beach house."

"Not bad. We're going to Cabo for spring break next week. There are, like, thirty of us staying in an all-inclusive resort. Hello!" Nothing like a little luxury to get Megan talking.

"Sounds pretty sweet. I thought coming to the beach would help get my mind off Mom." *And everything else,* I think to myself. *I also hoped sleeping extra today would help me escape,* but I keep that to myself too. "But she's still my mom. And I know she needs help."

"Kinda weird you called because my mom was freaking out a bit about your mom too. Mom got a couple of calls from creditors asking to speak to Libby Lassiter. When Mom tried to talk to her about it, your mom totally blew her off."

"Aaarrgghh! Sometimes I think it's not her fault. Other times I think she's addicted to the drama, hooked on the attention." I rake my fingers through my hair. "She makes me so angry. But then I get mad at myself for being mad at Mom when she's the one with problems."

"Sure, but her problems give you a major headache. She's so selfish." Megan sighs.

"She's lost," I say, correcting Megan. "There's a difference between selfish and lost, I think."

"Well, whatever. Anyway, Mom went there this morning to figure out what the—"

I interrupt before Megan can use her curse word of choice.

"To Cleveland? To check on Mom?"

"You got it. At least when I talked to her a couple of days ago that was the plan. As soon as I hear from her, I'll fill you in, k?"

"Yes. Please. That would be great, Meg."

"Sooooo, how should I get hold of you? Smoke signal?"

"Funny."

I give her Kat's and Palmer's phone numbers and hang up. Megan's not as bad as I once thought. In fact, she's been really good to me.

"Thank You, God, for Megan," I say out loud. When those words escape my lips, I realize it's the only thing I can do for Mom. Pray. And feeling the warm calm that comes from releasing things to God, I walk back to my bed and continue with my prayer.

God, please get Mom and me out of this. You are the only hope we have. I can't reach her. I half laugh at the irony. *I can't reach her mentally. I can't break through her walls. And I can't get ahold of her either. Please help Aunt Denise find out what's going on. Please help get Mom set back straight.* I look around the picture-perfect room. *I'm not trying to complain. My roommates are great. The beach is the most beautiful thing I've ever seen. I see You in the ocean, God. I know You are the force and beauty behind and in it, but it also makes me feel so desperate, so out of control, like I could get washed away any moment if I don't hold on tight enough. I don't want to end up like Mom, flailing and grabbing onto all the wrong things. But without Mom, or a place to live, I'm not sure what I'm even supposed to hold on to.*

Hold on to Me.

I feel the words, more than hear them, somewhere deep in my chest. But they're solid, as if I could reach out and touch the rise and fall of the *H* and run my finger across the curve of the *O*. I pull the covers around me. The comforter is soft and warm on my exposed shoulders.

Hold on to Me, I hear again.

I hold the comforter close, as if it contains a piece of God.

"My God, my rock, in whom I take refuge, my shield, and the horn of my salvation, my stronghold and my refuge, my

Savior; You save me."

I mutter the words to 2 Samuel 22:3, words on a prayer stone we got in junior high youth group. I repeat them again and again. "My rock. My refuge." *You save me. Will You save Mom too, God?*

So many times God has saved me flood my mind. I think of my roommates. God sent them to me just when I needed support the most. It's what got me through the rape, through all of last year.

I toss aside the covers, trade pajamas for my swimsuit, and weave my hair into a quick braid, knowing I need to find Kat and Palmer pronto. I grab a towel by the door and head to the beach.

Rock. Refuge. Safe, I repeat.

22
KAT

"Y'ALL WILL NOT BELIEVE WHAT I found on my run."
I drop between Palmer and Claire onto the empty lounge chair,
its slats hot from the sun.

"What?" Palmer shakes her head as if I've woken her
from a daze.

"Here." I hand Claire the neon yellow flyer I spied tacked
to the back of a bathroom stall along with a dozen others
advertising buckets of oysters and quarter beers.

"Get out!" Claire squeals.

"Wh-what." Palmer rolls her neck until it makes a sharp,
cracking sound.

"Were you asleep?" I ask, wiping the sweat from my brow
with the back of my arm before it can drip down and sting my
eyes.

"Kinda." Palmer sighs and stretches.

"A concert on the beach?" Claire shrieks.

"Looks like it. In two days." I grab the bottle of water I'd
stashed in my bag, and even though it's no longer cool after

sitting in the sun, I down half of it in one gulp.

"Fire Swamp?" Palmer asks, perking up a bit from behind her shades.

I flip the cap back down on my bottle. "Nicholas is gonna be jealous."

"Why did he go home for break, again?" Palmer asks.

"To save money, mainly." I shrug.

"We have to go!" Claire nods. "It says it's down by the dock of the public beach and the show is free. Free? Crazy!" Claire trails her fingers along the lines of type on the flyer as if she's reading Braille.

"They do it every year. It's some kind of promotion thing. A big corporate sponsor, like Coppertone maybe, brings in an up-and-coming band and passes out sunscreen samples. Fun. Fun. Fun," Palmer says. "And we can get a whole group to go. I ran into this guy I used to always hang out with on our vacations down here. He's with a bunch of his fraternity brothers from I.U. We could make a party out of it."

"Only you would be able to lure a group of fraternity boys to a concert." Claire nudges Palmer's leg with her bare foot.

"When did you see this guy?" I ask, mopping my face with my beach towel.

"This morning." Palmer yawns and covers her mouth. "I came out once my nails were dry. Claire was still snoozing, and you were off running a half marathon or something. You've been gone for"—she opens her mouth and yawns louder this time—"hours."

"Probably two hours," I say, tossing my towel down. "After stretching and doing some balance work on the beach, I ran eight or nine miles. I needed to clear my head this mornin'."

I do that sometimes, wake up not remembering, not wanting to remember, that Alex is gone. I think about texting him or calling him. I never know what will be the trigger. This morning it was the water. I looked at it and thought how much he'd want to swim here. How the waves would be some big challenge for him. But as I ran alongside the waves, it was almost as if Alex were swimming alongside me. Every single step I ran for Alex. Each step made the ground more solid and my vision more clear.

"Yeah," I say, sighing. "It was good. I think I'll do the same thing every morning while we're here."

"I had just come out and put my towel down when Tristan plopped in your chair," Palmer picks up where she left off. She starts using her hands, pointing to my seat as she talks.

"Tristan?" Claire asks in a sing-songy voice.

"Yeah." Palmer touches the edge of my chair. "Tristan. Hey, are you two thirsty? I'm craving an iced coffee."

"I'm in. I saw a coffee shop down that away." I point to the left.

"Java Junkies?" Palmer asks.

"That's the place. Looked cute."

"Love it. C'mon." Palmer stands and smoothes out her towel. She seems to sway for a moment, but steadies herself.

I can't read Claire's expression behind her sunglasses, but she seems to be studying her toenails.

"I don't need anything." Claire flips her braid from one shoulder to the other.

"Don't be silly. My treat." Palmer grabs Claire's hand and pulls her up.

"Really, I'm fine." Claire's voice is soft, unconvincing. "I think I have a Fire Swamp song on my phone."

"Me too," I chime in. "Dog downloaded it for me. You

have a docking station at the house. Right, Palm?"

"Of course. We can jam to them nonstop until tomorrow night and we'll know all the words." Palmer stops in her tracks and turns to us. "Why didn't I think of this before?"

Claire and I look at each other. Claire shrugs. I answer for us both. "Think of what?"

"A story about the Fire Swamp concert! It would be great for the magazine. If I could interview the band, I'd be golden."

"You're already golden." I laugh.

"That would be cool," Claire says. "Not that many people know about Fire Swamp yet. I always love discovering new bands, and Clarkston, well, besides Dog"—she looks to me when referencing my musician friend—"isn't exactly fresh in the music department."

"Spot on, sister." I shake my head. "If I hear one more Top 40 song playing in the Student Center I think I'll puke."

"Would you really be happy if every song you heard was something you'd never heard before?" Palmer shakes her head at us. "There's something super fun about knowing all the words."

"You've got a point," I say. "Hey, you still didn't give us the scoop on Tristan."

Our feet sink into the dry, grainy sand, leaving three sets of footprints as we backtrack the route I've just run.

"We're burning to hear your story," Claire teases.

"All right. All right." Palmer waves her hands at both of us, but I can tell by her smile and the excitement in her voice, she's eating this up. "Once upon a time, my family came here on vacation every year."

"Not to interrupt, but that's still goin' on." I laugh.

Palmer grins. "Anyway, the same families came year after year. All of the parents would go out to dinner together. All of the kids would ride bikes on the beach. But the last night of the week was always special. Almost magical. Especially for the kids."

"And one of the kids was Tristan?" I ask.

"So perceptive." Palmer laughs.

"Sounds like a movie," Claire says.

"It kind of felt like one. Especially the summer before freshman year of high school. We had this giant bonfire with hot dogs and marshmallows and then someone finished off a two-liter of Sprite and set it in the middle of our group."

"Spin the bottle?" I ask.

"Now it really sounds like a movie. In fact, I think I've seen it." Claire turns around and walks backward for a second so she can catch Palmer's eye.

"I know, right?" Palmer's voice is flush with the excitement she usually gets when telling a story. "So it's our last night, and I'm completely jittery, because I know my parents would kill me if they knew I was playing a kissing game. But all the kids we'd been hanging out with forever were there, and we were on the beach, and it was our last night."

"In or out?" I ask as we arrive at Java Junkies.

"Let's sit outside," Claire says.

"Great."

"Café au lait?" Palmer asks her.

Claire nods.

"Iced chai?" Palmer asks me.

"Thanks, sweetie. I'll get the next round," I promise.

"My new job at the dining hall cannot start soon enough. I'm sick of being a walking, talking I.O.U.," Claire says, raising her eyebrows.

"Stop!" Palmer waves her hands.

We order our drinks, Palmer pays, and we move down to

the pickup counter. While the barista's machine whirls, Palmer continues her story. "That summer Tristan had grown about three inches, filled out a little, and his voice had dropped into a smooth cadence that was almost like a tease with his innocent face. And somehow, even though his hair was still gold, his eyelashes were dark and heavy. When it was his turn, he spun the bottle, and guess who it landed on?"

I point at her.

She bows. She's bent over, almost touching her toes, when the barista passes over our drinks. I take them and hand Palmer and Claire theirs. "Thanks," I say, and we head to a small white table and sit. Sweat trickles down my spine as my body still cools down from my workout, and I wipe my forehead with a paper napkin from the holder in the middle of our table.

"And he kissed you?" Claire asks.

"Patience." Palmer smiles and takes a slow drink of her iced mocha. "Mmm. Now where was I?"

I swat her, then take a gulp of cool, spicy, creamy tea laced with orange. As the flavors tickle my tongue, my mind drifts to Nicholas. I love drinking tea with him. It almost always helps me unwind and center myself.

"I remember somebody saying, 'How long you been practicing that spin, Trist?'" Palmer's voice snaps me back to here and now, which is good. I shouldn't dwell on Nicholas. The last thing I need to do is get dependent on him. I was attached to Alex. And the letting go hurt too much.

Palmer's hands fly as she retells the details. "Someone else said, 'Tell me that wasn't rigged.' And I know my face flushed fuchsia. I was so nervous, because the first boy shoved his tongue down the girl's throat. It looked like they were just slobbering. And the next guy did the gentlemanly thing and just pecked his girl on the cheek. I didn't think I wanted either of those things to happen. But Tristan was totally different. He stood up, grabbed my hand, and pulled me up to stand beside him. He slid his hand behind my back, pulled me gently toward him, and kissed me softly."

Claire and I clap.

"And he's here?" Claire asks.

"Uh-huh." Palmer turns as red as she probably did that night at the bonfire. My mind slips back to Nicholas and how it feels when he kisses me. What if he were here today? What if he came to the concert with us? Where are we headed?

23

HANNAH

THE FELT STAR BEHIND THE glass looks like it could be a nametag for Vacation Bible School or part of a craft I'll have my students make once I become a teacher, but this six-pointed star with the word *Jud* written across it punches me in the gut and tugs at my vocal chords. I know, of course, that the Jewish people in Germany had to wear these stars. I read *The Diary of Anne Frank* in seventh grade. I was Maria in our high school's production of *The Sound of Music*. But actually seeing one, a real one, not a picture in a book or part of a costume, gives me horrified chills. I want to move on, away from this spot, so I don't have to look at this star and wonder for one minute longer who wore it and what awful tragedy they endured, but I can't move.

There are newspaper clippings and photographs surrounding the star behind the glass at the outdoor Holocaust Museum. The display case continues for what seems like miles, and countless visitors, way more than our student group, from all over the world, crowd the exhibition. It's cold and I huddle deeper inside my coat. There are graves behind me, too many to count. I picture Anne Frank in my head, and even though I can only recall one image of her, the black-and-white photo from the cover of the paperback, she's not that different from me. She had dark eyes and wavy brown hair. She might have had freckles. I'm pretty sure she liked to sing. There was definitely something in her diary about listening to music, and being worried someone might hear it. She had a sister. I haven't been able to chat with Sammie at all since I've been here. Is she mad that I didn't come home for break? Sad?

Nate's arms envelop me from behind, soothing my homesick heart and filling me with comfort. He smells fresh and clean and safe, the opposite of gasoline from tanks and gunpowder and musty hideouts.

"Pretty intense," he whispers out of reverence.

I nod.

"You okay?" he asks, rubbing my shoulders.

I try to say yes but the word catches, so I shake my head.

Nate squeezes me tighter. "Come here." He pulls me a few steps away, breaking my trance. "We need to give you a break. I mean, we *need* to see this." He emphasizes the word *need*, like it is an absolute truth. "But we also need to process it. Take in bits and pieces, not everything all at once." He turns me into his chest and holds me, keeping me safe from the swastikas and black boots. "It can be too much."

I drop my head into his chest, grateful for its solid strength. Should I pull back and show my own strength? I don't know if I can. I want to collapse into Nate and cry like when I was eight and found our hamster, Brownie, dead in her cage. My dad held me then. But I don't want to freak Nate out, don't want him to think I'm weak or needy. We've been together for how long, a month? Are we even considered "together"? He shouldn't have to shoulder my issues, but he's so strong and warm.

Dr. Wheeler weaves through the crowd and whispers to us, "Fifteen minutes, folks. When you're finished meet me by the entrance."

"I need to take a look at one more thing," Nate says quietly in my ear.

I burrow into him. I can't help it. His arms wrap around

me, so I know it's okay. The scent of his cologne, a kind of soapy, iced-tea smell, curls itself around me. I feel his body rise and lower with his breaths.

"It's okay. You don't have to see any of it." He pushes me gently a few inches back and turns me around so I'm facing the entrance, people coming and going, dark coats, no graves, no stars. "Wait right here."

And I do. I avert my eyes downward and watch black leather lace-ups, brown boots, the strappy, comfortable, Euro-looking flats most of Germany seems to wear and an occasional pair of gym shoes that shout, "American tourist," shuffling along the concrete. I wonder how many of our fifteen minutes have passed. I wonder what Nate still wanted to see. I hope I'm not hindering his quest for knowledge of the past. I smile thinking how his eyes light up when he discusses history. He is gorgeous. He doesn't hide how smart he is. And he's with me?

Allie taps me on the shoulder. "Hey, Anna. Bit of a bummer, huh?"

I gave up telling her my name is Hannah with an *H* after three times. It doesn't matter anyway.

"Gruesome."

"Want a smoke?" she asks, pulling out a cigarette.

"No thanks." I smile.

Allie tilts her head and perches the cigarette I declined between her lips. She lights it with a *whoosh* of her lighter, blows a couple of pungent smoke rings, and says, "Can you imagine being killed just because you have freckles or me, just because I'm a natural blonde?" She blows a long, thin stream of smoke to the right.

"No." I scrunch my nose.

"Total drag," she says.

I nod.

"Did you notice the tour guide for that Asian group?"

"Uh-uh. I'm focusing pretty hard on not noticing anything here. It's way too much for me."

"Got that. But he's a beautiful distraction. I'm dying to

see his eyes behind those sunglasses. Catch ya later."

"Yeah, later." Thanks for the uplifting thoughts, I think.

Laney is one step behind Allie, but doesn't seem to notice me as she frantically types notes on her phone and shakes her head. Assuming Rachel will be next with more morbid ideas, I turn slightly to avoid eye contact and return to my shoe watch.

With each pair of shoes that pass by, I hope I'll see Nate's familiar shoes. I don't know how much longer I can stand here. The parade of shoes seems endless. I consider counting them, one, two, three, four.

I hear someone sniff and the sound tugs somewhere deep inside me. I jerk my head half expecting to see my little brother, Owen, but instead see George standing strong and tall, looking full on at the wall while tears fall unashamed down his face. Seeing him confront this, unafraid but clearly affected, makes me feel stronger. Instinctively, I take a step forward. But as I glance down, Nate's gray shoes line up with the soles of my shoes. George and his honest strength fade to a memory. I look up from Nate's feet to our knees to our coats to his face.

"Thanks for waiting," he says softly and takes my arm.

24
PALMER

I SWEAR TRISTAN IS CUTER every time I see him, and I've seen him a few times over the last two days. The opening band, R.O.U.S., is cruising through an electric guitar solo that's louder and longer than I'd prefer, but Tristan sways to the sound, and when he leans right, his shoulder bumps into mine, sending a rush down my arm. I laugh and lean back into him.

It's strange. Michael and Tristan both have a magnetic pull on me, but they're opposites. Michael is all intellect and sophistication. Well, not *all*. He's also gorgeous and mysterious and commanding. But Tristan is funny and easy going. There aren't any games here. I'd stifle this smile with Michael, afraid he'd read something into it. With Tristan it just pops out.

"We're going to get some refreshments," Tristan's friend yells. He and Jacob, the guy with the New York accent, wait for Tristan.

Tristan leans into me and tells his friends, "Catch up with you in a few."

The next song is even louder, and the sound screaming

from the amps reverberates in my chest. I woke up with a headache this morning from drinking beer last night with Tristan and his gang after Kat and Claire turned in. I thought the combination of a shot of espresso, a couple of Advil, and an afternoon nap had taken care of it, but it seems to be resurfacing with each chord from the keyboards. *Stupid. I deserve this headache. I should have known better.* I shake my head and yell, "Too loud!"

"I kinda like their sound," Kat says.

I raise an eyebrow, not sure if she heard what I said or not.

"How cool they have a cellist," Claire adds. At least that's what I think she says, but with each passing second, I'm feeling increasingly crowded and affected by the noise.

"If you had been there when I was interviewing them this afternoon, you would not have been impressed with the cellist." I yawn.

"Why's that?" Claire asks.

"Let's just say his ego would not fit in his cello case. And he has terrible b.o."

"Really?" Kat asks. "He sure sounds good."

I shove my way a few feet to the left so my mouth is closer to Claire's and Kat's ears. "I'm going to get some air."

"Do you want me to come?" Claire asks.

"You all right?" Kat asks. "You've seemed a little out of it today."

"I'm fine. Just feeling overheated, probably too much sun this afternoon." I glance at the setting sun. "I'll be back in a few." I hope they can't detect that my smile is forced.

I weave my way through the sea of college kids in cutoffs, tank tops, and swimsuits.

"Excuse me. Sorry. Can I get through?"

I mutter these phrases again and again, not even sure if anyone can hear me until the crowd finally thins out and I can maneuver more freely. When I reach open beach, I stand still for a moment, relishing the room. I inhale the salty air and spy an abandoned lawn chair.

Claiming it for my own, I recline and close my eyes, grateful for the quiet of the waves and the space around me.

"You okay, pretty girl?" Tristan stands over me, his eyebrows drawn down in concern.

"Yeah," I sigh. "I usually love concerts. I just have a little headache." I tap my forehead.

"Maybe a cocktail to take the edge off?" Tristan asks.

"I'm afraid that might be why I have a headache in the first place," I admit. "I'm not a beer drinker."

"We call it hair of the dog."

"Eww! What does that even mean?"

He laughs. "I have no idea. But it has something to do with one more drink kills a hangover. Come on. We've got a full bar back at the house. Jacob and a bunch of other guys are playing bartender."

"Thanks." I put my fingers to my temples. "I don't think I'm up for a big group yet." I hold my hand up to stop him from trying to persuade me. "I will be. I just need a few more minutes of this—the waves are fixing my headache."

"Then you stay put. What's your poison? Kahlua? Greyhound? I'll be back in few with whatever sounds good."

I swallow. I'm not even sure what those things are. "You're sweet. But I'm fine."

"All right. You sit tight and be fine. I'm going to get myself a drink, and then I'll be back to sit with you, if you don't mind."

"Thanks." I nod, grateful for a moment alone and for his

offer to keep me company.

The sun sinks lower and the air starts to cool as his feet pad away. I allow my eyes to close and concentrate on the sound of waves *whooshing* back and forth. It feels like they're rolling from one side of my head to the other.

"Palmer? You alive?"

I jerk upright at the sound of Tristan's voice and run my fingers through my hair. Blinking a few times, I inhale deeply and square my shoulders. The sun is almost touching the water now. "I think the waves lulled me into a catnap."

"Worse things could happen." Tristan grins. "You couldn't have been out long. But it isn't a good idea for someone as gorgeous as you to be sitting here by herself. Good thing I'm back to guard you."

"Good thing." I slide my legs to the side to make room for him on my chair.

"So, I wasn't sure, but all the girls at I.U. drink this." Tristan holds up a bottle of Moscato in one hand, condensation dripping down the sides, and two plastic cups in the other.

"Mmm." I run my finger down the cold bottle. "That's something I do like."

"Great." Tristan opens the bottle and pours me a glass, then one for himself. We tip them together. The plastic makes a pathetic thud, but the wine is smooth and relaxing. Just the thought of it loosens me up a bit.

"Tell me about all the girls at I.U. Do you have a girlfriend?"

He pulls his cap down a little tighter on his head. "Not really."

"Not really?"

"Nah. I went to one girl's formal a couple of weeks

ago…Katelyn. We'd been hanging out. But she's pretty ditzy and kind of bugs me. I haven't hung out with her since." He fiddles with the edge of his cup.

"If she's really ditzy, why were you with her?"

"Honest?" he asks.

"Honest."

"She's really hot." His eyebrows go up under his cap. "I know that's shallow, but it's true. Every guy on campus seems to have a thing for her. When she started talking to me, it seemed like a no-brainer. All my buds were jealous and cheering for me." He laughs and spins his cup around in his hand. "It was fine for a couple of nights at the bars, you know? But after trying to have an actual conversation with her, spending the entire night with her at her formal—she doesn't even look cute to me anymore. I mean, like the image of her kind of makes my skin crawl." He does an overexaggerated shiver of his whole body. "You, on the other hand." Tristan lifts his cap up an inch so he's looking directly at me. "You, Palmer, I could hang out with for a very long time."

The wine is light and fruity and welcome after the bitter beer I've been drinking the last few days and the loud crowd we've left behind. Guitar chords strum faintly in the distance, and I wonder if Fire Swamp has come on stage. I should probably go back so Kat and Claire know I'm okay, but it's calm here. *I will*, I tell myself. *After one glass of wine. I mean, it was so sweet of Tristan to go get it for me.*

"Look, a bonfire." Tristan points far down the beach, where the flames dance in the distance. "You probably don't remember our last bonfire together." He takes a slug of wine like it's a Coke.

"I didn't think you would." I take a sip of my wine, looking down at my cup, avoiding his eyes.

"Right." He takes another gulp.

"You do?" I tilt my head to get a good look at his face. Light dances in Tristan's eyes. I take another sip of Moscato, letting the sweetness tickle my tongue. I think he's right. My headache seems to fade away with each swallow. I take one more.

"I believe it went something like this." Tristan finishes off his drink, sets his glass down sideways on the sand, and leans into me. His lips carry the apple flavor of the wine as they touch mine. I breathe him in and he kisses me again and again, and I forget about my headache and trying to prove myself to the magazine staff. I just let the warmth of the wine and Tristan's mouth relax me into a comfort zone where I too could hang out for a very long time.

25
CLAIRE

THE CELLO RIPS THROUGH THE air and into my heart, as if I have strings running up and down my interior that are being plucked and played. Deep parts of me that no one understands, that I can't say out loud even if I had words to match them, vibrate within. There is a buzz in the air, a hypnotic pleasurable trance where my mom, Hannah's absence, and the fact that I have no idea what I want to be when I grow up fizzle like popped bubbles, light and airy and unimportant. All that matters is this song and the words from the singer's lips. When he claps his hands I clap mine, and I am part of something. Something powerful.

Palmer and Tristan sidle into the group. His friends returned awhile ago. She's grinning, and she grabs my hands and dances with me. Everything seems good and right with her again. We lose ourselves in the music, in the movements, and our dance becomes the rhythm.

"I wish I could major in going to great concerts," Kat yells above the pounding bass.

"That is one of the most brilliant things you've ever said." Palmer grins. "And you've had some zingers before."

The three of us bump hips and sway.

Two guys make their way to our group, dancing as if they know us. Kat gives the one with espresso-colored skin a high five.

"Girl, you can dance too?" He laughs.

Kat shakes her head. "Hardly. Y'all want to kick the ball around again tomorrow?"

"We're leaving early for home," the blond one says. "But if you're ever in our neck of the woods." He winks at Kat.

"Have fun," Kat says as they keep dancing their way closer toward the stage.

I raise my eyebrows, waiting for her explanation.

"I met 'em while I was out running. Nice guys." Kat grabs my hand and twirls me around. Before I can grill her on how she can be so friendly and comfortable with everyone, she holds up her phone and videotapes one minute of musical bliss, then sends it. "Nicholas would love this. Had to text him."

She shows us his text back of a crazy emoticon dude with his hands over his face. As she responds, I return my gaze to the stage. I don't know this song, but it has a beat that pulls me in.

"Have you seen Fire Swamp before?" one of Tristan's friends asks. He has tiny, sparkly blue eyes that send out little lights from beneath thick, bushy blond eyebrows. He's tall, or at least he seems tall towering over all five feet one of me. I forget his name.

I shake my head. "They're amazing. I have a couple of their songs. But, wow, they're phenomenal."

"Yeah," he says. "I downloaded 'Hydrant' when it

released last spring. I listened to it all summer, but kind of put it away when school started. I forgot how much I loved them," he says.

Talking to unknown boys usually makes me extremely nervous. I have no idea how Kat does it. But music is something I can comfortably chat about.

"So many bands are a disaster when you see them live." I wind the end of my ponytail around my pointer finger. "But these guys sound even better in person."

"Right." He nods. "I'm Josh."

"I'm Claire, and this is Kat and Palmer." I nudge Kat and she looks up from her phone.

"Hey."

Palmer smiles and twirls in a circle and leans into Tristan.

"We all know Palmer. She's all Tristan talks about." Tristan is behind Palmer, his hands on her shoulders as they sway. I don't think they hear Josh. "Are you roommates?" Josh nods at each of us.

"Yup," Kat says, her eyes on her phone, reading another text from Nicholas.

"What are you majoring in?" Josh asks, keeping his voice loud so I can hear.

"Not sure," I yell back.

"She's a dancer," Kat says, stuffing her phone in the pocket of her jeans shorts. "I play soccer. The 'what we want to be when we grow up' thing. We're still working on that."

Josh seems to accept that with a grin, and Fire Swamp cranks into the opening strains of their next song.

I am mesmerized, hypnotized.

And then it's over.

The last chord echoes and reverberates until it is only a memory clinging to the edges of the evening sky. It's cooler and darker than when it all started, like the concert has actually altered the climate.

"That was sweet!" Josh claps his hands.

"Wow. All I can say is wow," Kat says, beating her palms together.

I clap until my hands actually ache but say nothing. No words will do justice.

Eventually, the applause fades and the lights go on, and the crowd breaks off into mini crowds and then into groups. Josh is back with a handful of frat boys. "We're going to Taco Bell, right off the strip. Wanna join us?"

"We're in." Tristan raises his hand, the one that's not attached to Palmer. She just smiles, big.

"Sure," Kat says before I can get out, "No thanks, I'm not hungry." Which would have been a lie. I'm starving, but it would have sounded better than, "No thanks, I'm broke."

But it's settled. Palmer and Tristan trail behind us. The rest of us blend together. The guys make friendly conversation, beer on their breath. Kat chimes in. I nod, shake my head, laugh when they're funny.

I've done the empty-pockets thing before. I know the drill. As everyone else files into line to order, I say, "I'm going to run to the restroom."

"Can I order you something?" Josh asks.

"No thanks. We ate all day. I'm not that hungry."

I stall in the bathroom. Washing my hands an extra time, readjusting my hair, pulling the lip gloss out of my front pocket and gliding it slowly across my lips. When I think enough time has passed, I wander into the dining area and find our crew crowded into a booth. Josh catches my eye, grabs a chair from an empty table behind him, and motions for me to sit by him on the end.

"Thanks," I say, turning my head to one of the other guys who's in mid-story about the last concert he attended.

Josh slides his chips toward me. "Help yourself. I over ordered," he whispers, trying not to interrupt his friend.

"Thanks." I nod and nibble on the salty chips while Josh inhales a giant burrito.

No one seems to notice that I didn't order. I'm relieved to have something to munch on, but I don't want Josh to think I *like* him, like him. He's nice enough, but we're all leaving soon. I ache to escape the glaring fluorescent lights of Taco Bell and return to the dark cloak of the concert. Away from cash registers and hot sauce and the nagging memory of a mom who blew all of our money and a boy I don't know how to handle and wadded up one-dollar bills and back to guitar chords and drum beats I can feel in my heart.

26

HANNAH

I SQUEEZE MY HANDS INTO tight fists as the steel slides across my forehead and I hear the sickening snip of blades. What if the stylist didn't understand what I meant when I pointed at the photo in the magazine? What if she cuts them too short? What if I look like an absolute dork and Nate doesn't like me anymore?

"Ya?" the girl who must be close to my age with bleached platinum hair in corkscrew curls and cherry red lips asks or announces, I'm not sure which, as she spins my chair around to face the mirror.

There I am. With bangs. But these bangs are so much more sophisticated than my high school bangs. These aren't bangs that look "so cute" with a headband. She's given me a side part, something I've never had before. And these bangs sweep sideways, dare I say mysteriously, over my right eyebrow, skimming over my right eye.

"Ya?" she asks again, tilting her head.

"Yeah." I nod, chewing my gum a little too ferociously.

I pay her the amount that flashes in blue lights on the register, feeling liberated, just like Germany. Free of something that held me, although I can't put my finger on what that was.

I feel crazy and daring as I walk out onto the busy sidewalk.

"You look fantastic." Nate points to me.

"Thanks." I feel myself blushing.

"No. Like, really good."

Maybe the day trip to Dresden has made us lose our senses. Maybe there's something in the air making us both feel daring. Nate pulls me against him and kisses me, one arm wrapped around my waist, the other running through my hair. Our lips part and connect and we kiss and we kiss and we don't care who sees, because we don't know anyone in Germany. There isn't anyone to gossip or judge or tease. His lips are warm and his arm is firm around my coat. A damp, cold wind blows against my face, drawing me closer to him.

After minutes or days or months, the kiss is over, but not completely. Nate slides his hand down my back and weaves his fingers between mine. We walk side by side along the brick street as if nothing happened, but I feel like everything's changed.

"What a great day. I was so ready to get away from my roommates."

"You do have an interesting room," Nate says with a laugh. "It's funny you ended up with Laney."

"Why's that?"

"Oh, we went out a couple of times freshman year." With his free hand, he runs his fingers through his hair.

"You did?" The back of my neck tightens. "She never said anything." *You never said anything.*

"It was no big deal. Believe me." Nate squeezes my hand.

"Okay," I say, but I don't feel okay.

"We had a class together second semester. We got grouped together for our final project and well, one thing led to another."

What kind of things? I wonder.

"And...?" I ask.

"And she's a bit of a know-it-all bore."

I nod. He's right.

"And way too tall." He laughs. "Plus, she looks at her

watch all the time. Don't tell her I said that. Any of that. There's nothing really wrong with Laney, just no spark, you know? We got together just because…I don't even know why we got together, looking back on it. Boredom, maybe."

This is the first time Nate has seemed at a loss of words around me. *Just because?* A thousand questions rattle around my brain, colder than the blades of the stylist's scissors, as we cross the bridge spanning the Elbe River. Who else has he dated? What are his parents like? Does he have any siblings? I don't even know! What else don't I know about him? Since he claims he never liked Laney, I try to sound casual as I ask, "When did you stop seeing each other?"

"End of school year last year. We turned in our project and there wasn't anything for us to talk about anymore. World politics was all we had. I never really liked her. Or her opinions about socialism, actually."

What opinions are those? I wonder. We stop in front of a golden statue of a man riding a horse, who seems to welcome us as we reach this side of the river. "King August the Strong," I read out loud as I trace the indented letters on his nameplate, buying myself a moment to gather my scattered thoughts.

"I like him." Nate nods. "I love this city. I love being here with you. *We* have so much to talk about besides class."

"We do, don't we?" I squeeze his hand now. His words coat the icy spot in my stomach.

"One dinner in Dresden," he says. "We should make it spectacular."

"Right." I crack my gum, revived by the turn in conversation. *He loves being here with me*, I repeat in my mind.

"Kat's dad told me about an incredible pasta place we should try here. Mr. Wiley has actually been to Dresden once for work. Who knew Germany would have great pasta, right?" I stop walking and try to look as serious as possible. "I can't manage one more meal of schnitzel or kraut."

"No more schnitzel or kraut," he agrees.

I smile. "I'm glad they gave us a free day. It's so much more fun to explore without a boring tour guide or a schedule." I skip two steps, intoxicated by the very word *free*. Nate laughs and lunges forward to keep up with me.

"And now we get to have a lovely dinner without any talk of allies and invasions," I add, but in my head I add Laney to the list of taboo topics.

Nate nudges my shoulder playfully with his as we walk. "I could listen to those talks all day, every day."

I tug my jaw backward, wishing I could pull back the awkward moments of our conversation. "I know you love that stuff. I'm just ready for a break is all."

Aaagh! None of my words are coming out right. How will I keep Nate's interest if I don't know how he feels about socialism? The whole thing bores me. I want Nate to like me for me, but what if I'm not good enough? What if next year he's telling some other girl that he doesn't know why he ever dated *me*? There's a widening in my chest, where I think I'm not getting air, because I'm definitely holding my breath. *Please tell me you still like me,* I silently plead with him, willing the spark inside me to return and burn away my insecurities.

"Come on. Lectures can be a drag. But history? Never!" Nate turns around to face the churches rebuilt after the heinous bombing in World War II and snaps his fingers, pointing at the beautiful architecture for emphasis. "Those two churches. Look at them. They are a crucial key to our future. All of Germany is." He shakes his head. "You plan on being a teacher, right?"

"Right." I nod.

"So think how cool it will be telling your students you've actually seen destruction rebuilt. A people who rebounded. That you've touched the Berlin Wall, walked through Checkpoint Charlie."

"We *are* actually here. I'm not sure how impressed my first graders will be." I tilt my head toward him and smile. "But you're right, Germany's story is interesting, awesome, really. But some of those tour guides!" I snort. "Now, if you were giving the tours, that would be an entirely different story."

"If I was giving you a tour, we might not get to too much

history." Nate leans over and kisses me softly, but long enough that I am revived.

"I definitely like your tours best." I smile.

"I definitely like being your tour guide." Nate kisses me again. "I also like dinner. I love pasta, and I'm getting hungry." Nate rubs his stomach. "Where is this place?"

"The Pasta Manufakturer. Isn't it weird how some German words sound so much like English? I had Mr. Wiley mark it on a map and send it to me before we left. Here, I've got the printout in my bag." I pull the folded sheet of paper, and easily identify the bridge and the statue on the map. "We should be just a few minutes away. I think down past these shops and then left." I point to the map.

"Look who's the tour guide now. Show me the way." He bows.

The light in the sky grows fainter by the moment and the streetlights illuminate one after the other like dominoes. I catch my reflection in a store window as we walk past, but don't recognize myself at first. It's a reflection of a girl with sassy bangs and an attractive, intelligent guy holding her hand, like they belong together, like they always have. I pull myself up straighter. *He's with me, not Laney*, I tell myself.

And for the first time in a very long time, I don't look at myself and wish I didn't have freckles, or that I was taller, or that all the heads in our group were turned toward me instead of toward Palmer. No, this time I love who I see. A girl full of adventure and possibility. A girl who travels the world and discusses history and knows about secret restaurants in foreign cities. A girl who *has* touched the Berlin Wall and who looks the part. I turn my head to keep an eye on that girl in the glass, and as I do, Nate catches my face with his hand, pressing his lips against mine again, sealing the deal.

27
KAT

LAST DAY AT THE BEACH means last early-morning run on the beach. It has to be a good one, because spring soccer training starts full force on Monday. I drop down on the wood-planked porch and do twenty-five quick push-ups. I will be stronger than any other player on the team. I have to be. Rolling over onto my back for sit-ups, I wonder how far I can run today. Today should be the farthest.

"That was the funniest thing I've ever seen in my entire life," Palmer says, her voice drifting from the house. I guess she and Claire are up.

"Like killer crazy. How many Banana Republics do you think Josh did?"

Not Claire's voice. A boy's voice, and it's coming from inside. At this time of morning?

"I have no idea. Tell me again what they poured in his mouth. One of them was banana schnapps..." So Palmer is having a conversation with the boy. Tristan. It must be Tristan. I do not want to know how he got here.

"And coconut rum, Malibu," Tristan continues.

"Right. It was surprisingly yummy. Like a piña colada Lifesaver."

"I've never had a piña colada Lifesaver." Tristan laughs loudly, then the house gets quiet. Thank goodness.

I hoist my right leg onto the rail of the porch and lean over it, stretching my hamstring. I wind tape around my healed ankle, around and around, for extra support. Their voices return soft and low now, over the breeze. I'll let them be. I switch legs to give my left side an equal stretch.

There's some creaking and a thud and a crash. What the what?

"Crap, I mean, ahhhh!" Tristan moans.

"What happened?" Palmer asks.

"I cut my hand. I was reaching for the bottle and must've knocked it over. Broken glass. Crap, I'm bleeding everywhere."

Palmer's a big girl and this is her house, but man, the guy's bleeding. Dang it.

"Y'all all right in here?" I ask, peering into Palmer's room. She's sitting on the side of her bed, her dark hair tangled down her back. She's wearing a tank top and red shorts. I should be glad she's dressed.

Tristan, who's shirtless but wearing shorts, sits beside her, resting his elbow on her shoulder for balance while holding his other hand, which does indeed have blood trickling down his fingers.

Why have I walked into an episode of *Girls*? This is so not how we do roommate life. Palmer's unwound and all, which is great, but I think she unwound a bit too much.

Palmer jumps at my voice. Her eyes, wide and wild, just stare at me for a long silent moment. She squares her shoulders and swallows before saying, "Kat, hi. I didn't know you were up." Palmer uses both hands to brush her crazy hair out of her eyes. "Could you grab a washcloth from the cabinet in the hall bathroom?"

"I'm on it." I turn as quickly as I can away from the scene. Palmer had Tristan over for a sleepover? And she's acting like it was no big deal. My heart pounds in my chest as I open the cabinet door.

"Preferably one of the burgundy ones," she calls.

"Sure."

I grab a neatly folded burgundy washcloth from a stack and walk back into the room, which smells stale and sweaty, the opposite of the floral cloud that typically clings to Palmer everywhere she goes. I hold out the cloth to Tristan.

"Here ya go. That looks pretty bad, though. Can I grab y'all Band-Aids, first-aid ointment? Palm, where do you keep all that stuff?"

"I'm fine, thanks." Tristan presses the cloth to his hand.

"Here, I'll hold it, baby." Palmer winks at him.

Hello, I'm standing right here. Baby?

"It's still bleeding. Like, a lot." Her voice is too slow and thick for her usual pep. "Kat, all the first-aid stuff is in the laundry room, over the washer, no, the dryer." She waves with her free hand in the general direction of the laundry room. "I mean, I'll get it."

I'm half out the door, eager to escape, when Tristan calls, "Really. I don't need any of that, but do you have super glue?"

"Super glue?" Palmer's a half step behind me. "I've got it."

"Great," I say with as much sarcasm as I can drum up and move toward the door, but Palmer grabs my arm.

"This is so *not* what it seems," she whispers, but her eyebrows and mouth look like she's shouting, she's so animated.

I shrug. "What's there to say?"

"Okay. So, yes, he slept over, but"—Palmer leans in so close to me her forehead touches mine—"it wasn't like that." She turns her head to the bedroom where Tristan waits.

I bite my tongue, trying not to judge, but as my eyes follow hers I have to bite down harder.

"You know he walked me home," Palmer says.

I nod.

"And we were making out." She throws her hands up in the air. "Not a big deal. I've seen you kiss Nicholas."

"That's not even close to being the same thing," I say, feeling a snarl tug at my lips.

"I know. I don't mean…" Palmer shakes her head, slides her arm around my shoulders, and pulls me out to the kitchen. She says loudly, "Just a sec, Trist."

"You and Nicholas are different. Got it. But I *do* like Tristan. And I have known him for ages." She rifles through a drawer and holds up the tube of glue triumphantly. "Anyway. It was just kissing, and we truly fell asleep. That's it. End of story. Nothing grand to report. Promise me you won't hate me?" She takes my wrist gently, like she won't let go until I reassure her.

I think of Nicholas's strong, broad swimmer's shoulders and how his arms feel wrapped around me. Sometimes I'd like to curl up in those arms and fall asleep, all safe and snug. I shake my head, not wanting to surrender.

"I get it. It's just…" I spin my pinkie ring with my thumb. "Weird. That's all."

"Super weird." Palmer giggles, releasing my wrist. "And so is the fact he asked for glue."

She tugs me back to her room, and I feel lighter knowing

things are more innocent than they appear.

"Thanks." Tristan smiles at Palmer and takes the tube of glue. He grabs the cap with his teeth, pulls it off, removes it from his mouth, flips it around, and punctures the tiny silver tube. He squirts glue on his cut, running parallel to his thumb, like it's a first-grade art project. The sharp scent of glue mingles with the other stench in the room.

My stomach tightens. I take a sharp inhale, but cannot pull my eyes off this process.

"That cannot be safe." Palmer runs her hand up and down his arm.

"Don't worry. We keep a couple of tubes in the fraternity house. It works. I've seen it before. Dries so fast none of the toxins can get in."

I take a step backward. "You two okay, then?"

"Oooh," Palmer groans. "I'm going to need to clean up the floor. Thank goodness none of it dripped on the carpet. Thank goodness for Pergo." Palmer scoots around Tristan and pauses to kiss the back of his neck.

"Mmm. Do that again. It makes my hand feel better," he purrs.

I exit before I gag, but I need to check on Claire. She's still sleeping, a small, quiet lump under her covers. Thankfully, sleep is one of her strong suits. I close her door so she won't be subjected to this madness.

The sea air hits me like smelling salts, reviving my senses. My feet are flying before I even hit the sand. I run as far away from the beach house as I can, letting the uneasiness in my stomach for Palmer and my longing and mixed emotions for Nicholas get lighter and lighter with each step as I focus all of my energy on my game.

28
CLAIRE

I DIP THE TOOTHBRUSH BACK into the beer can I found on the deck this morning. I've emptied it and rinsed it and filled it with a mixture of water and some Clorox I found in the laundry room. I don't know which smells worse—the stale beer or the bleach. At least there is something sterile about the bleach.

Kat and Palmer are down by the ocean, and I was, but I've had this idea brewing in my head all morning and I can't shake it. Had to do it. It's one thing to not have enough money to buy coffee or nachos. It's a whole different story to be in debt to my friends. I had to do something to repay Palmer and her parents for flying me here, for giving me a free spring break. And I won't collect that first paycheck for another month.

And this, cleaning rocking chairs, is a pitiful attempt to repay her, but it's something I know how to do. It's funny, ironic actually, that my aunt and Palmer's parents would have the exact same white industrial-strength plastic rocking chairs on their decks. And when I say plastic, I don't mean cheap Walmart specials. I mean special ordered. I mean the kind that come with the promise they were made with over twenty thousand recycled milk cartons and their paint will never fade or chip. I heard my aunt talk about them to anyone who would listen last summer. The only problem with the bright white, un-chippable chairs is that stark turns dingy in a hurry after feet get propped up on them, Cokes spill, and barbecue sauce drips.

One day last summer Aunt Denise asked me to clean the chairs. My way to pay my "rent" to stay at their mansion was by doing chores, which was the best deal that ever came my way. Between their cleaning lady who came twice a week and the caterer they hired every weekend to cook for parties, there wasn't really that much for me to do. But the chairs needed help, and I was it.

Denise had called the chair company, and they said it was as simple as scrubbing a little diluted bleach on the chairs. Sounded easy enough. But the problem with faux wood is it has all the crevices and cracks of real wood to make it look authentic. And every greasy hamburger and sticky plate of syrup made its mark in those grooves. Apparently it's not any different at Palmer's.

I swoosh the toothbrush round and round on the arms of the chairs, the dirtiest part, because they get the most use, like I'm brushing my teeth.

Swirl, whoosh, scrub, rub.

At first, nothing happens. The black goo likes the nooks and crannies it's found. It sticks, stays, and holds on for dear life.

But then, after several minutes of scrubbing some of the dirt lifts. I don't notice it at first, but the swirls are no longer clear but dingy, where the grime has released itself and the arms of the rocker are brighter. It's oddly rewarding. Knowing I am responsible for getting rid of something brackish. That I can aid in restoring something's beauty.

God laughs inside my head. A chuckle, really.

I make more circular motions with the brush, releasing more layers of filth and debris, slowly but surely.

I imagine all of my guilt and grime. The rape. Phillip's face. Mom not understanding. My resulting fears and insecurities, which most days seem in check, like these serviceable rocking chairs. They still work. They're just not at their best.

I picture Mom popping a small white pill from an orange-tinted bottle. I scour harder. Credit card bills heaped on the kitchen table, unpaid. My useless cell phone. My laptop, which is no longer mine. *Swoosh, swoosh, whoosh.* More and more particles of filth free themselves from the grooves of the faux wood. More and more bits of what clamps my brain, my heart, my mouth loosens, let's go.

If you can do that with a toothbrush and some bleach, think what I can do. God's voice whispers to me on the ocean breeze. It stirs the loose hairs that have escaped my braid.

Yes. Think what You can do.

I move on to the next chair. Dipping my toothbrush back into the solution. Shifting my weight. Scrunching my nose at a too-strong whiff of the bleach. I back up and look at the chair. Wondering where to start. I attacked the arms of the other one first. But on this one looks more stained, more in dire need of attention.

I exhale. *There are probably different parts of me that need more work than others too, right, God? And on any given day it could change, depending on what's been spilled on me lately. And where You start on me isn't where You start on Palmer or Kat or Hannah or anyone.*

Mom's face flashes in my thoughts. Her eyes, a mirror image of mine. *Right. You're working on her too. She has had a lot of crap flung at her, and it only makes sense that some of it stuck. I'm sorry I've been so insensitive to her. I just…*

I lean back from the chair and shake my head. Anger surges, taking over my calm, which makes me angrier, because I was in such a soothing place.

Don't worry about how I clean her. Just remember, I'm here getting rid of your pain and stains, one brushstroke at a time.

Just like my favorite painter, Monet—one brushstroke at a time.

"Oh my gosh, what are you doing?" Palmer's voice comes from behind, startling me so much I drop my toothbrush.

"I just…" I pick up the brush and shake my head.

"You look like Cinderella down there. I hope you don't think I'm the wicked stepmother. When I asked you to pick up your dishes, sweetie, I didn't mean this." Palmer pulls off her sunglasses and kneels next to me.

"I didn't think that for a minute."

"Need some help?" Kat asks, dropping her beach bag on the deck.

"Nah. Thanks, though. I'm just about done."

"Sweetheart, why did you do this? I mean, they look great! My folks will flip. They've been meaning to have those chairs cleaned all year. How did you even know how?"

"My aunt has the same ones." I laugh, more relaxed. "But I didn't want you to see. Didn't want credit. I just wanted it to be done for you, and for your parents. You know, as a thank-you."

"So unnecessary." Palmer shakes her head. "You blow me away, Claire Bear."

"You are about the coolest girl I know." Kat tilts her head toward me.

"Hardly." I sit crisscross applesauce.

"We were just planning dinner. We thought we'd cook up something scrumptious for our last night here." Kat looks at the house. "After a shower."

"I am so sticky I could scream," Palmer says. "Come on, Claire. We have three showers. We can all get cleaned up, cruise over to the grocery, get some fresh fish, and grill it up. Mmm. With mango-pineapple salsa. Does that sound good?"

"Sounds great."

Kat and Palmer stand and head inside. I gather my supplies and look back at my work. The chairs are not perfect. But who is? Actually, a little bit of light brown in the crevices makes the rocking chairs look more like real wood. The black stains are gone, less gunky, more genuine. They're brighter, fresher, but still a little lived in. Just like me.

29
HANNAH

NATE SQUEEZES MY HAND AND a current runs from my fingers up to my shoulders to my smile. I can't believe we left Clarkston a week ago. It feels like we've always been together, traveling the world, making new discoveries together, eating every meal with each other. This is how it should be. This is how it could be. This is what being married must be like.

"What ya thinking about? Must be something serious." Nate pushes his glasses up the bridge of his nose.

"Why do you say that?" I feel my cheeks warm. I didn't say the married thing out loud, did I? He seems to know exactly what I'm thinking. *Please don't know exactly*, I plead in my head. *Well, unless you agree. Do you agree?*

"Because you crinkle your forehead when you're thinking. And it's very cute. And the deeper your thoughts, the more you furrow."

"At this time, all passengers must fasten their seat belts," the flight attendant announces over the speaker.

"Man, I always forget to buckle," George says to no one in particular from across the aisle as he lifts his hips and searches for his seat belt.

"That's why they remind you." I smile at George, grateful for the distraction.

Nate fastens his buckle and reaches for mine. His hands brush the side of my waist, as if it's perfectly natural for him to be touching me, encircling me. He clicks me in. "There. Now what were your deep thoughts?"

"Hmm." I crack my gum. So Nate wasn't completely distracted. "Okay. Busted." I smile and put my head on his shoulder. Partly because it feels so nice and partly to buy a little time. "I was just thinking that in a way it's like we've always been in Germany, so it's really strange that it's over. Don't you think it's weird we're flying home. It felt like we were living there. I know it sounds silly." I hand the flight attendant my gum wrapper and a napkin as she walks by with a bag. "But at the same time, the week totally flew by. Weren't we just gathering around our tour guide and bumbling through our coffee order? Now we go there every morning. Getting pretzels and coffee, that's what we do. Greta is going to miss us." I laugh.

"'Time is the coin of your life. It's the only coin you have, and only you can determine how it will be spent.' Carl Sandburg said that." Nate smiles. "I'm glad you agreed to spend your coin with me."

This is why I swear I'm in love with him. And I can't say that out loud, because it's too soon, and he's my first boyfriend, and I'm supposed to play it cool. But hello! He's glad I spent my time with him? Who in their right mind wouldn't want to spend their time with him? And he quoted Carl Sandburg. Who does that?

"Thanks for suggesting I come," I say, flipping my gum over with my tongue to stop myself from saying the *L* word out loud. "I would have never taken this trip if you hadn't told me about it. I don't even feel like the same person I was before I came." I shake my head. "That sounds goofy, right? But there is such a ginormous world outside of Ohio, and it's awesome."

"That's the whole point."

Another flight attendant makes his rounds, checking

overhead compartments. I hold my breath, wondering if our jam-packed roller bags will pass inspection. Plus, he might not like the extra shopping bag I kind of stuffed to the side. He opens the bin opposite us and removes an enormous navy blue duffel that's been crammed in haphazardly and clearly doesn't fit, shakes his head, hands it to his partner who carries the dishonorable luggage off to the front, and continues his route through the aisle.

"Whew," I say, loosening my grip, realizing I'd clenched down on our armrests.

Nate laughs at me.

"What? What would we have done if he confiscated our bags?"

"He wasn't going to," Nate says.

"How do you know?"

"Because he has way bigger issues to worry about."

"I guess you're right," I say, internally relieved.

"You worry a lot about the little things," Nate says.

"Only if they can turn into big things."

"So now that we made it through luggage control, what will you worry about next?"

I know he's teasing, and he's right. I don't want him to think I'm a spaz. I blow my bangs and they flutter across my forehead. "This will sound crazy, but what happens tomorrow? I'll wake up in my dorm and go to breakfast with my roommates and nothing at Clarkston will have changed, but everything for me will have changed."

"We're not meeting for pretzels and coffee tomorrow morning?" Nate teases.

"Where could we even do that?"

"We could meet at Corner Cup or the Student Union, and we will. I hope. Lots. But c'mon, Han. We'll have classes and life too. We've got to take this and carry it around with us and use it in our real lives. Like new keys on our key chains. We don't have to use them every day, but we need to know they exist, in case we have to unlock something."

"Right." How did this conversation go from him being so

glad I spent my precious coin of time with him to going back to the real world? I don't want to go back to my real life. I like this one better, thank you very much. And if my key has to do with him, I *want* to use it every day.

The plane's wheels lurch beneath my seat. Like someone's tugging me from below. And as we roll forward, away from Berlin and toward Ohio, I lean toward the window and try to take a picture with my phone. But it's misty this morning and the view is a blur. The square gray and glass buildings could be of any airport in the world. They are not unique, or even memorable. A dreary good-bye making me question if the adventure was even real. I look at Nate, who's adjusting his backpack under the seat in front of him. His sandy hair. The way his glasses sit on his nose. His certainty about everything, even exactly how to line up his backpack. These past few days, every detail of him has belonged to me. But already, before we even get into the air, I question if they were ever really for me, or just on loan, just part of the trip, like any spring break romance. When we get back, will it be like *High School Musical*? Will I be the girl trying to fit in and Nate will be Zac Efron? Mmm, Nate's eyebrows actually remind me of Zac Efron.

He looks up as if on cue so I can get a better view of his eyebrows.

"What?"

"You have great eyebrows." I laugh.

Nate grins. He takes his index finger and smoothes it over one then the other of my brows, sending an inner zing to my eye sockets. "So do you." He pauses. "Actually, you have great everything."

The plane lifts from the ground at a surprisingly fast angle bumping our foreheads together. Nate kisses me. My stomach lurches, then we get bumped apart.

It feels like there are giant wads of Double Bubble inside of my eardrums. The pressure builds as the bubbles get larger and larger. Oh please, oh please, let them pop. But instead of a satisfying bang of relief, it feels like the bubbles are sucked back in, like my ears are inverting themselves.

And so does my life as I depart the spring break I never imagined and my fantasyland where only Nate and I lived in our own little world.

Whoosh.

We're headed home.

30
PALMER

"HOME SWEET HOME!" I ANNOUNCE as I swing the door to our dorm open. It smells flat and moldy, like it's been abandoned for months, maybe years, not the six days we were in Florida.

"Somebody light a candle, pronto." I set up suitcases near my bed and dig in my top dresser drawer for a contraband match.

"My legs are so tight from traveling, I've got to go on a run," Kat says, dropping her duffel in the middle of the room and bending over her legs in a stretch.

"It's getting dark out." Claire glances out the window.

"Don't worry." Kat bends her left knee. "It's not dark yet, and this'll be a quick one, just around the quads. I feel so lethargic after napping on the plane. I start practice tomorrow, so I don't want to wear myself out. But if I don't move, I'll implode."

Claire bites her lip.

I strike the match with a hiss and light an illegal oatmeal

cookie–scented candle—no fire in the dorms. "Better already."
I shake out the match.

Kat traded out her slides for her running shoes and pulled
her hair back all in the time it took me to light the candle.
"Outta here," she says.

"Suit yourself," I tell her. "A run is the last thing I need. I
feel like we've been running all day. I need to get unpacked,
acclimated."

"Travel makes me antsy." Kat slides her earbuds in her
ears. "See y'all in a bit."

"It's chilly in here." Claire shudders, unzips her bag, and
dumps everything in it on the top of her steamer trunk.
Hannah would die if she saw this. Well, actually, she'd
probably open up Kat's suitcase, fold everything from it and
from Claire's heap, and lay their clothes neatly in drawers, and
then die. By the looks of things Hannah's not even back yet.
Where is she?

Claire sits on her bed and tugs off her shoes. "I was
wondering if you would mind if I used your phone?" She looks
at me with her azure eyes. Hard to be too mad at her about
being messy when I know I'm really just ticked at Hannah and
feeling slightly off kilter from too many nights of drinking with
Tristan.

"Sure. Who are you texting? Josh? Because he was
heartbroken you didn't make out with him."

"I was thinking of checking in with Megan, see if she has
any updates on Mom. Josh is sweet. But the last thing I need is
a long-distance crush. No offense." Claire kicks my shin
playfully.

"None taken, although I do miss kissing Tristan. Already.
He is smokin'. I didn't even know a guy could be that hot." I
plop down next to Claire and hand her my phone. "So I dated

Keegan forever, right?"

"Right." Claire unravels her hair from a braid.

"And well, we went really far, too far, actually." I think back to all the times Keegan pressured me sexually and shiver. "I thought Keegan was the best kisser in the world, because what did I have it to compare him to? Not much. But Tristan, he makes me laugh so much that I don't worry about if I'm kissing him the right way, or if my hand should be behind his neck or on his cheek or on his back. He makes me feel free. I can just enjoy it. And there is so much to enjoy. He barely even tried anything on me, which is such a relief." I sigh out loud. "Just lots of kissing and his arms around me. Did I mention he smells soooo good?"

Claire finishes typing out a message to her cousin. "Wouldn't it be great if we knew ahead of time if a guy would try anything?" She asks, handing me back my phone. "When are you going to see him again? How did you two leave things? And"—she lies down and crosses her legs behind her—"does Tristan mean you don't like Michael anymore?"

"Good question." I unzip my boots and slide completely onto Claire's bed, grabbing a butterfly Pillow Pet to hold. "Tristan's working as a lifeguard at the beach all summer. I may ask my parents if I can spend the summer in Florida, or just go down for weekends. Summer's only"—I count in my head—"six weeks away. Plus, hmm, Michael is hot too, but in a totally different way. He was interviewing all of break, so I barely heard from him."

"Six weeks?" Claire hits the sheets with the palm of her hand.

"About."

"Not a lot of time to figure out my destiny."

"I thought you were going home …" I stop myself.

"Might be time for a change in plans. You could come to Florida with me." Even as I say it, I wonder if I'll even be in Florida. I hadn't thought about Michael, except in passing, until Claire just mentioned him. I kind of pushed him out of my mind, living in the moment. I wonder what he's doing this summer. And if I did hang out in Florida this summer, I'd want to be with Tristan. "Or you always have your rich aunt, right?" I throw out quickly.

Claire scissors her feet back and forth slowly. "She'd let me stay there again. At least, I'm pretty sure she would. And I could probably teach at the same dance studio. It's just I haven't asked either place, and it's so soon. Last year I arranged all of that before Christmas!"

She picks my phone off my laugh and checks the face. "Speaking of… no answer from Megan." She lies back down. "What do you think, God?" she asks the ceiling.

I rub the small of Claire's back. I have two houses to choose from. She's virtually homeless. "We'll figure this out." I lay down next to her. "Look at us. At Christmas break we thought we had summer all planned out. I was going home and working at the mall for shoe discounts. You were going home and making your mom's family room your room, and now we're completely undecided."

"Like my major." Claire sits back up.

"Hah!" I laugh. "It's confusing. There should be a book about how to spend your college summers. Really! It should talk about best summer jobs, internships, etc., based on what you're looking for. And list the top towns college kids should hang out in. And there should be a chapter about staying at home versus traveling or trying new adventures. And how relationships fit into all of that. You know, how to do the long-distance thing when you go home. How many times is the right amount to visit each other over the summer?" My brain is on fire with ideas.

"Why don't you write that book?" Claire asks.

The pipes clang deep from within the walls of our old dorm as the heater fires up.

I shake my head. "No. No. I'm more of a reporter. You know, news stories." But I do like the idea of a book.

"Seriously, that kind of book would be great. All of us could use it. Kat would want a chapter about summer workouts and having to come back to school early to train for college sports. You know Hannah's going to freak about not seeing Nate over the summer."

"If they're still together after their field trip," I growl.

"Don't you think they will be?"

"Who knows?" I wave my hands. "Anyway. It would be a good book."

"Then write it."

"I wish I had as much confidence in my writing as you do," I admit to Claire.

"Why don't you?"

I look at her, staring at me blankly, like she really doesn't know, like she really can't fathom I don't belong at *InkSpot* and *QuadAngles*. Like Claire hasn't considered I'm not good enough.

"It's not that easy," I say.

"Life isn't easy." Claire smiles, as if that's a positive statement.

"I could use a glass of wine." The words pop out too quickly. Wine has been softening the sharp edges of life lately. For me. Not for Claire.

She opens her mouth but stops.

"I was joking." I laugh.

"I've had wine before," Claire says as if she didn't hear me. "I didn't like how it made me feel."

"Really?" I hug my knees to my chest. "I couldn't talk about it with Kat or Hannah, because they've never even tried it. And I don't want Hannah to get all preachy at me. I mean, we're adults. We can vote and live on our own and get married. The drinking age is just silly."

Claire points her toes.

"Did you like how it tasted?" I ask, grateful for the chance to ask somebody who won't think I'm a fool for asking.

"It was okay." Claire reaches out over her toes, stretching. "It wasn't awful. The warmth was nice."

"It is. Comforting and soothing, almost."

"Almost." Claire rolls her ankles. "But it also made me feel a little uncertain, off balance. And I didn't like that."

"I think that's why I like it," I confess. "I think I work so freaking hard to do the right thing. To be a mass communications major instead of creative writing because my parents want me to earn a degree that I can 'make a career of.'" I make air quotes for emphasis. "And then busting it to get grades that matter, that will make *InkSpot* and *QuadAngles* take me seriously." I kick the mattress above with my feet. "Sorry."

"It's all right," Claire says. "I get it. I have to maintain grades for my scholarship, and the pressures in the dance studio are intense. Paige fainted last week because she hasn't been eating, and Brooke stepped in and started dancing Paige's part as if she'd been practicing it all along. It's ugly."

I scrunch up my face. "That is ugly. You all look so dainty and innocent."

Claire arches her eyebrow.

"Anyway. I'm a try-hard." It feels good to confess what I've always known. I try really hard to make it look like I've got it all together—too hard. "And I think the wine helps me try less and just enjoy. Does that make sense?"

Claire laughs. "It's funny. I feel like I'm grasping onto a ledge for dear life. Anything that would make me loosen my grip makes me feel like I'll fall. That's what wine did for me."

"So you're hanging on tight, and I'm trying to loosen my grip," I say. "There must be somewhere in between."

"There must be," she mumbles and taps her Bible peeking out from under her pillow. "I bet it's all in here." Claire sits up halfway and smiles at me.

"You're right," I say as I curl up next to her, surprised by how wiped out I suddenly feel. "I'm sure it's all in there. It's been a long time since we've had one of our roommate Bible studies. We should get back to those."

31

HANNAH

"OHMYGOSH, I'M BACK! I CAN'T believe it!" I call, entering my dorm room, a welcome sight after the cinderblock I'd stayed in with Allie, Rachel, and Laney all week.

"Hi," Palmer calls from our bedroom, then whispers something to someone else.

"Who's here?" I ask, rushing in. "Oh, I missed you guys so much!" I hug Palmer and Claire, who look like they've been napping, feeling a piece of my heart leap inside my chest. "My roommates in Germany were the worst. I hadn't even considered I'd have to live with someone else for a whole week. I guess they were actually nice enough, I just felt the whole time like we'd landed there from different planets. One of them had dated Nate before! Can you believe it? Where's Kat? Have you guys eaten dinner yet? I'm starving! Oh, and I have something for you. Something little."

"You got bangs!" Palmer shouts.

"Cute," Claire says, reaching forward and flipping my hair with her fingers.

"I'm right here," Kat says, hugging me from behind.

"Ew. You're sweaty."

"Sorry. That's my life." Kat laughs.

"How was your run?" Claire asks.

"Good. It was real good. Thanks." Kat kicks her leg up on the nightstand and stretches over it. "It just felt good to move. When did you get back, Hannah?"

"About five seconds ago. Ohhh, roomie hug." I grab her and pull her down to the bottom bunk where Palmer and Claire are still lying and tug them all into an awkward embrace. "Okay, wait here, just a sec." I dash to my bag and pull out the mugs wrapped in tissue paper I bought for them. "Okay, one for each of you."

"These are so cute," Claire says, running her finger along the smooth rim.

"Who is this little dude?" Kat asks.

"He's the traffic light guy." I laugh. "Isn't he cute as a boot? So there are two of him as a green light and one of him as a red light."

"I got the red one." Palmer raises her hand. "He's got his arm out in a tee, like he's about to do a balance for yoga. I like it. Thanks."

I exhale, just now realizing how much I craved these roommate moments, someone to hug and laugh and share stories with. I mean, I shared with Nate in different ways, but something was missing. "You guys are the best! I had a blast but totally missed you. Man, this trip made me appreciate you!"

"We missed you too," Palmer says with a bitter undertone. "We never heard from you. Not one text."

"Ohmigosh!" My stomach flips. "My phone." I pull it out of my pocket and wave it in the air as evidence. "My parents made me turn off the texting and calls. Too expensive. I tweeted you a couple of times and posted some pics on Pinterest, but we barely had Wi-Fi anywhere, and when we did, it seemed like there were a million other things going on. It was brutal. I tried to tell you. Well, that was the day you were so mad. I'm sorry, Palm. So sorry. Did you think…?"

"They did? You did?" Palmer asks, her features rearranging themselves on her face. "Me too." She nods and comes toward me. We hug for a long minute.

"Missed you," I whisper.

"Missed you too," Palmer answers softly, but then pulls away. I'm so relieved we made up. That's the longest fight we've ever had. But she still seems distant.

"Smart idea," Kat says. "I wish we could've heard from you, but those roaming fees are nasty."

"Yeah, so I just got texts from all of you when I landed. We so need to catch up."

"Not much to tell from our end." Palmer grins. "We just roamed around without any plans. It's a miracle we got anywhere or did anything or even ate without you there to keep us organized."

"Ha-ha!" I kiss her cheek.

"Did you say something about dinner?" Claire asks.

"Yes, please. Believe it or not, I miss dorm food! You guys had been chatting up how fabulous European food is. Someone forgot to tell the Germans. Except the restaurant your dad steered us to, Kat. I totally owe him one." I put my hand on her shoulder. "But if I never eat another pretzel again, it will be too soon. It's like all we ate every morning with our coffee. Which was…" I shake my head. "Trust me, you don't want to drink it."

"I missed you, Hannah." Claire slides out of the bed. "Give me about two minutes, and I'm ready for dinner."

"I need five." Kat drums her thumb ring against the metal frame of our bunk. "World's fastest shower." And she darts into the bathroom, then sticks her head back out. "The bangs really suit you. Nice."

"How about you, Palmer?" I ask. "What do you think?" I turn my head to get her opinion on my bangs.

"Didn't you just spend a year and a half growing out your bangs?" She steps over to the mirror and brushes her hair.

I bob my head. But feel like she's shot a poisonous dart at me. She's the one I really hoped would like them. She's the one with the style sense. Didn't we just make up? I blow a bubble and turn my gaze to our main room.

"Oh. Whose suitcase? Kat's, right?" I grab Kat's duffel out

of the middle of the floor and put it on her bunk for her where she'll find it easily.

"I knew that would bug you," Palmer says, glancing at me, almost like she's accusing me. Why is she being so harsh? I must be imagining it.

"No biggie." I smile, grabbing my own suitcase.

I start unpacking, putting dirty clothes in my laundry bag to take down to the machines after dinner and sliding the few clean items I have in my drawers.

"Stories?" Claire asks, tying a scarf around her hair.

"I'm not even sure where to start!" I shut my jewelry drawer. "Nate is absolutely incredible. He was so supportive and sweet every moment. I mean, it was a hard trip, you know? Having to face some horrific realities about humanity. Well, if I get started I won't be able to stop, but I'll give the full version at dinner. Short version—so glad I went. I learned so much, and did I mention Nate is dreamy?"

"I think you did." Claire grins and slides on her cowboy boots.

Soon we're all sitting at our favorite big round table by the window in our most visited dining hall.

"It's so weird, because this feels exactly the same as last week. I mean, here we are, and this is what I do, but I feel like everything has changed. Everything!" I take my gum out of my mouth and stick it on the edge of my plate, dip my fork in my mashed potatoes, and take a bite. "Yum! American food!" I call out.

"So the food was that bad?" Palmer sips her water through a straw. "We ate pretty well at the beach."

I strike my hand across my forehead. "I haven't even asked you guys about the beach!"

That's why Palmer's angry.

"I'm so sorry. I'm completely out of it from flying for, like, fourteen hours straight across the world. Was it great?" I ask.

"So great," Kat says.

Claire adds, "It was beautiful. I'd never seen the ocean before and it just overwhelmed me. In a good way. We missed you, though."

"Great time. Good music. Love runnin' on the beach. Palmer's place is unbelievable!" Kat takes a bite of her baked apples.

"Isn't it?" I stab my fork into my chicken, famished, realizing even the times we got decent food, I was so into Nate, I kind of forgot to eat. "Palmer, you and your parents are awesome to share it with everyone."

"Guess who we saw?" Palmer leans toward me.

"Who?"

"Tristan!"

"The guy with those crazy cool eyes and dark eyebrows?"

"That one." She bats her eyelashes.

"So did you guys hang out?"

"You could say that." Palmer smiles.

"Or you could say they were attached at the waist, maybe more at the lips." Kat laughs.

I start to ask how all of that came to be when I feel my phone buzz. "A text from Nate." I show them the screen. "He's such a sweetie. Just checking to make sure I made it back to my room and got all settled." We text back and forth for a few minutes.

"Earth to Hannah." Palmer taps me on the shoulder.

"What? Oh, sorry. I was trying to find that emoticon with the two hearts connected."

"Whatever," Palmer says softly.

"Why are you mad at me?" I ask, wounded by all the little jabs she's given me since I walked in the door.

Palmer looks directly at me. "I feel like you are letting Nate take over your entire life. You get home and blab blab blab about your trip, not even asking about ours, the one the other three of us went on, until we bring it up." She raises her eyebrows. "I start to tell you about Tristan, and you ignore me because you get a text from lover boy. And you don't just text him back politely, you completely disappear into your own little text world." She taps my phone. "We haven't seen you all week. What the heck is going on with you?"

I slide my phone out from under her hand. Tears loom, but I'm too angry to allow my hurt to show. I feel my vocal chords tightening and shaking. "I want you to be happy for me. I want to share it with you. I want you to like my bangs and ask about Berlin and think it's awesome I finally have someone in my life who cares about me. But instead you're mad." The tears sneak down anyway. I look at my tray to hide them. "You can talk about Tristan, but I can't talk about Nate?" I push out the words.

From my peripheral vision, I see Kat steal a glance at Claire. I'm sure this is awkward for them, but I can't help it. "I couldn't wait to tell you everything. I wanted to show you my haircut and my pictures. And—" I can't say anything else. My throat is too tight now and the tears sting too much. I grab my tray, pull the fudge cookie I'd saved for dessert off the edge, and dump the rest in the trash.

32
KAT

NINETY-FOUR, NINETY-FIVE, NINETY-SIX. I keep my ball in the air, tap after tap, juggling it with my thighs, laces, chest, whatever it takes. When I finally drop the ball, I notice a few of my teammates and our trainer, Johnny, starting to arrive. They chat as they line up water bottles and bags bulging with soccer balls along the bench. They're all talking and stretching, but I'm so pumped I have to keep moving.

Johnny calls, "Kat, let me take a look at that ankle of yours."

I dribble over to where he's set up his gear.

"All right, now, sit down."

I sit.

"How's it feelin'?"

"Good," I assure him, eyeing Coach DeLuca, who's just showed up wearing his black Clarkston fleece and red hat. "Real good."

"I'll be the judge of that." Johnny presses the palm of his hand onto the flat of my foot. "Press back."

I push as if I'm pedaling a bike. Then he has me do some side-to-side resistance tests.

"Okay, let me tape it and we'll see how it holds up. Careful on the grass. No balance exercises for you afterward."

"Okay." My chest burns. If Johnny won't let me do the balance drills, there's nothing I can do about that. I'll just have to prove to Coach I've completely recovered on the field.

As a team we dribble, pass, and shoot, Coach DeLuca scribbles on his clipboard. Time to show him what I'm made of.

We run laps, then weave in and out of cones dribbling the ball. Our assistant coach, Doug, pairs us off for Super 7 drills while Coach DeLuca takes more notes. For the last third of practice we scrimmage, our first time to play together since the end of our fall season. I'm a midfielder, always have been, but halfway through the match Coach switches me to defense.

I jog over and slap hands with Emily, but my brain screams, WHY?

"Kat, move up and out," our goalie, Molly, calls.

I grit my teeth. Furious I needed correction, I move into position before Coach sees. The ball drops back my way, and I boot it over the center line, but the ball lands right in front of Sarah, a freshman who's wearing a pinnie, which means in this scrimmage, she's my opponent. I can't make mistakes like that. Luckily, Latoya steals it from her and drives it down toward the goal, but the ball goes out-of-bounds.

I widen my eyes as far as they'll go, anxious for the throw-in, hating that I'm back here, knowing I have to do my best in spite of it.

Ginger, who's on the other team, traps the ball with her chest and drops it down to her foot. As she dribbles down the line toward me, I drop into position. She tries to cut left, but I step in front of her and steal the ball. Out of the corner of my eye, I see Latoya sprinting toward the goal. I pass her a long through ball. She fakes out a defender and scores.

"Yes!" I bounce on my heels.

When Coach Doug blows the whistle, I sprint to Coach DeLuca while others meander over out of breath. I'm winded too, but I will not be last. I must be first. Even if my lungs collapse.

"Decent work out there, today, ladies. Considering." His European accent sounds a bit scratchy from the cold, damp April morning. "But we have a long way to go before our friendly match against University of Kentucky in a few weeks, yes? You all will stay with Johnny and Coach Doug, who will lead you through your strength, agility, and balance training. I will see you back tomorrow."

Girls shove their hands in the center of our huddle for our closing cheer, but Coach isn't done. "I should have the roster for that match on Friday." He turns his back and strides away from the field.

My heart jerks in my chest. Friday? I clench my jaw. Friday. Man, that's soon.

"One two three, Cardinals!" everyone cheers. Every girl wants to be on that roster. Heck, every girl wants to start. But I want it more.

33
CLAIRE

"DON'T WAIT UP." PALMER GRABS her phone off the table by the door and pops it in her purse.

"Hey," Kat says, opening the door right into Palmer. "Sorry."

"No prob. Just on my way out."

"Hi, bye," Kat says, slipping past Palmer and into our room. "You look fabulous. Where ya headed?"

"Journalism happy hour." Palmer blows us kisses and latches the door behind her.

"Where's Han?" Kat looks around our room. "Wait, let me guess—Nate the Great?"

"How'd you know?"

"So, do ya think we should be at all worried about Diane Sawyer's drinking habits?" Kat motions toward the door.

"Maybe. I don't know." I grab a strand of hair. It's darker than most, almost brown, buried in the back where sun never hits it. I rub it between my fingers, trying not to judge Palmer. But I am worried.

"Yeah, me either." Kat sits next to me on our futon. "Claire, I declare, someone has done a dot to dot on your ankles."

"Cool, right?"

"Sure. If you say so. Is it some kind of tattoo or something? Clue me in, girl."

"I just got back from kinesiology class."

Kat wipes her forehead with the back of her arm. "And...?"

"We had to mark all the vulnerable parts on our feet. See, this blue dot is where my arch isn't really supported. And we had to draw lines up our Achilles tendons." I graze my fingers along the dark green marker line on the back edge of my heel. "I thought you'd love it."

Kat doesn't answer, just concentrates her gaze on my feet.

"With how much you depend on your feet for soccer, and then how vulnerable you learned they were when you sprained your ankle. For me, it's this revelation, about how I dance and what I expect my feet to be able to do, even when they're so vulnerable."

Kat leans over and touches the dots gently on my left arch. "Like here."

"That tickles." I laugh and wiggle my foot away. "But yeah. There."

"I've thought about it before, how we're both athletes," she says. "I've seen how hard you work your body. But I'd never considered how we're both so dependent on our feet. You know a lot of athletes are more reliant on their hands or arms."

"Our feet carry us. Literally and figuratively." I twist the strand of hair around my finger. "I love this class. I think I might become a kinesiology major. Now that would be cool.

Right?"

"What happened to pre-law?" Kat looks up from untying her shoes. "Kinesiology would be cool, though. Plus, you'd sound so darn smart. How do you even spell that? K-i-n…" Kat takes off her running shoes and peels off her socks. "Sorry," she smirks, grimacing at the smell.

"Mine have been worse." I shrug.

"I think I might major in history." Kat opens our window.

"Random."

"Very. But if you're actually picking a major, then I will too. And, well, I like history. A lot. When I was in Barcelona, my favorite part was the day I spent in Montserrat." She closes her eyes for a second, then looks at me. "For lots of reasons. But I loved learning all about how the monastery was built way up there on those cliffs and the history of the Catalonians in Barcelona, that they don't even declare themselves Spanish."

"The who? And they don't?"

"The Catalonians are the people who live in Barcelona, which is a giant city, but they consider it their own separate nation. Awesome, right?"

"I sometimes think I'm my own separate nation." I smile at the thought. "Then it's settled. Although, it sounds like you should major in world cultures instead of history. But whatever. We're going places."

"Great places." Kat shoves her stinky socks into her shoes. "But back to our regularly scheduled program. Your feet!" Kat goes back to staring at my bare feet.

I stretch them out in front of me so I can look too.

"All right, so I'm not joking, this class is awesome. I realized I need my feet. As a dancer, I rely on my entire body. It has to function properly. But without my feet I can't even stand."

"Even when I'd rather someone else carry me." Kat leans back and closes her eyes.

I wonder if she's thinking about Nicholas or about how much she misses Alex or how her mom has gone AWOL mentally. Maybe her mom would get along with my mom.

"Wouldn't that be nice?" I sigh.

"Wait. Don't you have guy dancers who lift you up and twirl you around every now and then?" Kat asks.

"Every now and then, but rarely. Thank goodness. I'm always a basket case, thinking of trusting them enough, you know, actually jumping up into a random guy's arms and trusting he'll catch me."

"So maybe it's a good thing we don't have that in soccer." Kat laughs, but keeps her eyes closed. "Not to mention how ridiculous we'd look."

I laugh and lean back next to her, closing my eyes too.

We sit in silence for a minute or two. It's a nice quiet. I can tell Kat's thinking. And my mind flits from the blue and green marks on my feet to how vulnerable I am. Especially now. If Mom was supposed to be the dancer who caught me, she failed. I jumped and she didn't put her arms out, or she put them out and then let me slide right through them. I'm alone on the dance floor, awkward, twisted, a little bruised, and not sure how to gracefully get up from here.

An image of strong arms outstretched to me appears. Not the bare arms of my dance partner. Long, loose sleeves billow around these arms. I don't see who they belong to, but I don't need to. I sense warmth and assurance that God's arms are always ready to catch me and twirl me around. He'll never drop me. I love how safe that feels. I wish life didn't make me forget who is really holding me.

You've been holding me a lot lately, God, I pray in my head. *Thankfully no spinning. But thanks for keeping me up, stronger this time than in the past with Mom. Distance from her seems to help some.*

Plus, you're getting stronger, I feel Him telling me. *When a ballerina is being held by another dancer, she still needs to be strong enough to hold her pose.*

I picture the end-of-year production we're rehearsing and the move Ms. Kladinski has suggested for the end of my duet with Bartholomew. What if I were strong enough?

"Shoot. Speaking of feet, I'm supposed to be doing these blasted balance exercises." Kat abruptly jumps up out of her quiet place. "My ankle wasn't strong enough before, but it is now, so I'm behind."

The words "strong enough" echo inside of me.

Am I? Strong enough?

A warmth flares in my heart. God reassuring me, once again.

Kat stands on her left leg, extending her arms out like an airplane. "You do this in ballet, right?"

I tilt my head to take her in, foot flexed, body wobbling. "Umm. Sort of." I stand and touch her abs gently. "Pull in here, like you're locking them into place."

"Uh-huh."

"And pretend you have an imaginary string pulling you upward from your head." I mime a string with my hands.

Kat lifts her head and leans too far to the right. I spot her, pulling her weight back over the center of her left foot. "You just have to stay centered."

"Right."

Centered, I tell myself.

34
HANNAH

"I DON'T KNOW WHAT'S GOTTEN into you, young lady, but you are not nearly as high and mighty as you seem to think you are these days." Mom's voice is so sharp it could cut my phone in half.

I have no idea what she's talking about, yet my hand trembles, making my phone bump against my ear. My cheeks flame, like when I was in third grade and Mr. Steinberg would always say in his creepy, quiet voice, "Eyes on your own paper." My eyes were on my own paper, but just the thought that he might think they weren't scared the daylights out of me.

"What do you have to say for yourself?"

"I…I…I'm sorry. What did I do?" I ask, pacing around my room. Palmer and Kat exchange looks. I walk out into the hallway. More pacing room. And privacy.

"What is today, young lady?"

"April 15," I spit out automatically. Which means what. "Tax day?" I try.

"Not funny. What was yesterday?"

"April 14," I say, afraid this sounds a bit sarcastic.

"Bingo."

I search my brain. April 14? April 14! "Oh no, Mom, is she mad? Is she there? What did Sammie say?"

"She tried to be brave. She blew out her candles and opened her presents, and just kind of looked around to make sure she hadn't missed anything. Which she hadn't. Because you didn't send her anything. Really, Hannah? Not even a little trinket from Germany? You didn't even call."

She might as well be saying, "Shame on you." Because that's what I feel. Shame.

I open the door at the end of the hallway, feeling suddenly cramped and crowded and longing for outside. Rain trickles over the eaves and drips onto the porch from the overhang. I sit on the cold brick and listen to the drizzle.

"I'm so sorry. I can't believe I forgot."

"Quite frankly, neither can I."

"I feel horrible. Like, awfully, totally horrible. How can I make it up to her?"

"I don't know, but you better think of something. We're all doing everything we can here to make your college experience the best it can be. You better make sure it's not so good that you forget about home." Mom's breath is heavy in my ear.

"You know I love you guys."

"We love you too," Mom says in her fed-up mom voice. "Think it over, Hannah, and call me back."

"I haven't forgotten," I sputter into the mouthpiece. But I had. And Mom's already hung up.

I shiver and go back inside away from the rain and the chill and the accusations.

"What was I doing yesterday?" I ask Palmer and Kat

when I get back to our room.

"I wasn't around much," Kat says. "Practice early. Weight lifting afterward. Then class."

Palmer is filing her nails. She doesn't look up but says flatly, "You were gone all day. Something about studying with Nate *and* eating dinner with him, since you two were already together."

"Dang it."

"Why?" Kat asks.

"It was Sammie's birthday, and I totally blew it! I swear I'm still off kilter from Germany. You know how it is, Kat, time change, jet-lag, culture shock, and all of that." I realize the travel comment directly to Kat might be a mini-jab at Palmer. Aarrgh!

"It does get you out of whack." Kat shakes her head. There's a ripping sound as she unwinds tape from her ankle.

"Wouldn't know," Palmer comments. "But Tia would be upset if I forgot her birthday. Heck, I'd be upset if she forgot mine."

I grab a piece of gum from the drawer in my desk and pop it in my mouth, allowing the mint to wake up my tongue.

"I forgot my sister's birthday. I mean, I bought her a cool scarf in Germany just like the one I got myself, but I didn't mail it. I didn't get a card. I didn't even send her a text. What kind of a jerk am I?"

"A distracted jerk, that's all. You've got a lot on your mind. Classes are kicking us in the behind this year, plus the travel. I think we're all in over our heads a bit. I know I sure am." Kat wads up the ball of tape she removed and tosses it in the trash can. "Nothin' but net," she says.

"What are you in over your head with?" Palmer looks up from her nails.

"Soccer. Please. We find out Friday who starts for the first spring game." Kat shakes her head.

"And it will be you. For sure." Palmer tosses her hands in the air.

"No 'for sures' about it," Kat answers.

"Sheesh. I thought I was the only one worried about positions." Palmer shakes a bottle of nail polish, slapping it lightly against her palm. "Every word I write for the magazine seems like garbage. I am completely out of my league with those folks. They are so smart and sophisticated. I can't seem to keep up with them."

"You have never had a problem keeping up." I sigh, blowing my bangs out of my eyes. "You've always been two steps ahead."

"You should see how ridiculous I look in a roomful of reporters." Palmer shakes her head.

"I'm not buyin' it." Kat laughs.

"Believe it, lady." Palmer sets down the polish.

"And I don't want to complain. I can't complain. I can't believe I have a boyfriend and that Nate likes me, but I don't know what I'm doing. I've never had a boyfriend before. Kat, you seem so natural with Nicholas. And, Palmer, well, like I was saying. You're two steps ahead. Maybe five."

Palmer laughs, shaking her head.

Kat snorts. "Hardly. I haven't even called Nicholas since we've been back. How's that for natural?"

"Get out. Really?" Palmer asks.

Kat nods. "Sad but true. Tryin' to stay focused on soccer. Is that awful?"

"No." I shake my head. "Me? I either talk too much or not enough. I want to let Nate know how I feel, but at the same time I don't want to come across as clingy, so I bite my tongue. I change the subject, and then I wonder why I didn't say something. I am an awkward loser around him." I sink into the futon. "And now I've forgotten my own sister. And I didn't buy Owen a single Lego and there was this giant Legoland place. And I thought about it. I really did, but then Nate wanted to check out some architecture that was brilliant, and I never got back to the Legos. I'm a jerk."

"Not a jerk." Palmer joins me on the futon and places her hand on my knee. The first time she's seemed like my old friend since before spring break. It gives me a strange comfort, like my blanket when I was small. "Just overwhelmed," she adds.

"Way overwhelmed." I lean my head on her shoulder, and it feels like everything will be okay.

"Mail her the scarf, but also get Sammie something fabulous and have it sent to her school, like roses or a cookiegram or something, a big production. She'll love it, and she'll get over the tardiness in a heartbeat." Palmer beams.

"You have the best ideas!"

"That is a good idea," Kat agrees. "I should file that one away."

"I think I'm going to use it for Tia's birthday," Palmer says. "It was a pretty fabulous idea."

"Okay, Miss Fabulous." Kat looks at her. "Now for Claire's birthday. We have to plan something pretty fab for that too.

35

CLAIRE

I HEAR PALMER'S VOICE AND Hannah's giggles and a loud, "Dang it all!" from Kat. They claimed they all needed to do something in our bedroom at the same time while I'm studying on the couch. On my birthday. So I'll play along.

"*Happy birthday to you. Happy birthday to you. Happy Birthday, dear Claire Bear. Happy birthday to you.*" Hannah's beautiful voice carries the tune while Palmer carries a plate of cupcakes frosted bright blue with big icing eyes and Oreos for mouths.

"Cookie Monster!" I squeal.

Kat waves a pom-pom around in the back of their little parade chanting, "C is for cookie, that's good enough for me."

"These are the cutest things ever," I say. I knew they were up to some sort of birthday surprise, or at least I suspected it, at least hoped it, but somehow all of them standing in front of me with goofy grins and Muppet cupcakes overwhelms me. One fast, hot tear shoots down my right cheek.

"Whatcha waitin' for? Blow out the candles, already," Kat encourages, sitting down next to me. "We don't want any wax on our cake."

"Make a wish," Palmer says.

I hold my breath and look inward. My wish is really more

of a prayer. *Dear God, please help Mom out of this downward spiral, chemical-infused high, serious funk.* But that wish seems tangled, like not enough, like the wrong words or the wrong order of words, making this magic spell defunct. I blow and all but two of the twenty candles go out, proving I got the magic wrong.

Hannah leans forward and blows them out before I even finish my breath, then sings, "And many more."

"They are fantastic," I say. "Look at their eyes."

"Right?" Palmer chimes. "I got them at Schneiders, no surprise. I wanted to make you a cake, but we don't exactly have the equipment." She waves her hands toward our mini fridge and coffee maker. "But next year? Look out! When we have our own apartment, with our own kitchen, I will be dangerous."

"I hope they turn our tongues blue!" Hannah peeps.

It's a relief to see Hannah and Palmer getting along. The tension between them seems to have mellowed. With my new job, ballet, and classes, I haven't been home much the last few days, and to be honest it was nice to escape the strain between those two. Good to have friendliness back in the air, even if it's just for my birthday. We could all use a calm, safe place.

"They're almost too cute to eat." I pick up a cupcake loaded with frosting.

"Almost, but not quite." Palmer raises her eyebrows.

"Let's dive in." Hannah produces paper plates with Elmo and matching napkins as well as plastic forks from her secret stash of party supplies. I have no idea where she gets or stores these things.

"Ahhh." I close my eyes, letting extreme amounts of sugar fizzle on my tongue. "This is the most delicious cupcake I have ever eaten, ever."

"You have to open your present too," Hannah says, pointing to the small silver box next to the forks. I'd missed it all together.

"You guys. Cake was enough. Plenty. More than enough." I look to their three faces, amazed really. "You didn't have to get me a present too."

"Sure we did." Kat hands me the box.

My fingers shake as I untie the pink ribbon and open the lid. Inside, nestled in a square of cotton, is a silver chain with a square wooden charm. I pick it up, feeling the texture of the tile on my fingers, smooth on one side, bumpy on the other. I flip to the bumpy side inscribed with the letter *C*. "A Scrabble square! That is really clever." I turn it back to the smooth side and examine it closely. It's a postage stamp, French.

My thumb glides over the charm as I feel my forehead scrunch. "Where did you find this?"

"At an art festival over the summer!" Palmer says. "It just screamed, 'Claire.' I mean, really, a French stamp on a *C*. It was too perfect. I bought it on a whim, texted a pic to these guys. And we all agreed. It's been so hard to keep it a secret for months and months."

"It also screams *C* for Cookie Monster," Kat adds.

"You were thinking of my birthday way back in the summer at an art fair?" I swallow.

"Sure."

"Let's put it on you," Hannah offers, gently taking the chain from me. She slides it around my neck and fastens it under my hair. "There you go. Take a look." She points to the mirror on our door.

"It's perfect." I hold the pendant to my chest, feeling my heart beat right under the charm.

"Best present you got today?" Kat asks.

"Yeah." I smile. "Only present I got today, but still the best. By far."

"Get out!" The growl that sometimes emerges from Kat lets loose.

"Your mom didn't send you anything?" Hannah is at my side.

I shake my head. I wasn't going to tell them. I didn't want a pity party. I just wanted them to know how grateful I am for what they did for me. For caring that much. For planning that long ago.

"She probably sent you something in the mail. I haven't

checked it yet." Hannah smiles, trying to reassure all of us.

"I checked. Just in case." I suck in my lips and look at the ceiling.

"So uncool." Kat stomps her foot.

"Mom's in denial of everything right now. I called Aunt Denise after we got back from the beach and she said Mom acted like everything was grand when she visited. Mom was busy with all of her usual distractions. I'm guessing my birthday wasn't on the top of her mind."

"A card?" Palmer asks.

I shake my head again, feeling the warm sting of tears. "It's fine. Really. She just…I can't explain. What you guys did…" I suck in my lips again, to hold back the shakes. "Totally awesome. Best birthday ever."

36
KAT

THE GIRL NEXT TO ME hacks so loudly, I think she might be losing a lung. It doesn't matter how much she tries to cover her mouth with the crook of her elbow. I'm pretty sure some of those germs found their way over to me. I check the time on my phone. Again. I've been sitting here for twenty-three minutes. Twenty-three! And it feels like years. How can this be happening? This cannot be happening.

My sweat has turned cold and damp, clinging to my shirt, which now clings to my skin. I shiver in my plastic seat, willing my ankle not to hurt. But it's killing me. I tap my pinky ring on the armrest like there's a spasm in my finger.

"Katherine Wiley?" The student worker, who apparently has the unfortunate job requirement of wearing scrubs, looks up from her file.

"That's me." I stand and wince at the sharp twinge in my ankle when I barely put any weight onto it.

"I'll take you back to room three. Do you need help?" She looks at me with bright eyes, like she honestly feels badly for me.

"I'm fine," I practically growl. Not that it's her fault. But I do *not* need help. I can't need help.

"You sure?"

"Mm-hmm," I say as the pain shoots up my leg.

"Okay. Have a seat in here and the doctor will be here in a minute." Her eyes seem less bright, probably because I was rude. I didn't want to be. I'm just fuming at myself. It's all my fault.

Sorry, Alex. I don't know why I feel like I let him down, but I do. The rational part of me knows he's not even here. The irrational part of me wonders why I think he'd care if I rolled my ankle. And I am just calling it a roll, because it cannot be a sprain.

Because I'm running for him. In a way it's true. I run and I run and I run some more. I know I'm doing it to be in great shape. At first it was to earn a starting spot on the lineup. Which Coach announced on Friday that I have, at least for the scrimmage. But that's not enough. Now that Coach has awarded me a starting spot, I'll run to show him I belong there and I need to stay there. Coach has to see that my injury last fall didn't slow me down. But don't I also do it to show the world that the passing of my brother didn't slow me down? Don't I do it because Alex can't?

"Are you okay?" Nicholas peeks his head in my door.

I exhale, wondering how long I've been holding my breath. "Thank the good Lord you're here! I was about to implode."

"What happened?"

"I got myself in a major tangle. After practice, I decided to run the trails home, and I must've hit a branch." I scrunch up my nose, because I will not allow myself to crack.

"This one?" Nicholas bends over my leg and gently runs his hands down my knee to my left ankle.

I twitch.

"Sorry." He pulls back even though he barely touched it.

"I came here straight away. 'Cause if something's wrong, I need the doctor to fix it...now."

"How bad?" Nicholas asks. Only now do I notice his red hair is standing straight up in places.

"Not bad. Can't be." I shake my head. "Sorry I woke you.

That was dumb of me to text you at—whatever time it was. I'm just full of dumb ideas this mornin'."

"It was almost nine. Not that early." He smiles crookedly. "And I'm glad you woke me, even if I don't have class until eleven today. I haven't seen you since you got back from break. A guy could get a complex." He takes my hand, which is trembling a bit, but less so in his warm grip.

My throat tightens. "Nick, I'm sorry. I..." I shake my head, searching for a legitimate excuse, but I know I don't have one. "I told you I'm dumb. I'm just really stressed about soccer right now." I squeeze his hand, maybe to steady mine. "I missed you."

"What have we here?" the doctor asks, opening the door. He's young with broad shoulders and gelled hair. I was expecting an old guy with glasses and bushy eyebrows.

"I rolled my ankle running on the trails." I look him in the eye, daring him to tell me otherwise.

"Let's take a look." He pushes back his sleeves and sits down on the stool designated for him. "Push back on my hand." He grabs the bottom of my foot and I do what he tells me. The same thing I do with Johnny. "Any pain?"

I shake my head. I can do this, and it doesn't hurt. Ha!

"Then let's try this." He moves his hand, giving opposing force to the outside of my foot. "Now push."

I bite my lip.

"Sore?"

I nod.

"Okay, let's try the side."

I push against his hand from left to right without difficulty.

"Okay, it looks like it's just what you said. You rolled it. You've had sprains before?" He raises his eyebrows.

"Yeah. I'm a soccer player. Had a pretty nasty sprain at the end of the season in October."

"You play for Clarkston?" Dr. Biceps asks.

"Yeah." I smile. I love being able to answer that. "Yeah, I do."

"Do you wear a brace or tape?"

"Both. I've just been taping it lately."

"This doesn't look bad. Just a tweak, but always a good idea to have it checked out, especially for an athlete."

I breathe, realizing I'd been holding my breath. Not bad. Just a tweak. *Thank You, God.*

"DeLuca has you doing trail runs?" He tilts his head as he asks.

I look at Nicholas, who narrows his eyes.

"No, sir," I answer.

The doctor raises his eyebrows again, his eyes fixed on me. So are Nicholas's.

"I was running home after practice and took the trails. Dumb. So dumb. Totally my fault." I strain my face muscles to hold back tears.

"You don't need me to tell you this, but from what I've heard, DeLuca works you pretty hard."

I nod, still freezing my face like stone so I don't let any tears sneak out.

"Then after practice, take it easy. Walk home. Or get a ride. And avoid those trails. Too uneven." He rotates his wrists, demonstrating what a trail can do to my ankle.

"Lesson learned," I say.

"Today's Thursday. See how you feel in the morning. If you're up for it, go light on it tomorrow with your brace on. Take a complete break over the weekend. No activity. See how you're doing. If you feel stable again, you can go back to tape, but if you question it at all, I'd keep the brace on." He looks at me. "Make sense."

"Great."

"Come back for a follow-up in two weeks, or sooner if you need me. That's what we're here for." The doctor looks at me, waiting for a response.

"Got it. Thank you."

"Sure thing." He picks up his clipboard and exits.

Nicholas rubs my back. He understands how important this diagnosis is. The tightness in my shoulders and spine unwinds. A stubborn tear pushes its way out of my left eye.

"You okay?" Nicholas brushes the tear away.

"Yeah. I think maybe just relieved."

"Maybe it's a little more than that?" Nicholas asks, rubbing his hand through his wayward red curls.

Maybe it is more, my heart seems to say.

"I think I've been going pretty hard, to try to, you know, do it for Alex," I confess, my words heavy.

"I get that." Nicholas leans back. "I do, Kat. But maybe it's time to focus on what you have, not what you've lost."

I look down at my ankle.

"I don't mean stop thinking about him," Nicholas whispers. "Just that, maybe, like your ankle, there was a season to rest, to stay off of it. But now spring training's started. Time to get back to running life, slowly and carefully, but still being part of it, not running away from it."

I sniff, wiping another tear. Nicholas says things I could never get my head around, but he's always right. I have him. I have an ankle that's rolled, not sprained.

Number one and number two on my gratitude list for the week.

My roommates and I used to keep weekly gratitude lists and compare them. We've gotten out of the habit. Maybe I should get everyone doing that again.

"Maybe you're right." I stand and kiss the top of Nick's curls. "Maybe I should get back on track."

37
HANNAH

"AND NUMBER 18 UP TO BAT for Clarkston," the announcer booms.

"The sun feels incredible," I say, stretching my legs out in front of me in the soft grass to soak up the warmth. "Yikes! Look how pale I am!"

Palmer sips her soda. "You could have been laying out with us in Florida. Sunnier than Germany, I'm guessing." She stretches her legs right up against mine. In the winter, her skin is a lovely olive against my snowflake color. Now, even though she's been back from the beach for almost two weeks, she looks like an Islander. Her comment feels heavier than the words sound. I just want things to be normal.

"Palm, I'm sorry I bailed on Florida. But I had a chance to go to Germany. You'd have done the exact same thing. I thought we were through with this. Can you stop being mad about it?"

"Who says I'm mad?" She shrugs. "Just saying you could be tanner if you wanted to be. Geez!" She snorts.

"C'mon girls," Kat interjects. "We're all here together. It's a gorgeous day. The sun feels amazing, and I got y'all to another sporting event. Think about the tan lines I'll get from this thing." She lifts her left foot sporting a medical-grade ankle brace.

"I think it'll be all the rage. You're basically a trendsetter," Claire says and lies back. I think her eyes are closed, hard to tell for sure under her shades.

"Oh, Kat, where can I get one? I want a crisscross tan on my ankle too." I smile, determined to let Palmer's jabs go. Am I overthinking this one? Is she just jealous I have a boyfriend? A real one. I love the way that sounds. I have a boyfriend! I slide my phone out and text Nate.

AT THE BASEBALL GAME MISSING YOU.

He texts back: IS CLARKSTON PLAYING? WHAT INNING?

"What inning are we in?" I ask out loud.

"Second," Kat answers. "I can only stay through the fourth, though. Then I'll need to go study for my Spanish exam, even though it's not until Monday. I stink at verb conjugation."

"Me too." Claire sits up and tosses her hair over a shoulder. "My French is decent, but I always speak it in the present tense, even when it's supposed to be future perfect."

"What if we could make our futures perfect, just by talking about them in the right way?" Palmer asks.

I have so much to say on that subject, but I need to text Nate back. I'm not sure why he's asking about innings, pretty sure he had a meeting, but maybe, just maybe he'll show up, since there's still a lot of game left.

SECOND INNING. AND IT'S GORGEOUS HERE! WHATCHA DOING?

STUDENT GOVT MEETING. OVER IN 30 MINS. I'LL TXT

THEN.

DEAL.

I check the time on my phone. It's 5:11 now, so at 5:41 I should hear from him. I haven't seen him in two days and I feel like I'll bust. At least we have class tomorrow, but that is far from intimate. "How long are innings?"

"Totally depends," Palmer says. "If the pitcher strikes out three batters in a row, it's bam bam bam, just a few minutes." She extends her fingers like she's counting one, two, three. "But if there are a ton of balls and singles it could take forever."

"Who knew you were so up on your sports facts?" Kat lowers her sunglasses on her nose and peers at Palmer.

"Keegan played baseball. I've been to a zillion games." Palmer's voice sounds distant.

"Do you ever miss him?" I ask, because it sounds like she might.

"Not really." She takes one last loud slurp of her drink, quickly stands, and walks toward the trash can. She's back in a minute, minus her cup and her smile.

"How long did you date?" Claire asks. "I should know, but the only time I ever saw Keegan was at Alex's funeral. Sorry, Kat." Claire puts her hand on Kat's shoulder.

"It's all right," Kat says. "It's where we all saw Keegan last. It's okay to talk about it. It happened." She picks a few pieces of grass, each piece making a slight popping sound, and tosses them lightly in the air. And then she picks some more.

"Almost three years." Palmer shakes her head like she can't believe it.

"Is it hard to come to a baseball game?" Claire asks. "We could have done something else."

"It's fine." Palmer shrugs. "It's just baseball, for crying

out loud. It's not like I can avoid our national pastime just because my ex played. I don't miss him, you know, because Keegan was so evil at the end, but I miss the fun, which we had a lot of. I don't know…"

"But you have Michael, and Tristan too. That's not a bad gig. You're in high demand." I smile, trying to lighten the mood.

"Yeah." Palmer's gaze goes back to the game.

"What's the word from Tristan?" Claire asks.

Palmer pulls out her phone, hits her text icon, and faces the screen to us, which without reading, I can tell is hundreds of texts from Tristan.

"He's always been smitten with you," I say.

"And it's a Clarkston home run!" the announcer calls while John Fogerty's voice croons, "Put me in, Coach—I'm ready to play today."

Kat winces. "There's gotta be a more current song that has to do with baseball. Please?"

"Pretty bad," Claire agrees.

"Keegan loved this song." Palmer puts her hands to her ears. "See, I told you I don't miss him. It's worth breaking up, just so I don't have to listen to his awful taste in music anymore."

"My dream boy would love all the best bands." Claire slides her sunglasses on top of her head.

"Mine too," Kat sighs.

"Mine would be"—I picture Nate in my head—"really smart and interesting and romantic and handsome and old-fashioned." Something twitters inside me as I picture Nate in his glasses, explaining the strengths and weaknesses of the current German government.

"How about you, Palm?" Kat asks.

"Well." She leans back on her elbows. "He'd be, hmm, what would he be?"

"A little tug of war between Michael and Tristan?" Kat asks.

"I'm not really dating either of them," Palmer answers.

"I thought you really liked both of them," Claire says.

"I did. I do." Palmer shakes her head. "I have no idea what I'm doing. In a way it was easier to date Keegan, because I didn't have to think about who to like or who to text, it was always just him."

"Michael's here and Tristan's at I.U., right?" I ask.

"Right."

"Well, does that make it easier? Tristan is adorable, and he was always a sweetheart, but long distance is really hard."

"How would you know?" Palmer asks, her voice icy.

"I wouldn't." I hesitate. Why is she mad? What did I say now? "I just saw what you went through last year with Keegan."

"You never truly got what I went through with Keegan." Palmer stands and smoothes her top. "I've gotta get out of here." She turns her manicured toes in their leather sandals toward the exit and leaves.

"Ouch," Kat says.

"Is she mad because of Keegan or because of me? Is this still about me not going to Florida with you guys? We've kinda been through that, like, a thousand times. She so would have gone to Europe if she'd had the chance. And now it's like she's mad I have a boyfriend. She's mad at me all the time. You guys understand, right?"

Claire rubs my knee. "She's all knotted up about these two boys. Plus, she's not handling the pressure from *QuadAngles* well. She puts too much pressure on herself."

Claire glances at Kat. "And apparently she's missing Keegan a little bit too. I get that. Sometimes I miss my high school boyfriend, even though I haven't seen him since graduation and would never, ever want to get back with him. Just the sweet moments of having someone's hand to hold, ya know?"

I think of the surge I feel when Nate holds my hand, like I'm stronger, prettier, safer, almost invincible, like I've been infused with superpowers. What if we broke up and I didn't have that hand to hold anymore? *No, Hannah, don't think it,* but yes, I'd be desperate for that feeling again.

"Makes sense," I say. "I didn't know she was blue about Keegan. She seems so wrapped up in Michael and Tristan and her new magazine friends. I didn't think she was lacking anything."

"But y'all know Palmer. Always perfume and smiles on the outside. Even when she and Keegan broke up last year—" Kat starts.

"She is like that," I interrupt. I hear Kat saying something, but I intentionally speak louder to cover her up. Claire and Kat need to know I'm not okay with Palmer blowing up at me. Even if she is having boy trouble, and honestly, two boys don't seem like much trouble, so I continue at a higher volume. "But even if she's deciding between two boys, poor thing, that doesn't make it okay for her to keep saying snarky comments to me. Did you hear her? About my tan and I wouldn't know about long-distance relationships. Those hurt. And she knew it. She said those things on purpose, because she knows me. She knows they'll sting, and it's not fair."

I come up for air and see Kat and Claire watching me, not with anger, I don't think, but with concern. Their faces look soft.

"Hey." Kat picks a handful of grass and scatters it on my

calves. "You and Palmer are like sisters. You've both gotta let this go."

I pull my knees up and hug them to my chest, letting the grass tumble to the ground. "She has to let it go. I haven't done anything wrong."

Claire breathes in, then says, "Hannah, I love you *and* Palmer. And you, Kat." She smiles at Kat. "She's passionate. She has a temper sometimes. I know Palmer says stuff she doesn't mean, but you know that better than I do. You said so yourself a second ago, 'she knows me.' She does. I can't stand to see you two fight. Palmer looks so perfect on the outside, but I'm worried. I think she has a storm brewing down there somewhere. I don't know. I've been praying for her." Claire pulls her sunglasses back over her eyes, making it hard for me to discern her expression.

I blow my new bangs. *Praying?* I haven't done that in a while. I feel a stab of guilt. It hurts more than Palmer's comments. I was the one who started our roomie Bible study last year. What happened to it? I guess I got sick of always rallying everyone and organizing all of it, and we just stopped. I should try again. But Palmer probably wouldn't even do it. And it doesn't seem like Claire even needs me for it. "Storm, Claire? I don't notice anything wrong with Palmer but her attitude."

"Hey, gorgeous." Nate's voice is rich and thick like hot caramel sauce. I feel his lips warm on the back of my neck before I can turn and see his face.

"Yay! I was hoping you'd come," I say, and mean it with every cell of me. My inside self jumps for joy. I lean over and hug his neck, feeling the smile overtaking my face as he situates himself between me and Claire.

"My meeting let out early." He puts his arm around my

waist. "What's the score?"

"Five to three, the bad guys." Kat jerks her head toward the scoreboard.

I turn to Nate. "So how was your meeting? Anything interesting come up? Are you changing the last day of school or canceling finals this year?" I snuggle into him, getting as close as I can, soaking in his Nateness and the sweet, soapy scent of his cologne.

"Fourth inning," Kat says. "Sadly, I gotta scoot. Unless you actually canceled those exams?" She looks to Nate, then steadies herself on my shoulders to stand.

"Maybe next term," Nate says, grinning.

"How about next week?" Kat raises her eyebrows.

"Sorry."

"I'll go with you." Claire stands up. "I have to get to work."

"Have fun, ladies." Nate waves. I love how comfortable he is with my roommates. That he totally fits in with us, almost like he's our fifth roommate. It's that natural having him around.

"Adios." Kat waves. "That's Spanish for good-bye. See, I'll barely have to study. I might be back for the ninth."

"Bye, guys." Claire waves.

My throat relaxes as they disappear.

"I missed you," I whisper in Nate's ear as soon as they're gone. "I'm sick of all the girl drama. Plus, you smell so good."

38

PALMER

I WILL NOT TEXT MICHAEL. I will not text Michael. I will not text Michael. I haven't seen him alone since before spring break, just at a happy hour and a magazine meeting. He flirted, we even kissed, plus he's texted a few times, so he's not totally blowing me off. But I thought we had something going on and he hasn't even taken me out for coffee. My hand grips the side of my phone so tightly I might crush it.

Of course that's why I was thinking of Keegan. And Hannah, the one person I thought I could count on to understand, acted like I was talking about losing a bracelet. I finger the spot where I used to wear the artsy green bracelet Keegan got me right before I came to college. "Aarrgh!" I scream out loud as I march down the street from the stadium to our dorm, passing a group of three large guys in Clarkston tees who turn their heads. I wave and smile at the must-be football players. They all wave back. "I don't know you," I say in a sing-songy voice, waving some more as I turn the corner.

I hate boys.

Someone should warn Hannah. She doesn't know what she's gotten herself into with Nate. I know she's been pining for a boyfriend since the third grade. I'm sure that's why she dove in head first, but I'm afraid she'll drown.

I could text Keegan. NO! I will not text Keegan. I will not text Keegan. I will not text Keegan.

What is wrong with me?

I make another quick turn to the Formal Gardens, which I've passed but never truly ventured into. The thick smell of tulips and daffodils overwhelms me as I hide among the green hedges.

Quiet. Finally.

It's so quiet in here. The only sound is my sandals clacking against the pavement. I slow my gait. It's like a labyrinth surrounding a castle. The hedges wrap around a giant rectangle with zigzagging walks. The walks are bordered with yellow daffodils and red tulips, so vivid. The primary colors bombard me. Giant redbud trees spread their branches over this sanctuary covering it with purple blooms.

I stop and breathe.

A butterfly flits past my nose. I follow it slowly as it weaves back and forth, finally deciding to turn the corner to the next section of the flora maze. It lands on a waxy purple tulip, surrounded by white daffodils, then flutters away.

The late-afternoon sun is warm and soothing. I allow it to penetrate my skin as I sit on a green slatted bench. It's spectacular in here. Why haven't I ever come here before? It's exactly what I need.

I allow my anger at Hannah to float away with the butterfly. It's not her fault I feel like a necklace chain that's all knotted. I'm immediately more relaxed, just by letting go of our tiff.

Why am I so knotted, God? Nothing bad happened. Yet I feel like I don't even know where to start loosening the tangle.

Start with Me, comes the obvious answer from God.

But it isn't that easy, my brain shouts back. I like Michael. He's so different from Keegan. He's brilliant, and he does seem into me because of our journalism connection because we can share that, talk about it.

I pull out my pink leather journal from my bag and open to the page marked with a ribbon. On the left page I write *Michael,* taking extra time to thicken the letters, give them depth. Under his name I write:

Brilliant.

Journalism thing.

Dad would love him. Mom too. "Full of potential," they'd say.

Sophisticated.

Almost unattainable. Almost, but that's hopefully changing.

Seems like he's ten years older than Keegan. Which I love, which I crave. I could learn so much from him!

An incredible kisser.

I can almost feel his hand around the back of my neck, the way he pulls me close to him, not rough, but strong, like he needs me.

Blink. Blink. Blink. Whew.

Cool down, girl.

On the right-hand page I write *Tristan* in bubble letters. His list comes quickly:

Adorable.

Sweet.

Mom and Dad already like him. At least they like his parents. That counts for a lot. They never liked Keegan's parents.

Funny and fun. Should that be two lines or on the same line? Same line.

Likes me for me. Maybe likes me too much? Maybe too easy. Is that a bad thing, because it shouldn't be, should it?

Not a bad kisser. Understatement. I practically sense his tan arms around the lower part of my back and the salty taste of his lips.

And he wants me to spend the summer at the beach with him. He always says he loves my eyes.

I don't even know where Michael's going. I write a giant question mark on his column and set my journal down. I pluck a smooth, shiny leaf from the hedge and rub it between my fingers. Michael doesn't know either. He's still waiting to hear back from a magazine in DC and a newspaper in Austin, Texas. Which both sound incredibly cool. How can I figure out what I'm doing when I don't even know where he'll be once he graduates? Not that he's asked me to join him. But what if he did?

As a thick cloud covers the sun, the sky turns a shade grayer, as if it's put on sunglasses. I let go of my leaf, letting it float to the path. Bumps prickle my arms with the lack of rays. I rub them up and down with my hands.

I jump as my phone blips, so sharp and mechanical sounding amidst all this quiet. I read: GOOD NEWS ON THE JOB FRONT. PUT ON SOMETHING RED-CARPET WORTHY AND I'LL PICK YOU UP IN AN HOUR TO CELEBRATE.

My heart jumps higher than it did when my phone buzzed. It's like an omen saying I'm supposed to be with Michael. He wants to celebrate his good news with *me*! Maybe Hannah was right when she talked about him being here. Tristan feels like he was just in one of my dreams, not reality.

I type back: CONGRATS! SOUNDS FUN. YOU'RE LUCKY I JUST HAPPEN TO BE AVAILABLE.

LOOKING FORWARD TO IT, he zips right back.

I slide my phone back in my bag and sling my bag over my shoulder. The sun is still behind the cloud, and it looks like more clouds have sprouted out of nowhere. Still, I love this place, and I only saw about half of it. How romantic would it be to go for an evening stroll with Michael here?

All right, girls, I think, answering my roommates' question from earlier as I stand and imagine walking arm in arm with Michael down the rows of flowers, *my dream guy would be tall, dark, have a way with words, be mature, cultured, and have a job*.

I bend over and stick my nose in a particularly bright daffodil, inhaling its heady perfume. The petals tickle my nose. I step away, enchanted.

***

"YOU DO A GREAT JOB following directions," Michael whispers in my ear. His lips tickle.

"Meaning?" I ask.

I'd be lying if I said I wasn't shocked when, after picking

me up, he pulled into the parking lot of Summer's apartment building. Or when we walked into a group of nine—I counted them—other literary types apparently all gathered to celebrate Michael's job choice. So much for moonlit walks in the formal gardens unless we want it to be a group hike.

"The paparazzi would go wild if they saw you," he says, his voice low.

I glance down, glad I selected my dress with the black ruffled top and leopard print skirt. Heat rises up my neck and flushes my cheeks. Looking back up, I see him watching me, grinning, approving.

"Very red carpet, indeed." He smiles.

I shift my eyes sideways, then back at him, unable to hold his intense gaze. Plus, he might just notice my eyelash extensions if I flutter them at the right angle. I'm so jittery, my lashes might fly me right up to Summer's skylight.

Michael, a glint in his eye, opens his mouth, but before his words escape, April bounces over. "Please tell me you're going to Austin. Because my older brother goes to UT and I could so come and visit you."

Where is the wine?

"I'd tell you, but I'd have to kill you." Michael leans in toward April, too close for my liking.

I step backward, glancing toward the counter where Summer had wine at our *QuadAngles* meeting. Jackpot.

I have to take small steps in my black strappy heels, but I'm by the counter before April finishes laughing.

"I'm Wayne. Can I get you a drink?" asks a tall guy with whitish skin and hair greased back like a vampire.

"Sure, wine, please. White. Moscato if you have it. Thanks." I look away from Wayne and try to sneak a glance at Michael and April. He's moved away from her, which is a good thing, and is now shaking hands with Ahmed. But Van just pranced in the door, and if her neckline plunged any deeper we'd all see her belly button.

"Pinot noir looks like the only wine of choice tonight." Dracula hands me a glass that looks like it's full of blood. "I didn't catch your name."

"Palmer. Thanks." I raise my glass and gulp down half my drink. Donning a fake grin that I hope Count Waynecula can tell means "not interested", I start to turn.

"I've seen you around, you know." He raises his eyebrows, which together form a weird V shape.

"Oh," I say.

He grabs my arm, roughly. His clasp is cold and strong. "Here, let me top off you're wine, and you can tell me what you're writing."

"I'm good." I shake my head, tugging my arm. But he doesn't let go. Instead, he fills my glass. "I'd really like to get to know you better."

"There you are." Michael slips his hands around my hips from behind. I suck in my stomach, conscious of him touching my waist. "Are you hungry?"

"No," I lie as Wayne lets go and slips into the woodwork. I skipped dinner to get ready and I'm pretty sure I've had too much wine too fast without any food to absorb the alcohol. But all I want to do is get away from Wayne's grasp. "Whew."

"You okay."

"I am now. That guy, do you know him?" I ask, taking a series of short sips so I'll stop shaking.

"Yeah. He's the editor of the student newspaper. Genius. A little out there, though. And I didn't like him pawing at you."

I laugh nervously, but it feels more like a shiver. "Me either. He was creeping me out." I keep my voice low.

"Really?"

"He wouldn't let go of my arm." I shudder.

"Wayne's all right. You're just so hot, Palmer. It's hard for guys to see you and not want you. I'll make it clear that we're together. He'll back off. I promise."

A mallet drums against my chest. *Hot? Want me? Is that how he sees it? Does he even like my writing?* I settle my hand on top of Michael's where it sits on my hipbone. His grip is warm and adventurous as he wraps his fingers around mine. *Make it clear we're together. Together. Together?*

I take another long draw of the wine as I see Wayne leering at me from the other side of the room like I'm an ice-cream cone.

Michael turns to me, slips his fingers behind my hair, along the nape of my neck, and kisses my top lip, then my bottom lip. Our lips feel sticky, like they don't want to let go of each other. He kisses me full-on, pulling me gently closer until our bodies are up against each other. It's not right to kiss in the middle of this room. I know that. The lights seem too bright and the music blares too loud and Michael's body feels too close. I've got to get something to eat. I should push him away. But is this Michael's way of showing Wayne and the rest of the world we're together? That can't be a bad thing, can it? And his kisses are so tingly.

"Rock and Roll" by Eric Hutchinson plays through the speakers, lightly teasing, "If you want to rock, you rock." I feel lighter, like I'm full of helium. The wine has gone straight to my head, but I'm glad. I do want to rock and roll and completely let go and let Michael kiss me here in the middle of this room and not worry about anything else. Michael's mouth closes on mine and his chest is warm against my ruffles and Vampire guy can eat his heart out. And so can April and Van and Summer.

Michael exhales sharply. "You are like a drug," he whispers before kissing me again. "I think I'm addicted to you."

"Down boy. I know you're celebrating, but it's not New Year's Eve." We jump an inch apart at the interruption. I open my eyes to see Summer standing before us. Excuse me, we were kissing.

"You're killing me with the suspense, Michael. I can hardly hold still. Your job?" Summer claps her hands together, her scarlet bob bouncing. "Announcement, everybody." Her voice could quiet a heard of rhinos. "We're all gathered here tonight because one of our very own Clarkston literary figures is taking his expertise out into the world, and we want to celebrate."

Michael still has his hand cupped around my neck. He kisses me again, one long second of lips and heat, even though he knows all eyes in the room are on him, on us. It's awkward. It's uncomfortable. It's exhilarating, like I'm soaring, like I can't get enough. Maybe I'm the one addicted to him.

He gently slides his hand from my neck down my side and takes my hand. One side of Michael's mouth goes up in a grin. He strokes his trimmed beard. *Our babies would be so beautiful.*

Did I just think that?

"I do have an announcement. But I'm not sharing my story tonight to brag. No, this is to help you all in search of careers in the literary world. There are writing jobs out there, people. You just have to look for them."

"I'll drink to that," Van cheers and a few people clap.

"Cheers." Michael holds his glass up. Everyone is eating it up. "I had interviews in DC and in Austin. I also had a phone interview with this artsy music and happenings paper in Atlanta called *Creative Loafing.*"

"What a great name." My knees bounce against each other. I empty my glass to busy my hands and lips while he speaks.

"*Creative Loafing* wanted to make me editor of The Arts section. An editor fresh out. How could I pass that up?"

"Atlanta is way happening, dude," Brennan calls from the corner. When did he get here?

"Definitely, but I decided to check out who I'd be working with. Did a little Facebook stalking, because everyone's Linked In profile looks exactly the same."

"And...?" Van has inched forward until she's standing in front of us.

"And they're a bunch of hippies. A bunch of brilliant, creative hippies, going for it, putting together a really top-notch paper. It's been around forever, and is revered as the nightlife and weekend bible for all the up and comers in Atlanta. For one of you"—Michael points out to the small but captive crowd—"it would be amazing. But it's not a good fit for me. I need somewhere where I can learn the business." Michael rubs his chin, so comfortable in the spotlight. And I don't even care where he says he's going as long as he'll kiss me again. I watch his lips form every word and imagine them on mine.

"I don't have much knowledge of the *industry*. I need that. Of how to hone a story for AP publication. How to get interviews with major politicians or decision makers. I need to understand better typical deadlines and resources for major breaking stories. I need someone to mentor me. I value that experience. Which is why..." He pauses, raises his glass, and motions for me to do the same.

"Which is why you decided?" Summer asks.

"Which is why I decided on the *Washingtonian* in DC. I start June 20, just in time to get all the Independence Day hype."

Everyone cheers and Van does a weird little dance, shaking her behind. Summer clinks her glass on his and Michael smiles, which sends a hot ember down my throat. I sway a little in my heels but grab the counter behind me for balance.

"Congratulations! You will be fabulous." That was the right thing to say, wasn't it?

"It's a killer opportunity." He looks at me. "You need another drink? Hey, you look cold."

"I am. A little." I wrap myself in my arms, not convinced it's a temperature thing. "I was at the Formal Gardens today, which are gorgeous. Have you spent much time there? And the sun went behind some clouds." I hear myself babble but continue anyway. My tongue feels thick and funny as I speak. "I've been shivery ever since."

"Here." Michael slides his sport coat off his shoulders and sets it on mine, holding it firmly in place with his hands for a second. He lifts my hair and kisses my neck. I'm surrounded by his musky scent, like flannel and fresh cotton and red wine. "You weren't shivering before Summer interrupted our kiss, were you?"

Wayne is back making a show with his glass, clinking against Michael's and then mine. "DC is where it's at," Wayne says. "I'll have to keep an eye on Palmer for you when you take off next year."

"That won't be necessary." Michael jerks his chin up and slides his arm around my side, pulling me toward him until our hips touch.

Wayne looks me up and down. "I'll catch you later then. Just remember, I'd be happy to help out." He walks away.

I cringe, sinking deeper into Michael.

"Should we get out of here, grab something to eat?" Michael asks. "Would that make you less shivery?"

"I think so." I search his dark eyes, wanting him to know I'm grateful he got rid of Wayne. I'm expectant, excited, oddly nervous. I smile, feeling it creep from the center of my mouth to both sides, flashing my freshly whitened teeth and letting it spread all the way up my cheeks and to my eyelashes, which I bat an extra time for good measure. Hoping this smile will convey all of my thoughts and more.

"Perfect, because I'm famished and a bit bored with this crowd," Michael whispers, then laughs, a low, sweet laugh that makes me think maybe he understood. He finishes off his wine and sets down his glass. Warm and slightly shaky, but stabilized by Michael's arm and his self-assurance, we walk toward the door.

39
KAT

"WOW! NICK. WHAT ARE YOU doing here? It's awfully early."

"Oh, hey, Kat," he says casually, as if it's not unusual for him to be on my doorstep at 6:30 a.m. But even though Nicholas's words are relaxed, his usual positive energy seems drained.

My body longs to plow past him and outside. Get a light run in before practice. It would be easier. Easier than confronting him or confronting that I've been blowing him off. But when I see Nicholas, my heart aches. I didn't realize how much I missed him. Which is why I want to flee.

"You okay?" I ask, still standing half in, half out of our dorm, the heavy door pressing on my shoulder.

"Yeah. Great." He shoves his hands deep into his jean pockets. "The girl I'm crazy about, who happens to be my best friend, went away for spring break, and in the weeks since she's been back I've seen her for about half an hour, which I might add was when she was at the clinic and desperate for help. I'm grand."

I let go of the door, feeling its weight swing shut behind me. "I'm real sorry," I scramble to say. "I just…" I exhale.

"You just what, Kat?" Nicholas stares at me with his shamrock green eyes.

"I just feel out of whack, ya know. Unsettled." I plead with my eyes for him to understand, to let this go.

But his usual forgiving smile is gone. So is his ever-present warmth and the way he gets me. He looks blank, like a drawing of himself.

Unsettled, I twirl the ring on my left index finger with my thumb as I try to explain. "It's everything. It's not you."

He sits on the brick steps of Tomarken Hall's front entry. I take a step to sit too, but the green grass of the quad is so inviting. I really need to run. Torn, I stand beside him.

Nicholas's eyes are turned downward and his eyebrows seem lopsided. He doesn't say anything.

"Okay, I'd really like to talk about all of this today, but I need to go for a run. I'll explode if I don't. You know that about me. And if I don't go now, I won't be able to squeeze it in today. We have weights after practice. This is my day with three classes. I have a group meeting at the library for a project in earth science. And I've got to study."

"If your whole day is crammed, when were you planning on us talking?"

"Right." I shake my head. "I don't know." Defeated, I sit next to him, but when I bump my knee against his, for the comfort and steadiness his touch brings me, he pulls it a centimeter away. It might be nothing. He might have just moved or flinched or breathed, but it feels intentional and cold and hollow and I hate it.

"You know I'm horrible at talking about stuff I don't have a handle on." I look to him for encouragement. Blank stare. *Please be normal*, I beg in my mind. "I'm in over my head right now. I took a light course load in the fall because of soccer. So this semester I'm taking eighteen hours, and they're all hard-core classes. I need to train like a maniac to get back in shape. I get to start in the first scrimmage, but I've gotta be prime. Daddy's been real busy with work and trying to keep Mama straight, and Mama's a mess. Spring break needed to be far away, you know, no chance of having to hang out in Columbus with my folks for even a day. I don't think I could do it right now. And I'd be lyin' if I said I never missed Alex." It all pours out in one jumbled heap of words and gulps.

Nicholas puts his knee back against mine. I sigh and sink my shoulders at his touch.

"I'm wound too tight. I'm sorry." The tears come hot and sharp. Partly for the mess I am. Partly because I can tell he's wounded, that I wounded him. "I'm really bad at all of this. That's why I tried to take things slow. I'm not good at relationships. Heck, I'm not even good at my relationship with myself."

"I'm not grading you, Kat." Nick's voice is so quiet I can barely hear him over the airplane flying overhead. "I just need you to talk to me. To hang out with me. When you head out of town for spring break like that without even asking what I'm doing…When you get back and don't make any effort to see me…When I show up unexpected…" He tilts his head to the giant white door. "When I show up and you look like you still want to take off, that's painful. If you don't want to be with me, Kat, just say so. But don't tell me you need me and then make me your last priority."

"You are *not* my last priority." I shake my head, knowing how much I need him to steady me. "I need you."

"Prove it," Nicholas says.

"All right." I tap my thumb ring against the steps. "Let's go out this weekend. Something date-ish."

Nicholas takes my hand in his. Maybe to stop me from spasmodically tapping my ring. "You don't get it, Kat. That's not what I mean."

I squeeze his hand, because I'm not sure what will happen if I let go. "What do you mean? You don't want to be with me?" My voice is louder and squeakier than I want it to be.

"I do want to be with you. That's exactly what I want. I want you to be my best friend and my girlfriend. I want to talk to you every day. I want you to tell me what's going on. I want you to trust me. I want to be important to you." Nicholas takes my other hand in his, which stops it from shaking, but also makes me feel a little trapped. "I know you told me way back before you came to school that you weren't looking for a boyfriend. You were just looking for soccer. And I'm thrilled you have your game. I get that it means the world to you. But that same day I told you I was ready for a relationship and I hoped it would be with you. I have lots of patience. I have been patient. But I'm at my limit."

I can't swallow. I can't move. It feels like tiny needles prick my eyes in thousands of places. Determined not to let him see the flood of tears, I whip my head forward, staring out to the quad.

"I know that," I say tightly, squeezing the words out of my swollen throat.

"Really? Last we chatted, we talked about you getting back on track. Living again. You have a life to live, Kat."

The words "Alex lost his" are unspoken, but we both know they're there.

"I know that too."

"You don't act like it. I see it in you. Even now, you want to bolt. You'd rather run until your muscles scream than deal with this, than deal with me or your parents or anything else."

"Stop being so mad." I pull my hands away from him, keeping my eyes trained forward.

"I'm not mad at you."

I hear him sigh, softly. I sense his body sagging next to me, like some of the air's been let out.

"I'm not mad. I'm sad." Nicholas sniffs. I don't dare look at him to see if he's crying or just sniffing. *Please don't be crying. I'd hate myself if I made your precious soul cry*, I think. "If it's too hard to deal with, you just run away, literally, Kat. You just run and run farther and farther, but everything is still here; school and your parents and the fact that Alex died, and life, and me."

He sniffs again.

"I know." I nod my head, too hard, because several tears spill.

"Come back, Kat, because I miss you," Nicholas whispers.

I miss you too, I think. *So much. You are the sweetest person I know. You understand me better than anyone else. I love you.* But I don't tell him. I don't know how, and the idea of telling Nicholas terrifies me. My heart tries to jump right out of my chest. If it had legs it would. It would jump out and run a marathon by itself, just to get away from the potential overwhelming emotion sitting here on this step.

"I just need some time to myself." I choke the words out and take off running before he can say anything else. Running away faster and harder, trying to catch my heart that got a head start, pounding all of my emotions out against the pavement, leaving everything I need to consider far behind.

40
HANNAH

I LOOK AT THE CLOCK on my phone again. 5:28 p.m. That's not too late to make plans for Saturday night, is it? I mean, Nate's super busy, and probably isn't even back to his dorm yet.

"Earth to Hannah." Kat tugs on the sleeve of my cardi.

"Yeah. Sorry. Just thinking through what I need to get done." I'm so distracted I stumble over the crack in the sidewalk that runs through the academic quad.

"You okay?" Claire asks.

"Fine. Just clutzy." I laugh.

"So whaddaya think about dinner?" Kat asks.

"I don't know." I try to draw out my words. I am so hoping I'll be eating dinner with Nate, but I'm running out of time to make that a reality. "What did you have in mind?" Stall. Stall.

"You really were spaced out." Palmer clicks her tongue.

"Guilty." I blow my bangs out of my face, like they were blocking the conversation from my ears.

"Maybe Bagels R Us. I have a buy one-get one free coupon," Claire says. "Something cheap, please."

"I don't care what it is as long as I don't have to eat one more meal at the dining hall." Kat kicks a small stone like it's a soccer ball, dribbling it between her feet, then passing it to her invisible teammate in the grass.

"How about we order Chinese?" Palmer asks. "We haven't done that in ages and they deliver. We could—" her perky voice continues.

I interrupt. "I swear that's Nate's roommate, Oscar, the one with the buzz cut, outside of the library. I'll catch up with you guys in a few." I wave and take off. A few steps down the walk I turn and say, "Whatever you decide is great."

I trot over, calling, "Hey, Oscar."

Oscar turns. "Hannah," he says, tucking a pencil behind his ear.

"Hi. How are you? Isn't this a gorgeous day? A little chilly, though, with the sun going down." I hug my arms. "Do you happen to know where Nate is?" I ask, feeling the wind skim the layers of my skirt.

"He's in there." Oscar shrugs toward the library doors. "He'll be out in a few."

"Great." I try to act nonchalant. "So, do you have any big plans this weekend?" I investigate for hints of Nate's schedule.

"Nah. Just the usual."

Of course I have no idea what the usual is for Oscar.

"Right." I nod. "How about homework? Do you have a lot?"

"I have a paper to write for poli-sci. It'll take most tonight and tomorrow. But, you know, sleep's overrated. I'll probably pull an all-nighter Sunday to finish."

"I'm kind of big on sleep," I say. "I mean, I never sleep late—can't do it, wake up every morning like that." I snap my fingers. "But I love to go to bed. I don't think I could pull an all-nighter if I tried. What's the paper about?" Oscar is not Mister Conversation. How long will Nate be in there?

"Free and fair elections." Oscar scratches his arm as if that says it all.

Not a lot to go on. Like in the U.S.? Or in other countries? I want to shake him. At least try to converse. But instead I say, "Everyone deserves free and fair, right? You know Nate and I just got back from Germany." I pause to see if he has anything to say about Nate. He doesn't. Surprise, surprise. I continue, "And to think of how Hitler basically took over by bullying people. It's really scary. Nothing free or fair about that. And that kind of thing still goes on in so many parts of the world. It's insane."

"Right," Oscar says. Okay, Oscar, this was your topic!

"Want a piece of gum?" I ask, reaching in my bag.

"Sure."

"I only have peppermint, because that's my favorite kind. Although my roommate Claire thinks it's too spicy, which is funny to me, because I've never thought of mint as spicy before, have you?"

"Nope."

Thanks for the single syllable. Very helpful. I pop open my container of Mentos and hand him a piece. His hand is hot and sweaty, which is gross. But I killed, what, another whole minute?

"O-man." Nate gives Oscar five. "Hannah. You're a nice surprise."

Finally.

"Hi." My heart beats faster than I can chew my gum. I lean forward and kiss him quickly on the cheek.

"That's worth coming out of the library for." He tucks his arm around my waist, strong and warm and solid and even worth non-chatting with Oscar for.

"What were you working on in there?" I ask.

"Group project. It'll take the rest of my weekend. We're just taking a dinner break. I think we all hate each other already, and we didn't want to have to eat with each other too."

"That bad?"

"Nah. Just a lot of drama. One of the guys used to date one of the girls, but now he's dating her sorority sister. Ugly. And, well, dramatic."

"Awkward." I pop my gum.

"Extremely. We present on Monday, and it's our major

grade for the semester, so we'll just have to plow through it."

"I guess I'll write in our room, then, man." Oscar pulls the pencil out from behind his ear and taps it like a drumstick on the bike rack in front of us.

"Sure. I'll be mostly out of your way." Nate adjusts his backpack on his shoulder.

"So when do we get to squeeze in some time?" I nudge him playfully. "Dinner break? I'm free." I half lie, but not really lie, because I didn't commit to anything specific with my roommates.

"Oh, Hannah." Nate shifts his eyes away from me and to Oscar's drumming.

"What?"

"Well, Oscar and I are grabbing dinner back at the dining hall, and then I'm right back with the group. I'm just buried this weekend."

"Oh." I swallow.

"Oscar, keep the beat, my friend. Give me two minutes, okay?"

"No prob." Oscar continues drumming by himself as Nate steers me by the waist over to a giant maple tree.

My throat feels swollen. And I feel heat behind my eyeballs, like tears threatening to show up, but almost too angry to make their appearance. He's grabbing dinner with buzzhead who doesn't even speak? That'll be a thrill. Instead of with me? I chew my gum harder.

"Hey." Nate puts his hand under my chin and lifts my face.

I shift my eyes away from him, because those tears aren't just threatening anymore, they're sneaking into the corners, and I don't want him to see. Don't want him to think I'm being a baby, or clingy, or I don't understand. But I don't. Understand.

"Hey," he says again, softly. "I know this stinks. I mean, Germany was a fantasy world, but we both knew it while we were there. I wish we could hang out together all day, every day, but life isn't like that. I have commitments and classes and a GPA to keep up, and a roommate." He tilts his head toward

Oscar. But I don't look, can't move my head. It's too full. "And you do too. That's one of the things that drew me to you in the first place. You're so organized, pulled together. Every time I saw you around campus you were surrounded by those roommates of yours. Showed you weren't one of those girls just out to get an M.R.S. degree. That you had a life of your own. That you're not needy. You know, a lot of girls are. You're so grounded, Hannah."

I snort and laugh and brush away a streaming tear all in one clumsy motion.

But I am one of those girls. I do want to get married. I want to marry you. Is that the worst thing in the world?

"I don't get to see you at all this weekend?" As soon as the words are out, I know I sound ultra insecure. I try to salvage it. "I mean, I totally get the busy thing." I nod my head several times to show my total agreement. "My roomies are great and we're having a movie night tonight and I have a presentation in American Sign Language and an exam in art history on Monday, so my weekend is slammed too." I take a deep breath. "I just...We just...I knew things would be different when we got back, I just liked getting to see you all the time. I miss it." I dare to peek at him. His response to this is critical.

"I miss you too."

Nate kisses me slowly and gently. My back is against the tree, its bark rough and solid behind me. Our kiss definitely takes up more than the two minutes Nate borrowed from Oscar, but I could stay here forever and don't care, and I let myself become dizzy with Nate and his warmth and the way his chest leans against mine as if we actually share heartbeats.

"Yeah, Germany was good." He slides his glasses back up on his nose. "But campus is good too. We'll find our rhythm here, you and me. We just got back, and it's such a crazy time in the semester. But hey, I got to see you now." He leans back into me and kisses me again. And I'm more relaxed, feel more upright, and the breeze that tickles my hair is no match for the way this kiss tickles my heart, making it jumpy and wiggly and happy.

"Gotta go." He leans back and taps my nose. "Thanks for the treat. Wish it was longer, but it's not. Next weekend, though…" He turns his hand and points his finger at me. "Next weekend we could get very cozy." He leans in and plants a wet, fast kiss on my lips, but I'm turned so inside out I can't even kiss back. "Good luck with that paper. Text me." He grins and walks back over to Oscar.

"Thanks. I will," I say. Meanwhile my brain wheels are spinning too fast to form thoughts. I can't process here. I can't stay glued to this tree trunk. I will my feet to step one in front of the other in the opposite direction of Nate and Oscar, even though it would be more direct to walk a little toward them to get to Main Street, where I'm sure my roomies are by now. I can always backtrack and double over after I exit this quad and am hidden by the giant brick buildings.

As I walk, my brain wrestles with itself, tossing all of the information back and forth.

He misses me. That's good, right?

But he's still having dinner with Oscar The Grouch instead of with me, his girlfriend?

I am his girlfriend, right?

That kiss was amazing. Times two. But then he just walked off.

He's too busy to see me all the time, even though he says he'd like to. He doesn't want a clingy girl and likes me because of my relationship with my roommates. That one is really confusing. I haven't been spending that much time with them lately because I've wanted Nate to be my priority. But he doesn't seem to want to do the same. Why doesn't he want to put me first? The tears release themselves, hot and thick, sliding down my cheeks. My phone buzzes. It's Kat.

WHERE ARE YOU? WE DECIDED ON CHINESE? WANT US TO ORDER FOR YOU? MEET US AT HOME?

YES, PLEASE. ORANGE CHICKEN AND AN EGG ROLL. I'LL BE THERE IN A FEW.

Nate doesn't want to have dinner with me, but somehow, even after how jerky I've been—and I have been, haven't I?—

my roommates still want to have dinner with me.

41

PALMER

IF SUPPLY GOES UP, AND demand remains constant, then prices drop.

If demand rises, and supply remains the same, prices increase.

I repeat these facts over and over again in my head, tapping on my econ book with a four-colored pen to reiterate their truths. Note to self. I stink at econ.

I flip through to see I have three more chapters of text I need to memorize tonight before tomorrow's test.

I check my phone. I've been in this crammed nook at the library for an hour and a half already. I almost hit the Instagram icon, but restrain myself from the distraction. I have got to somehow commit this all to memory.

I allow myself a five-minute break to stretch my legs, use the bathroom, and get a drink of water. Returning to my desk, I see Michael. I haven't seen him since he took me home after his celebration party at Summer's and our dinner at La Fiesta a couple of nights ago, and now he's practically nose-to-nose with April. I've speculated a hundred times about why he hasn't called. Maybe I gobbled way too many nachos. But I was famished and had to anchor the buzz that had overtaken me that night. When we were done eating, I was so tired I could barely keep my eyes open. I'm sure that didn't win me any extra points either. Still. Michael chose *me* as his date. He kissed *me* in front of everyone. And he left with *me* on his arm.

April tosses her hair and laughs, then punches Michael lightly in the ribs and walks off. Maybe not as intimate as it first seemed.

"Palmer," Michael says, spying me spying on him. Awkward.

Nothing to do but smile and wave.

He walks toward me. "Imagine finding you here."

"Was that April?" I ask.

"She's hilarious." He laughs. "What're you working on?"

"Econ, and it's a nightmare."

"Micro or macro?" he asks.

I push my glasses up my nose, not sure if I'm glad he sees me with them on or not. They definitely don't make me look "hilarious." "Micro. Which means I have macro to look forward to next year, if I pass."

"You'll pass. You have great insight."

"Apparently not when it comes to sheaves of wheat and pork bellies."

Michael smiles. "How long are you staying?"

"At this rate? Forever." I open my hands.

"Tell you what. I have a team meeting that should last about an hour and a half. Why don't I find you when I'm done and we'll go out for a drink?"

"Tempting," I say and mean it. He did say I had great insight. "But I honestly don't know if I'll be done."

"If you're not, bring your notes, and I'll quiz you. Where are you sitting?"

"Over there." I point to the corner where my nerdy pen and twenty-pound book await me.

"Great. See you in a bit." He puts his hand gently on my shoulder and walks away. Like we always do this. Study, then go out for drinks. Like there's nothing weird about the fact he didn't call. I probably overanalyzed. Hanging out with him tonight might be enough inspiration to crank through those chapters.

42

CLAIRE

"OUCH!" I DROP THE SCORCHING ladle and it clatters as it bangs against the metal pan of gravy.

"You okay?" a guy with a bandana tied around his head asks from the other side of the cafeteria line.

"Yeah. Fine." I shake my hand and scan the counter for hot pads.

"So, do I get to have that gravy or what?" the guy in front of him with shaggy hair and eyes that bore into mine, asks.

"Sure. Just a sec." I turn around and look behind me. My hand still stings. Where the heck do they keep the hot pads? Nowhere, apparently. "I'm not supposed to do gravy. I'm the meatball hoagie girl." I shrug. "She'll be back in just a minute. Sorry."

"Do you have any chicken sandwiches left?" the do-rag boy asks me in a gentle voice, which I can't express how much I appreciate.

"Sure. Spicy or regular?"

"Regular, please. Three if you have 'em."

"Here you go." I pull three foil-wrapped chicken sandwiches from the warmer with my plastic-gloved hand and pass them across the counter.

"Thanks." He smiles, blue eyes twinkling.

"You're welcome." I smile back.

"I thought you only did hoagies," grumpy gravy guy snarls.

"And sandwiches, sorry." My throat feels quivery. He's just standing there, glaring, and there is no human way for me to touch that ladle again without protection.

Nancy, the actual cafeteria lady, returns with a fresh pan of chicken sandwiches stacked on top of a tray of breadsticks. She's wearing the hot pads.

"He really needs gravy." I gesture toward our angry customer.

"Gravy?" she asks him, holding up the deceptively innocent-looking ladle in her covered hand.

When the line slows down to a trickle, Nancy says, "I'll start shutting down here in a bit. Doesn't look like anyone else much is coming through."

"Okay." I try not to sound too eager to be finished.

The two last dinner customers stroll right past us to the salad bar. I look to Nancy expectantly. "Yup, I'll get it from here. You can grab one of those buckets by the sink. They should be filled with soapy water, and there'll be cleaner and rags next to them. Go ahead and start washing the tables. After that, we'll see if there are any dishes left. Then for the good part—we get to eat. They told you we all get a free meal with each shift, didn't they?"

"Yeah. Thanks."

The free food sounded like a perk when the university told me the only campus job they had available this far into the semester was in the freshman dining hall, but if that means meatball hoagies, it's lost its appeal. It's pretty clear why this was the only job left. I don't mind working. I've always worked. And I didn't expect it to be completely easy, just a little surprised by some of the dirty work. Like the tables. Don't they have custodians? But I am grateful. I can do this. I can work a couple of evenings a week. It's pretty mindless, and it will help me pay Palmer back. Maybe I'll be able to afford counseling again.

I find the supplies just as Nancy described, not sure if I should spray or use the soapy water, but since they've given me both, I guess I'll use both. My first two shifts there was no table cleaning involved, just wrapping sandwiches, putting blobs of cookie dough on pans, and stacking napkins and silverware. I survey the room filled with countless chairs and plastic-coated tables. I head to the back corner, figuring I can work my way down the rows so I can keep track of what I have and haven't washed. I spray the top of the most remote table, the one I probably would've eaten at, watching the clean stream from the bottle. I dip my hand holding the rag into the bucket.

"Crap!" Boiling water seers my hand in all the same places the ladle did.

"You okay?"

I turn my head to see who's talking. Tears of pain fill the rims of my eyes. It's bandana head again.

"Uh-huh," I say, but I feel how pinched my expression is.

"Is your job always this dangerous?"

"I sure hope not," I say, grabbing the rag I'd thrown to the table, cooler now, and wiping off the surface.

"On a scale of one to ten, ten being the most dangerous, what is today?"

"Don't know. I hope ten. Then it can only get better. It's only my third day." I move to the next table, but it's still close enough to blue eyes to continue the conversation. If he wants.

"At least you get to wear a cool hat." He finishes off the rest of his milk.

"Ha!" I reach the bill of the Clarkston ball cap they issued me as part of my uniform. It's stiff and tall, and looks more like a hat a grandpa would wear than a college girl. Although Kat could probably pull it off. I feel awkward and plastic in the Clarkston golf shirt and hat. "Don't forget the shirt." I tug on my collar.

"What's wrong with the shirt?" He's wearing a faded gray Notre Dame sweatshirt. It looks soft. I'm jealous.

"I can't pull off golf shirts." I shrug and spray another

pungent burst of pine-scented cleaner.

"I'm Brady," he says. He looks down at his hand. "I'd shake your hand, but…"

"Got it." I laugh, seeing as my hands are burned, full of cleaning supplies, and smell like meatballs.

"And you're…?"

"Claire."

"Nice to meet you, Claire. I'd love to stay and chat, but I have a chem test starting in about"—he slides the bar across his phone—"fifteen minutes. That's why I ate here. No one ever bugs you at the freshman dining hall. Figures I got distracted anyway." He gathers his tray and his backpack. His hands look soft and have dark hairs on the knuckles. Brady flashes those crystal blue eyes again. "See you around."

"Good luck on your chem test."

"Thanks."

To avoid staring at him, I concentrate on wiping tomato sauce off the table. How could someone smear that much sauce and not even attempt to wipe any of it up with a napkin? Gross! I clean it all up. Now what? Dip that disgustingness back into my bucket? Ew.

He said he got distracted here. I guess I did too.

43

PALMER

"HUH?" FEELING A HAND ON my shoulder, I turn around, my brain full of graphs and colored lines.

"Very nice." Michael points to a diagram on my notebook.

"Thanks." I click the green end of the pen down.

"C'mon, let's go." He tilts his head toward the exit.

"I thought you'd never ask. Over three hours of econ has got to be enough." I close my book shut and slide it, my notebook, my pen, and my phone all into my backpack. "Where to?"

"I have an idea." Michael raises his eyebrows as we exit the side entrance of the library.

"It's way colder out here than when I got here," I say. "Hang on a second." I put my bag down, unzip it, and pull out a scarf and wrap it around my neck, missing the warmth of the Florida sun. Thinking of the beach triggers Tristan's face to flash in my mind.

"How did your meeting go?" I ask to change the subject in my brain.

"Well, there's one bossy girl in our group who likes to hear herself talk. Two dudes who are praying this project will raise their grade. And me."

We walk along the tree-lined sidewalk out of the academic quad and toward Main Street. "The way I figure it is, this girl and I can carry the project. She's bossy, but she knows what she's doing and she's not afraid to speak in front of the class. We can get the two guys to do the grunt work. I'll write it all up and we'll get an A. No problem."

"Sounds like you've got it all figured out."

A guy from my econ class passes on our right.

"You ready for the exam?" he asks.

"I hope so." I smile and keep walking.

A few steps later Zach, a chatty guy who trailed after Hannah last year, stops in front of us. "Hey, Palmer, I haven't seen you all semester. How are you? How's Hannah? I never see her. I hate not having class with her. She is so great! Did she change her phone number? Tell her I'll call her. Okay? Okay. Good to see you."

"Do you know everyone on campus?" Michael looks at me.

"Hardly." I wave my hand, but inside I smile. Not a bad thing to show Michael that people know me. People outside the writing circles. People he's never even met. I mean, he basically showed the world we were together by making out at Summer's, but he hasn't called since. I feel like I'm on a trampoline bouncing up and down with emotions and mixed signals about who and what we are to each other.

"Here." Michael motions down an alley. In a few steps we're at the neon orange front door of The Brewery.

"I'm not legal," I whisper to Michael.

"Not a problem." Michael shakes his head. "Hand me your ID."

I dig in my bag and hand him my driver's license, which clearly states I am not twenty-one.

We walk through the door, into my first college bar. For all the mystique behind these places I have to laugh. It looks like an unfinished basement—concrete slab of a floor, light bulbs screwed into exposed fixtures, wooden picnic tables scattered about jammed with students and overflowing with pitchers of beer. Radiohead jams from the speakers so loudly I'm not sure if people can hear each other. It smells stale and sticky. And I am sure I don't want to be here. Not even with Michael.

"Hey, Mike," a burly guy with a faded yellow T-shirt says.

"Hey, Chris." Michael hands him our licenses, mine under his. Chris glances at the pieces of plastic in his thick fingers, but doesn't even slide mine out from under Michael's. "We're headed outside," Michael informs him.

Thank goodness.

"Good idea. That table in the corner's a little rowdy." Chris hands Michael back our licenses and points to four guys who are actually standing on a table doing shots. Then he stamps both of our hands. Michael puts his other hand behind the small of my back, and instead of guiding me back out the door, we charge through the masses.

"I thought you said outside." I raise my voice so he'll hear me.

"I did." He continues behind the table standers where an open door that looks more like an emergency exit than a passageway is propped open. Once through we're on a patio surrounded by trees and dotted with heat lamps. Just a few people sit at some of the tables, holding what appear to be actual conversations.

"How about here?" Michael motions to the only table without any discarded cups or bottles on it. "I'll be back in a minute."

I unload my backpack on the bench and sit on the edge of the seat as close as I can to the heat lamp. The seat wobbles and I wonder if I shouldn't just head home. Where did Michael go? There's a group of girls two tables to my left huddling around a phone, clearly checking out pictures. A few tables away three guys all dressed in black and smoking cigarettes are studying. I wouldn't have thought of coming here to study.

"This is more like it." Michael sets down a bottle of white wine and two plastic glasses.

"I had no idea this was back here," I confess. The warmth of the lamp starts to seep into me. I roll my neck, relaxing.

"Most people don't. Most people don't want to venture out

of the mayhem inside. But I prefer quiet. It's a good place for thinking." He pours wine up to the rims of both of our glasses.

"Cheers." He holds up his cup.

"Cheers." I tap back lightly and gladly take a deep drink, knowing already it will help me loosen my grip. My brain buzzes with equations. My writer's soul wants to record all of the strange and surprising details about The Brewery and my conscience wonders if I can get arrested for under-age drinking. Plus, I'm feeling stressed about how I'll do on the econ exam.

"So think of it this way," Michael says, leaning back. "What if there were a pair of designer sunglasses that were so hot, they sold out in just a few hours at one of the downtown shops."

I smile, curious as to where he's going with this. "Continue."

"Would you pay more for the last pair if you knew it could be yours."

"Of course," I say. "Well, only if they were awesome." I take another sip. "And which shop?"

"The most awesome." He winks. "And hypothetical. This is econ."

"Then, definitely." I wink back, feeling lighter already.

"That's supply and demand in a nutshell." Michael pours more wine into my glass. "If someone really wants something and there aren't that many of that something, the seller can charge basically whatever he wants. If the same great pair of shades were being given away in the dining halls to every student who came through the line, you wouldn't pay extra for them; in fact, you'd be angry if you had to pay for them at all."

"Right." I take another sip. "You make it sound so easy."

"It is simple." Michael stands and slides over to my side of the bench.

My phone buzzes and I glance at the screen.

CHIPOTLE IS PLAYING FIRE SWAMP. MADE ME THINK OF THE CONCERT AND THE BEACH.

Tristan. I blush. I would love to go back to that concert, or to those minutes when Tristan and I were talking on the beach. That was all so simple. But here I am with Michael. That's what I want, isn't it?

I drink another swallow of wine, enjoying its warmth and the filmy way it makes everything look.

Michael doesn't even ask about the text. Instead, he leans over and kisses me. I taste the wine on his lips and on mine. His kiss is so different from Tristan's. So determined and confident.

We drink more wine and discuss more economics and kiss more and drink more wine and kiss more. My eyelids are heavy. My brain is heavy.

***

"THAT'S ME IN THE SPOTLIGHT, losing my religion, trying to keep up with you…"

The old R.E.M. song plays through my head, or is it from the speakers?

It is hard to keep up, I think to myself. *I don't know if I can do it*, my thoughts continue and R.E.M. sings.

Who am I trying to be? What am I trying to prove?

I open my eyes, but it hurts so much, like someone has shrink-wrapped my face. I see Michael, but can't keep my eyes open. He pulls me closer to him, but my ears feel like there are wads of cotton in them. I snuggle into him, but I'm so freakishly thirsty.

I pull away, and oh no, oh freaking no, we're on a couch in an apartment I don't recognize! It must be Michael's place, right? We talked about coming back here, to get a sweatshirt for a walk in the Formal Gardens. Didn't we? I'd gotten up the nerve to suggest it. But we're not there. We're here. How long have we been here?

Lowering my feet to the floor, feeling dizzy, I squeeze my eyes back together. I open them to the dim room. What time is it? And where, please tell me, is the fridge? I slide as quietly as I can off the couch, trying not to disturb Michael. He makes a sound and rolls the other direction. As I weave my way through the hall, someone snores loudly in another room. I find the bathroom, which has no cups, so I drink straight from the faucet. The water feels incredible on my throat, but instantly sloshes in my stomach, like it doesn't know where it's supposed to go. I pee, wash my hands, and shake them dry, because apparently there aren't any towels either, or toilet paper.

I have got to get out of here.

I tiptoe back through this brown, plaid nightmare of a room. I glance around desperately, trying to piece together how I got here. I remember making out. How far did we go?

Dark, stark anxiety covers me like a cloud covering the sun.

Anything might have happened. What did?

I push up the sleeves on my sweatshirt…well, his sweatshirt. We put the sweatshirts on. Then what? *Thank You, God, that I'm still fully dressed.* Except my shoes. I exhale, realizing I had stopped breathing all together. Where are my shoes? What did we do? I'm way too frightened to know. The details after suggesting we get sweatshirts are fuzzy. I don't even remember walking here. Please tell me we didn't drive. I've got to get out of here. Now.

I find my boots under the coffee table, slide my backpack over my shoulders, lean over to kiss Michael's check. His beard is rough and prickly. "Deadline," he mumbles.

Feeling like my ears are so full of gauze it's starting to crowd my throat, I find the fridge. Three cans of Coke, an empty pizza box, mustard, a jar of banana peppers, and a box of baking soda are the entire contents. Someone's mom undoubtedly put the baking soda here at the beginning of the school year.

Coke equals good.

I am outside, but I'm not sure where. I don't think we ever talked about where he lived. It must be within walking distance of The Brewery. But in which direction? What if Michael wakes up and sees me out the window not even knowing where to go. How stupid would I look? I march across the parking lot like a girl with a purpose. A girl with cool boots and a purpose. But it's all an act. Just like most of my life lately.

Once across the lot, I pause to open my Coke and take a sip, an excuse to get my bearings. My economics exam is at ten in the morning. I will so need to clear my head before then. The Coke tastes good. Sweet and strong. I survey the street and recognize a bank under a streetlight. Not my bank, but one I've seen. One I'm pretty sure is just a block north of Main Street. Streetlights glow in the night sky in that direction and the salty smell of grease, maybe onion rings, confirms I'm headed toward downtown. I turn left like I know where I'm going. Where do I want to be going? Home? My roommates will freak.

Halfway down the block I feel seasick, like the wine and the Coke and Michael's kisses are a giant wave and I'm in a boat they're about to crash into. I trot faster to try to outrun the wave. But I can't. Hot foam overtakes my stomach and I throw up in the grass.

Oh please, Michael, world, anyone, everyone, please don't have seen that. But I get the feeling someone did. Like even if no one else knows, I know. Like God knows.

I keep walking. Fast. To the strains of the R.E.M. song still playing in my head.

"Michael's spotlight might be too shiny," I whisper. "And scorching. And it makes me see little spots, blurring everything. I can't even keep up with myself."

***

IT'S THREE A.M. AND HERE I am, back by the bench in the garden where I was a few days ago. Was it just days? It feels like months. Somewhere between Michael's apartment and my dorm, I knew I needed to journal. Needed to. But I remembered I haven't seen it in a while, and the last time I remember writing in my journal is here. I should be concerned someone else found it, discovered my secrets, my pros and cons, the daily calorie intake Mom made me list over Christmas break (or close to it, I mean who counts M&M's as actual calories), my story ideas for *QuadAngles* complete with checks by the ones I've submitted and stars by the ones Summer's accepted. But even though those thoughts flash across my radar, I'm way more concerned with getting my journal back so I can write in it.

I feel hollow when I spot the green wooden surface of the empty slatted bench.

Gone.

It has been days. How many people come here in a day or a week? A small lamppost reminiscent of the one in *The Lion, the Witch and the Wardrobe* shines a pinkish glow along the path.

Pink?

Is that...? A spark jumps inside me.

It is.

Under the bench, tucked under a piece of curling ivy, is my journal, as if it was safely hiding until I came back to claim it.

Bending down, nausea rolls from my scalp over my face. I steady myself, placing one hand on the bench. Inhale. Exhale. Better.

I slide the journal out carefully from its hiding spot. The ivy gently releases its hold. Moonlight and lamplight illuminate the pages I open to, the one the pink ribbon marks, but it's not the one I thought I'd marked—the place I'd last been writing, with Michael's and Tristan's names. Instead, it's near the beginning, from the first week of second semester, when we actually held a roommate Bible study.

Hannah had baked brownies, thick and gooey and smothered in fudge frosting, at the end of break and brought them from home as a welcome back to school treat. We devoured the whole pan that night. The furnace smelled like a fireplace with a hint of rust from not being used most of December during break. Kat had downloaded the new Matt Maher CD with an iTunes gift card she'd gotten in her stocking, and we were listening to it over and over again.

And here's the Bible verse from that night. I jotted it down. I can still hear Matt Maher's deep, soulful voice in the background as I wrote the words on the fresh blank page.

What I'm trying to do here is to get you to relax, to not be so preoccupied with getting, so you can respond to God's giving. People who don't know God and the way he works fuss over these things, but you know both God and how he works. Steep your life in God-reality, God-initiative, God-provisions. Don't worry about missing out. You'll find all your everyday human concerns will be met. Matthew 6:31

What have I been preoccupied with? Everything. Because I have been worried about missing out. Desperately. About missing a chance to be published. About missing a chance with Michael or Tristan or an opportunity to belong at *QuadAngles*. I feel like God created me to write, that He put this in me. *So is that so bad, God?* How have I been fussing over it? Through Michael? Through his approval? Does he even approve? Or am I his flavor of the month? Arm candy for his announcement? The way he kissed me in front of everyone was exciting, but unsettling, unnatural. Like an exhibition.

I thought I had been relaxing. Using the wine to unwind, to tap into my inner strength, so I wouldn't waver. Right?

I beg myself to be right, but it's freezing on this wooden bench in the middle of the night. I'm grateful for this sweatshirt. What does it say on it? Harvard? Didn't I see Summer wearing a sweatshirt like this before? I feel like I'll throw up again. It doesn't matter if it's hers at his place or if Michael let her borrow it. It's the same either way. I don't feel relaxed or empowered, just chilled and alone. *My everyday human concerns aren't being met right now!* I dare God in my head. I feel like nothing's being met.

Have you turned any of those concerns over to Me? He dares me right back, but His dare is much gentler, no sharp edges, just concern.

I shake my head, angry at myself for my answer. I curl into a ball on the bench, clutching my journal to my chest, pressing the words into my heart.

44
KAT

EXHUASTED FROM THIS MORNING'S PRACTICE and lifting, I pop my phone into the docking station and turn on my "chill" mix. Holly Starr's melodic voice fills our room. I lie down on the carpet with plans to do one hundred sit-ups. But I'm tired. So tired. And her voice soothes me as she sings, "He makes me lie down in green pastures," her rendition of King David's Twenty-Third Psalm. *He makes me lie down.* I smirk at the irony. Here I am lying down, which is a rarity. *You want me to lie down, Lord?* Something inside, my shield, cracks, a thin line down the middle, then shatters into countless fragments as warm tears slide from my eyes, sideways into my ears. It's time to lie down, to stop going, to feel again, to be refreshed.

"Halleluiah," Hannah sings along as she walks into the room wearing her glasses. Her voice is a perfect harmony to the recording.

I wipe my eyes with my sleeve before she sees. "What are you doing here?" I ask. "Don't you have class?"

"Canceled today. I was just in my bunk. Studying." Hannah holds up her text book.

"Since what time?"

"I think it was five thirty." She laughs at herself. "You

know I don't pull late nights. But early mornings, those I thrive on." She smiles, then starts singing again, "Hallelujah."

"So you crashed before Palmer got home?" I ask.

Hannah stops singing and sinks into the beanbag chair. "I've tried to text her maybe fifteen times. I don't know where she is. I don't think she came home." Her voice trembles.

"Your voice is beautiful," Claire's voice peeps.

I prop myself up on my elbows and spy her in a heap on the couch, huddled under her comforter. "I didn't even notice you when I came in."

"After Hannah went to bed, I stayed up waiting for Palmer. I was worried about her." Claire yawns. She tilts her head to the docking station. "I will fear no evil," Claire whispers along to the psalm. "No evil. That means none, right? You think Palm's okay. I couldn't text her."

"Did you check her bed?"

"Twice. Just in case. And the bathroom." Hannah busies herself organizing binders and books on her desk, still singing. Easier than talking about how Palmer is M.I.A.

A few minutes later Palmer pushes open the door wearing a baggy sweatshirt I've never seen before. She's rumpled. Her mascara is smeared. "Can you turn the music down?" she asks.

An entire tank of oxygen seems to escape my lungs in relief. "Hey, girl. You all right?" I croak.

"Palm?" Hannah runs to her and hugs her. Palmer collapses in Hannah's embrace.

Claire and I gravitate toward them.

Claire smoothes Palmer's hair. "What happened? Are you okay?"

I catch Claire's sapphire eyes, wide and questioning. She gives me a quick glance. Knowing I had a lightening flash moment where I wondered if Palmer was still alive, I wonder if Claire had an instant wondering if Palmer had been assaulted. Our fear factors are hypersensitive. My tears increase with sadness for how disconnected we've been, love for Claire, concern seeing Palmer, who's always pulled together, disheveled. "We're all so not at our best right now. We used to be at our best when we were together," I say, swiping a tear from my cheek.

Palmer whispers, "I'm okay," and buries her head in Hannah's shoulder, shaking it back and forth.

"We still are better together," Claire says quietly but steadily.

Hannah gives Palmer another quick squeeze, then goes over to the docking station and puts the song on repeat. "Palmer's okay. We're all here."

Claire narrows her eyes at Hannah. It's subtle, but I catch it and Hannah must too. "What?" Hannah asks.

Claire pushes back her hair, not answering.

I speak for her, the unsaid words that have floated around our room all semester, all of us too frightened to grab them and consider what they may mean. "We're just not together that much lately." I swallow the accusation, bigger than I knew it was.

Hannah freezes and a squeak comes from Palmer.

"I didn't mean for it to be like this." Palmer's voice wavers as she flops next to where Claire has slid over on the couch. Claire lifts her covers and wraps the corner around Palmer.

"Like what?" Hannah asks.

"I just want to write." Palmer takes a deep breath. "I want to write, and for people to believe I can do it. It's all I've ever wanted, really." She looks up at the ceiling.

"You can write without drinking and without spending the night with fill-in-the-blank." Hannah's words are razor sharp.

Palmer's round, dark eyes fill.

"Penalty," I call, trying to stop them before it gets too ugly.

"She's right. Look at me." Palmer lets her eyes scan down her body to the toes of her boots.

"What happened?" Claire asks.

"I don't know. I mean, I was at the library studying and saw Michael, which was fine. When we were done studying we went out for a drink." She grabs a Kleenex from the coffee table and blows her nose. "We said something about going for a walk and the next thing I knew I woke up on his couch. I don't know how I got there. I'm not sure what we did." Her eyes are full of fear.

"Did he drug you? Are you okay? How did you get home?" Hannah asks.

"We were getting sweatshirts." She tugs on her shirt. "I must have passed out. I've been out walking for a long time. And praying. Trying to find myself again. Trying to find God again."

"I think we're all looking for something," Claire whispers. "Looking for still waters. For something to restore our souls."

"I could use some restoring," I say.

"Me too," Palmer squawks.

"Me three." Claire's lips curl gently on the ends.

I join them on the couch.

"Me four," Hannah sighs, and her chipper expression melts as tears run down her cheeks too. "I thought I found it. In Nate. All I ever dreamed of was a boyfriend. And when I got one I thought that was it. And somehow, in Germany, it was enough. It was just us. But that wasn't real. I know that now. He's not enough. I'm still missing something. And I've totally ditched you guys. Which is so not fair to you." She chokes out a sob. "I'm so sorry." And covers her face with both hands.

Palmer opens her mouth, but instead of words a loud racking sob explodes from her.

Hannah joins us on the couch. We are one crowded, crying heap. "I'm sorry, Palm. I'm so sorry."

Palmer gulps. "I haven't been a good friend. I haven't been a good anything." She lets out a jagged exhale, her breath stale and sweet from the wine we all know she drank last night.

"I've been running from everything," I offer. "I've been running away from my memories of Alex, and some from y'all, 'cause you give me comfort, but mostly from Nicholas. I've been awful to him." I swallow. "And it was like I didn't want your love or Nick's. I needed to be in control, to be stronger and tougher than all of it put together." My vocal chords wobble in my throat. "But I'm not."

Claire leans her head on my shoulder. "I know the feeling."

"Thanks."

"For me," Palmer gasps, then says, "it's been like I'm trying to prove myself. With Keegan, in high school, I had this identity. I was—"

"Gorgeous. Popular. Adored," Hannah interrupts.

Palmer splays her palms. "But what does that even mean?"

"It's what everyone wants." Hannah's voice is softer now. "We all want to be adored."

"Of course." Palmer rubs Hannah's knee. "But I never wanted to be adored because I was Keegan's. I wanted to be adored because I was me."

"I adore you." Hannah finds a hint of her smile.

"Really?" Palmer asks. "Even after the way I've acted? I've been a selfish witch."

"No matter what." Hannah's voice is thick. "And I've been more selfish."

"Back at ya." Palmer winks.

"I told you we were at our best together," Claire says.

"Definitely," I agree. "But there's more."

"It's not just being together. It's sharing." Hannah's green eyes light up. "Like, Kat, you should totally talk to us about Alex and Nicholas. We love you. You're not weak for talking to us. And, Palmer, you don't ever have to prove yourself to us. And, Claire, I wish I knew more about what was going on with your mom. I want to help." Hannah exhales, and her new bangs kind of dance across her forehead from the blast of air. "And talking to you guys about Nate gives me perspective. I've been floundering by myself, and that doesn't work."

"More than that," I say, feeling in my heart the thing I was missing all along, what I fear Hannah's still missing.

"His rod and His staff comfort me," Claire says.

"Bingo."

"We need each other, but we need God with us." Palmer squares her shoulders. "There is no way I can do this without Him. I don't know why I'm so stubborn about it."

"I think I win the stubborn trophy," I snort. "I've been trying to do it on my own. I totally pushed Nicholas away, and he's the best thing that's ever happened to me. Except y'all."

"I thought a little wine would help me relax and not feel the pressure. Add in a couple of parties, some glamour, and two beautiful boys for distraction, and that's the same thing as trying to do it on my own." Palmer traces her lips with her index finger.

"I've just been trying to keep my head above water." Claire half laughs and half chokes.

"I've been really happy." Hannah stands up and walks to the window. "Mostly."

"We're really happy you've found Nate," Claire's says softly. "But we miss you. I miss you." She readjusts her comforter.

Hannah turns back. "You do?"

"We all do." Palmer reaches her hand out toward Hannah.

Hannah eyes it for a second, then takes Palmer's hand and sits back down with us.

"We do," I agree.

"I didn't mean to ditch you guys." Hannah wrinkles her nose. "I didn't notice…" She shakes her head. "I didn't realize…" She exhales loudly. "I was swept off my feet."

"And that's a good thing." Palmer smiles. "A great thing, Han. Just don't let it be your only thing. I speak from experience."

Hannah brushes more tears from her cheeks.

"Everything okay with Nate?" Palmer asks.

Hannah shrugs. "I guess. I don't know."

"We're supposed to keep God as our main thing. Man, why is that so hard?" Palmer asks. "I know that, down deep, but then everything else rushes around me, and it's like I can't even hear Him, or won't let myself hear Him. But when I do stop and listen, like now to that song, it is more powerful or comforting than anything, you know?"

"It's not enough just to lean on Him." Claire clears her throat and I turn toward her. "We also have to remind each other to depend on God. That's our job. It's like He entrusted us to one another, because He knew we needed each other."

"He is so clever." Hannah smiles.

"We figured that out our first semester together," Palmer says.

"Right," I say. "But we forgot."

"We haven't been helping each other enough lately." Claire pulls a bobby pin off the shelf behind her and uses it to pin back a curl. "I've been trying so hard to trust God with what's going on with my mom that I haven't been strong for you guys."

"Oh, Claire," Hannah says, "you're always there for us."

Claire shakes her head. "I pray *for* you guys all the time, but when was the last time I prayed *with* one of you?"

"When was the last time we did our Bible study?" Hannah bites her lip.

"When was the last time we even tried to?" Palmer asks.

"Why not now?" I ask.

"Well, we usually do them on Wednesdays..." Hannah seems to be trying to pull a calendar out of thin air the way she's furrowing her brows.

Palmer snorts.

Hannah swats her lightly. "Well, we do."

My playlist has ended and the heater clicks off. Silence overcomes the room.

I lean forward to get on the floor and do some sit-ups, but Claire shifts her weight and I stop myself.

Or maybe God stops me. Maybe He's telling me I don't have to fill every silence with exercise. It won't fill my holes. We were talking about our Bible study. Why was I so quick to dismiss that, to push it away?

"Let's grab this chance for us to reconnect. While it's on our minds," I say. "We've all been flailing. All of us. Look at me. I've shut everyone out? Hey." I reach out and rub Hannah's elbow. "Bible study never was an assignment. There's not a due date or there aren't any expectations. This is just us trying to grow. Just us trying to lean on Him more and ourselves less. I, for one, could use some of that right now."

Hannah clicks her fingers, then waves her phone, opened to

her Bible app. "I'm pretty sure we were on Colossians, but how about we skip around and read the Twenty-Third Psalm?"

45

HANNAH

"REMEMBER, YOUR EXAM WILL be on Tuesday morning in Boyce Hall, not here." Dr. Wheeler points to his desk. "I'll post it on Blackboard as a reminder. The format will be all essay. I'll distribute blue books as you enter. Come prepared. Class dismissed."

"I've heard his exams are easy." Nate tilts his head toward the white board where we've spent the last hour reviewing everything I ever wanted to know about world studies and then some.

"Maybe for you." I raise my eyebrows. "But for us non-majors, not so sure."

Nate picks up his books. "We'll study together. I'll quiz you."

"I need to spend some time alone with my notes before I'll be ready for your quiz." I sigh, sliding my notebook into my bag. We file behind the herd of students out the door.

"I like time alone with you." He winks. "I have a study group Sunday afternoon, and I promised Oscar I'd study with him Sunday night, so let's get together Saturday night."

I blink in the sunlight, startlingly bright after the dim of the classroom, then close my eyes, allowing the light and warmth to seep in. "It finally feels like spring," I say, inhaling the warm air. "Saturday night?" I ask, eyes still closed, hoping Nate won't sense my hesitation and that he won't be mad at me.

"Yeah, Saturday." Nate nods and gently takes my hand.

Although I open my eyes, I don't notice the campus around me. Instead, I picture Nate and me cozied up on a beanbag in a make-believe room, snuggled over our textbooks. I shake my head and the image. "I can't."

"What?"

"Kat, Claire, Palmer, and I are all having dinner, then studying together Saturday night. We knew by Sunday we'd be insane cramming, and we all finish on different days and are basically headed home as soon as we're done." My words fly faster than usual and I feel my palm sweating against Nate's. I let go and face him. "Sorry."

The glare of the sun on his glasses prevents me from seeing Nate's eyes. My heart hammers. I need to keep my commitment with my girls. I want to. I'm looking forward to our night, but when will I see Nate before we leave each other for summer? *Thump. Thump.*

"We could do Saturday afternoon. What time are you guys doing your thing?" he asks.

It's that easy?

"Uh, five thirty or six. Sure. Um. Saturday afternoon's great."

"Cool. Then we'll just get together around two? Is that good?"

"Two o'clock. Perfect." I'm nodding. Too much.

Nate takes my hand back, and we continue walking down the tree-lined sidewalk. I look up to the sun, the source of my external warmth, and to the Son, my internal warmth. *Thanks,* my heart calls.

46
CLAIRE

SHOVING MY ILL-FITTED baseball cap on my head and pulling my ponytail through the opening in the back, I rush through the door to my place in the cafeteria line. I toss my bag on the employee rack and slide on plastic gloves before Nancy has a chance to remind me.

"Hey there, Claire. You're working the salad bar today."

"Hi, Nancy. Okay. Should I check out what we need to refill, or did you have something else you wanted me to do?"

"You're a good kid." Nancy punches the foil covering the dinner entrees we'll start serving any minute with her giant metal spoon. Steam seeps out of the slits. She turns to me, putting her hand on her hip. "I know we're low on crackers. We're always low on crackers. I swear kids shove piles of 'em in their backpacks."

"Got it." I laugh. "Should we put up a cracker surveillance camera?"

"Not a bad idea." Nancy laughs too. "Although I don't blame them. Just wish they'd refill it themselves."

I duck into the storage closet, scanning the shelves for Saltines. I like Nancy. And I've decided I don't mind this job. I might even apply for it again next school year. Finding the crackers in the back right corner near the floor, I slide out the plastic bin that holds hundreds of packages of Saltines and carry it into the dining hall.

It's only four thirty, so there isn't a crowd, but a few students are scattered throughout the room, poring over notes in preparation for finals.

The crackers, as Nancy predicted, are depleted. I switch out the near-empty bin on the bar with my full one and take mental notes that we're also low on applesauce, sunflower seeds, and ranch dressing. ASR. I repeat my acronym to myself. ASR.

Winding my way around the tables back toward the kitchen, I spy Brady in a navy blue bandana. He's scrolling through something on his tablet, his forehead scrunched up in concentration. I feel a tickle in the back of my throat, but he doesn't see me. I could go back to the kitchen and he'd never notice. But why? I'd like to talk to him. Wouldn't I? I liked talking to him before. I can't avoid all guys forever, although I've been trying. I've been protecting myself, and cautious is good, but I'm sick of allowing Phillip to continue violating me by stealing my sense of security.

Time to be strong, Claire, God nudges.

I'm not really the strong type.

Baby steps, He reassures me.

It's only a few strides over to Brady's table. I set my bin down on the edge and hold up one of the few remaining packets of Saltines. "May I interest you in some slightly smushed crackers?" I manage.

Brady looks up. The line in his forehead disappears and the corners of his eyes turn up. "Finally. Some service around here."

"Yeah, well, as you can see, it's pretty busy." I motion to the near empty room.

"Jammed. I mean, it's Friday night after all." Brady keeps looking at me and smiling. But there's this pause, and I have nothing to offer other than crackers, and maybe I shouldn't have come over here.

But then he rescues me by laying his palm out flat and saying, "I could really use the salt to help me memorize."

I lay the crackers in his palm, grateful he didn't grab them, that I didn't have to flinch, that he's making this easy. The cords in my neck relax. "I didn't know salt could help you memorize things. I should keep a shaker near me this weekend."

"I read it in one of my mom's health magazines one time." Brady raises his eyebrows so high they disappear under his do-rag. "I'm not sure if I buy it, but it can't hurt."

"Well"—I shift my weight—"here's to salty exams."

"Cheers!" Brady holds up the salt shaker from his table.

"Cheers." I laugh and pick up my bin.

"Claire?"

"Yeah."

"This'll sound weird, 'cause the semester's over. But I'd love to buy you a coffee sometime or go on a walk or"—he looks around the dining hall—"chat somewhere besides here."

"That would be nice." I smile, not my nervous smile of the past year, but my old smile, the one I had back when I found out I got into Clarkston, when I received my letter confirming my scholarship, when Mom first told me we were going to Paris, when my life was full of possibilities.

"Can I have your number?"

I laugh again. "Long story, but I'm kind of between phones." I shrug. "I'm staying with my aunt and uncle this summer. I'll give you their number."

"Cool." Brady nods and slides his phone over to me. My fingers hesitate for a second before punching in my contact info, but I figure he'll never call over the summer anyway. If we were still going to be here for a few weeks, that might be different.

"Hey, that's a Detroit number," he says when I turn the phone back toward him.

"Yeah."

"I'm interning in Detroit this summer."

47
KAT

THE LUMP IN MY THROAT is as big as a soccer ball as I stand outside his door. He's probably not in there anyway. I knocked. I waited. Time to roll. I should have gone to weight training. I can't believe I skipped.

"Yeah?" Jack, Nicholas's roommate, opens the door to their dorm room with a tremendous case of bed head. He blinks at me, then drags his fingers through his dark brown hair, which only makes it stick up more.

"Is Nicholas here?" I ask. My voice sounds noiseless in the hollow hallway.

"Man." Jack shakes his head.

"Is that a yes or a no?" I tap my thumbs against my thighs.

"Hang on." Jack closes the door.

Two guys Nick introduced me to one afternoon at the library amble down the hall.

"Hey." I half smile at them, feeling awkward standing outside his door and not remembering their names.

"Hi, Kat. Right?"

"Yeah." I nod.

"You done yet?" the skinny guy asks.

"I still have one tomorrow."

"Me too." He shrugs. "See ya."

"See ya."

The stockier guy holds his hand up in a wave.

My eyes follow them as they make their way down the hall, and I hear the squeak and bang of the door. How long should I stand here? Should I knock again? Does Jack have any idea how long I debated about coming here?

"Are you okay?" Nicholas asks. "Don't you have training?"

I start at his voice and turn to see him standing in his doorway, half in, half out. His nose is crinkled, his eyes the bright green of Mexico's home jerseys. I open my mouth to say, "I'm fine," but all that comes out is a thick gasp. I tap my foot and look away as the tears well up like pools full of my screw-ups. I'd prepared a speech. A whole litany of what I've done wrong, how sorry I am, how I'll make changes, how I am making changes. I'd even rehearsed it in my head as I walked the opposite direction of the weight room to be here instead of at our final training session. But I can't get any of it out. I just shake my head and collapse against his chest.

"Hey." Nicholas smoothes my hair with his warm hand, strong and safe and sure. His voice is soft, a river of calm. "Hey, what happened?"

"I'm sorry," I blurt out. "It's all my fault. I miss you. Every day I miss you."

48
PALMER

"HERE'S TO THE SENIORS!" April holds up her glass. We all raise our drinks and a cacophony of clanks fills Summer's almost-empty apartment. Without the leather couches and mod bar stools it's pretty much a white square with wood floors. Funny how different things look when you change perspective.

I take a sip of my water and watch Summer walk to the middle of the circle. Her eyes are bloodshot, and her usually sleek bob is in a stubby ponytail. "Finals just about killed me this year," she starts. "But I survived."

There are a few obligatory laughs and snorts.

"Working on this magazine has been amazing, but now, I leave it to you. I leave it to you guys to keep writing quality pieces, taking stunning photos, and making sure every Clarkston student reads every issue cover to cover."

We all clap. Somebody whistles.

"You'll need to recruit the best of the best next year. And once you've gotten them on board you'll need to make them prove themselves. That's how we got all of you. That's how we got here." She motions to the other seniors, minus Michael, standing behind her.

He texted me yesterday, or was it the day before—exams have made my head spin—saying he wouldn't be here. He was done with finals and headed home to get ready for his move to DC, and asked if I wanted to go out for one last cocktail.

I was tempted. But I texted back that I needed to study for econ, which was true. What I didn't say was that one last cocktail sounded an awful lot like he had no plans for me in his future. It also sounded like the only way he liked to hang out with me was with a drink and a make-out session. I'd be lying if I said I didn't have to give my phone to Hannah to refrain from texting back, but she buried it for me while I made thousands of colored supply-and-demand graphs. By then it was 1:00 a.m. and I went to bed. And for the first time in a long time I woke up refreshed, not foggy, no headache, but clear and ready for my exam.

"Happy Hour at the Frosty Frog in about..." Summer glances to where the chic clock with Roman numerals used to be mounted on her wall, but it's not there. It's probably packed up with the rest of her roommates' furnishings either in a U-Haul headed home or in the pile near the side window.

"Well, how about in an hour?" She grins.

More cheers and clanks of glasses.

"You going," Ahmed asks me as I stick my journal in my bag.

"Nah. I have an emergency brownie date with my roommates."

"Sounds fun. Let me know if you have leftovers." He nudges me.

"We won't." I laugh. "We've never had leftover chocolate."

He smiles. "Sounds like you have good roommates."

"The best," I say.

EPILOGUE
PALMER

"THIS IS THE MOST DELICIOUS thing I've ever tasted!" Kat leans back against the futon.

"Palmer made them." Hannah points to me.

"Well, *you* found the recipe on Pinterest." I motion to Hannah, giving her the credit.

"I am in love with them." Claire licks her lips.

"I thought you were in love with Brady." Hannah snickers.

"Ha!" Claire grabs a pillow and swats Hannah. "I barely know him!"

"Careful, Claire Bear. I don't want to spill a single crumb of this brownie-in-a-mug. Plus, I was just kidding. You know that. I think it's fun you have a nice boy in Detroit for the summer. Wild how things work out."

"I haven't had much time to think about it. I know you're done, Han, but I still have another exam tomorrow." Claire scoops another chocolaty bite with her spoon. "I don't really know what to expect this summer."

"Right there with you, sister." I sigh, licking rich fudge off my top lip. "I still have another exam and I have no idea what to expect this summer. Taking a class at OSU will be weird. It's huge, and I won't know anyone."

"But you make friends so easily," Claire says. "They'll love you."

"I think it's awesome you're taking a creative writing class." Hannah's spoon clanks against the bottom of her cup.

"Yeah." I nod. "It feels right. I need some distance from journalism."

"I wonder how *long* distance will work?" Hannah stares at the bottom of her empty cup. "I haven't even gotten the hang of *close* distance yet."

"Neither have I." Kat snorts. "Man, the car ride home is gonna be strange tomorrow afternoon."

"You'll do fine." Claire puts her hand on Kat's knee. "You can always be yourself around Nicholas."

Kat sniffs. "Yeah, I guess. I've just got a lot of damage to undo. It's a miracle he agreed to drive me home."

"If you hadn't noticed, he's in love with you," I remind her.

"I used to think that." Kat looks off.

"He still is." I reach out and tuck a stray chunk of her dark hair behind her ear.

"I've got to prove to Nicholas that he's important to me and that I'm going to be less of a maniac about workouts." Kat squares her jaw and nods, as if convincing herself.

"You will," Claire affirms. "I know you will."

No one says anything for a minute. Like we have to process. I know my mind is packed with my mistakes of sophomore year. The way I turned inward, but not toward God. It's crammed with the questions of what summer will bring and stuffed with hope for next year.

"I'm sorry," I finally break the silence.

Claire twirls a strand of hair. Kat remains frozen in her determined stance. Hannah's gaze is turned out the window toward the quad. It takes them a minute to register my apology, to return to me and our room and our us-ness.

"Me too," Hannah and Kat blurt almost simultaneously.

Claire nods. "You guys would never believe it, but I used to be independent."

Hannah turns toward us and sits up. "I remember when I

saw you for the first time ever—in the bathroom during freshman orientation. You were so you. So cool. So cool to be you."

Claire laughs. "I'm going to try to get back to feeling good about me. I think spending the summer away from Mom will help. She has some things she needs to fix on her own. And, Aunt Denise is nudging her."

"Feeling good about me. That should be our motto for junior year." Hannah bounces up and down.

"I don't think it's as easy as coming up with a motto." I shake my head.

"Right." Kat swallows. "We need a plan."

"A plan and a whole lot of faith," I add.

"Faith," Claire whispers.

"And great roommates," Hannah says.

"And more of these things." Kat holds up her mug.

"Definitely more brownies junior year!" I roll back my shoulders. "Only we'll have a real oven in our apartment and be able to bake them in a pan."

"I have zero complaints about what you created in the microwave." Claire scrapes a smudge of whipped cream from the rim of her mug with her finger and licks it.

"Feeling good about yourself through faith, roommates, and brownies," I say.

"That sounds like the name of a blog." Hannah grins.

"A blog? Sounds like I might have my next writing project."

"I'm done with projects." Kat laughs. "But I'm ready for fresh starts."

"Fresh starts that include brownies." Hannah puts her arm around me, and we all lean together for the last roommate hug of sophomore year, stronger and closer than when we began.

WANT TO KNOW HOW IT ALL BEGAN?
ENJOY THIS EXCERPT FROM
IT'S COMPLICATED, BOOK ONE OF
THE STATUS UPDATES SERIES BY
LAURA L. SMITH

It's Complicated

"YOU HAVE A TEN MINUTE break before your parents rejoin us for the dormitory tour." The peppy girl at the front of the room sounds like she's leading a cheer. All she needs are pom-poms. She smiles and closes her notebook with a light thud.

That's my cue to head to the bathroom. Mingling is not my thing. Especially in a group like this, where I don't know anyone, where I'm not sure if I belong. I mean I'm really excited to go to Clarkston University—considered the best state school in Ohio—this fall. I was nervous about getting in. Now that I'm in, I'm nervous about fitting in. Everyone here seems rich and beautiful and smart and totally pulled together.

I'm the smart part, I guess. But pulled together? I work hard at just trying to keep it together. And rich? Not even close. Mom and I struggle to get by. I'm here on partial financial aid, partial academic scholarship, and partial wing and a prayer.

I adjust my floral tank in the mirror and tighten one of my long, sandy blonde braids.

"I love your hair!"

"Thanks." I smile gratefully to the girl with sparkling hazel eyes, wavy auburn hair, freckles, and a wide grin.

"I could never get away with it." She shrugs. "My hair is so crazy and out of control. It would just look poufy. See?" She grabs the ends of her hair and pulls them outward past her ears.

I can't help but laugh. This girl wearing silver bangles, the sundress I swear I saw in the window of J. Crew, and pink nail polish that matches the pattern in the dress perfectly is one of the girls I'd labeled as "totally pulled together."

"I copied it. Have you heard of Holly Starr?"

The girl wrinkles her forehead. "Actress?"

"Musician. Anyway, I love her music, and she always wears braids with big, cool headbands." I straighten my own headband.

"What kind of music does she play?" It's getting crowded by the mirrors, so smiley girl leads the way, and I follow her out of the bathroom to an empty space along the wall.

I'm not used to girls like this starting up conversations with me, let alone continuing them. "Upbeat and slow. A little of everything. She inspires me."

"Cool." The girl nods. "I like a little of everything. I'm Hannah, by the way."

"Claire." I manage.

"There you are, Hannah." A PTA-ish looking woman wearing white capris, a turquoise silk top, and pearls slides her arm around Hannah.

"Hi, Mom. This is Claire."

"Nice to meet you." I give Hannah's mom a quick handshake.

"Hello, Claire. Nice to meet you too. How do you girls know each other?"

My cheeks warm. I was trying to get away from conversation, not dive into it. "We just met. I'm from Cleveland."

"Hi, I'm Lauren Lassiter." My mom appears. I cringe. I

never know what Mom will say or do, but it usually makes me uncomfortable.

"Polly Trager." They shake hands, sizing each other up.

"Last names starting with A–K follow me," calls Cheerleader Girl, who ran our last session about dining halls.

"Last names L–Z follow me," announces the boy with Clark Kent glasses and plaid shorts, who helped with the opening session.

"They must be alphabet top heavy," Mom says. She looks like she could be a student with her broomstick skirt and chocolate brown tank. Since Mom's so young, for a mom, and we're both petite, we share clothes. It stretches our budget and wardrobe. Bone structure and clothes are hopefully all people think we have in common.

"Yay, we get to be together!" Hannah cheers, tipping my balance as she hooks her arm in mine. "Plus, we get the cute tour guide. So, this is what I know about the dorms," she starts, while our moms chat two steps ahead of us. "My best friend, Palmer, was here last week for orientation. We couldn't come together, long story. Anyway, they have doubles, which are like military barracks, or they have these sweet four-person suites."

"Sweet suites?" I ask, feeling a little awkward walking arm in arm with this girl I hardly know, but also a little relieved she's leading and talking and apparently in the know.

"Well, for one thing, they have their own bathroom, so you don't have to share the locker room style showers down the hall. Nasty."

"Nice." I nod.

"And, for another, they have two rooms, plus the bath, so it's like a little family room and a little bedroom. So cute. I guess they're both small, but it gives you a place besides your bedroom to hang out."

"Space is good," I say as we cross the street. I picture a room with bright beanbag chairs and posters on the walls, like something out of a Pottery Barn Teen catalog.

"Palmer and I are going to room together," Hannah

continues, chomping on her gum. "We were going to go lottery for two other roommates, so we could live in one of those suites, but what would *you* think about being our third?"

My heart jumps inside my chest and I feel my face flushing. I'm sure I can't afford the more expensive room, but am grateful someone as nice as Hannah wants to room with me. I thought it was going to be so hard to meet people. "*Umm*. Wow, that would be cool, only I d-don't," I stammer.

"Here is the standard double room, complete with trundle beds that fold into couches, giving you more living space," our guide says. "Feel free to break up and peek in any of the rooms in this hall."

Hannah drags me into a room on the far right. "See. They are itty-bitty. Living space? Hardly! No place to run, no place to hide, and you'll gag when you see the community bathroom."

"The trundles are cute," I say.

"What do you think?" Mom asks, rubbing my back. I stiffen at her touch interrupting a rare "me making a friend" moment. "They're bigger than your bedroom."

I tense tighter. "They're fine," I answer. Did Mom have to point out how rinky-dink my room is at home?

"Hannah's mom has been telling me about the quads. They're a little cheaper and give you some options for living space." Mom's voice quivers. I can tell she's worried about something. Maybe the higher rent? Wait. Did she say cheaper?

"Cheaper?" I almost spit out the word in surprise.

"Yeah, isn't that hilarious?" Hannah laughs. "It's like a sale at Macy's on designer shoes. The cooler rooms cost less."

"Some weird University accounting." Hannah's mom swings her purse. "Anyway, Hannah and her best friend, Palmer, are getting a quad. College costs a fortune. It doesn't hurt to save a little where you can."

"And Claire." Hannah grins, squeezing my elbow. "She's our third. Right? Promise me you'll be our third!"

"Yeah, sure." I smile, twisting one of my braids. "Is that okay, Mom?"

Mom exhales, and even from behind her giant sunglasses I can tell she's relieved. I exhale too. Cutting costs is a good thing. Mom agreeing to let me room with Hannah is an even better thing.

"Now, we'll take these stairs to the second level, where you can see the other option of four roommates," Glasses Guy says.

"He's so cute in a nerdy, collegiate kind of way. Don't ya think?" Hannah whispers in my ear.

"Not my type." I smile. "But, cute. Definitely cute."

Back on the street, our tour guide gives one last spiel about how to log in online to sign up for dorm and roommate preferences.

"Now, you're all free to roam around our downtown area for lunch. I suggest Mr. Burger—the best hamburgers anywhere!" He smiles. "Next session is in two hours back at the main room of the student center. See you there."

"I'll be there early." Hannah bats her eyelashes in his direction, even though I don't think he hears her.

"Care to join us for lunch?" Mrs. Trager asks.

"That would be great. I'm famished," Mom agrees. "Since the girls are going to be roommates, we should probably get to know each other."

"How about we skip Mr. Burger." I'm a vegetarian. "I bet every last person in orientation will swarm there."

"When I went to school here there was a delicious bagel shop. You could get anything you wanted on them. I hope it's still here. How does that sound?" Mrs. Trager asks.

"But, you went here a jillion years ago, Mom." Hannah wrinkles her nose.

"Sounds de-lish." I smile, thrilled to avoid a crowd and beef at the same time.

"You went here?" Mom asks.

"It's where I met my husband. It's special to have Hannah carry on the tradition." Mrs. Trager gives Hannah a squeeze. Hannah rolls her eyes, so just I can see. "How about you?"

"I got my degree from Ohio State," Mom answers. "I

teach high school history."

"Hey, I know that girl." Hannah motions toward the other side of the street. "She was new at my high school this year. I didn't know her very well, but she always seemed sweet and laid back, you know? Her name is…something cool…oh what is it…Karly, no, K-K-Kat."

"Kat Wiley!" Hannah calls.

The girl with dark hair, pulled back in a ponytail, sporting Umbros and a Clarkston Soccer T-shirt stops and looks around.

"Kat, it's me, Hannah from Hoover High." Hannah waves frantically.

"Hey." She crosses the street toward us. "Are y'all comin' to school here, too?" she drawls.

"Go Clarkston!" Hannah cheers, pointing to Kat's shirt. "This is my new roommate, Claire. We're rooming with Palmer Ruscilli too. Do you know her? We're here for orientation and all that. Do you play soccer here?"

Kat nods slowly. "I know Palmer. The gorgeous one, right? We had Calculus together. And, yeah, I can't believe it, but I made the team. We're trainin' all week every week, but I've been headin' home on the weekends to hang out with my folks. Coach can't officially call it practice 'til August." Her voice is slow and sweet and Southern.

"That is so awesome! Making a college team is like ultra hard to do." Hannah grins. "Do you get to hang out with the football players?"

"There are athletes all over the place. And, yeah, I'm amped. Clarkston has some strong players returning this year. We should have a great season."

"You don't by chance, have a roommate yet? Do you? Please tell me you don't have a roommate," Hannah grabs Kat's arm.

"I've been thinkin' about livin' in the athlete dorm." Kat tightens her ponytail. "But I don't know. The girls I play with seem great and all, but I might need a break from the intensity sometimes, ya know?"

"We need a fourth!" Hannah can barely contain herself. She's actually jumping up and down. "You can be our fourth. We'll have one of those adorable quads, and it will be so much fun!"

"For real? Y'all need a fourth?"

I nod.

"For real!" Hannah jumps again.

"I'm in." Kat gives us each high fives.

"I have to text Palmer!" Hannah squeals. "She'll be *so* excited!"

ACKNOWLEDGEMENTS

Jesus, you are my one true addiction. You fill every hole, every void in my heart. Thank you for your constant love and for words and for stories. I pray this book will touch hearts for Your glory.

Brett, I wish I could explain to Hannah, Palmer, Claire and Kat that there truly is a Prince Charming waiting for them, that they don't have to settle for anyone less than their ideal, that there is someone who will love and cherish them for exactly who they are, who will support them and cheer for them and even call them out when needed. I wish my characters knew what true love looks like, but they can't because they haven't found it yet. I've found it in you. And for that, I can never fully thank you.

Mom, you are my biggest fan. You always have been. Thank you for putting my stories up on the fridge when I was in second grade and for reading every one of them since.

Amy Parker, you have consistently cheered me on, believed in me and my stories and my topics and my characters even when it felt like I was hitting dead ends. Thank you for giving me strength and energy and endurance at all the right times and in all the right places.

Laura Kurk, because you are so eloquent with words it is near impossible to explain what your friendship and writing support mean to me. You fit somewhere into my soul like a lost puzzle piece.

Tammy Bundy, my beloved writing "twin", you make my words ring truer, my characters more alive, and my days shine brighter.

Julie Breihan, you are a wordsmith extraordinaire. Thank you for your meticulous editing and precise shaping to take this story from a manuscript to a book (with an actual ending).

Jennifer Murgia, Stephanie Morrill, Rajdeep Paulus I am honored to write alongside you. You are role models and inspiration to me daily.

To my OBF fellow journeyers, thank you for praying me through this past year of writing. The things you have taught me about life and God will impact me always.

To Birch House Press, thank you for providing my stories a beautiful home.

ABOUT THE AUTHOR

I believe in God. I believe in true love. I believe if I bang hard enough on the back of my wardrobe I'll get to Narnia someday. I believe eating chocolate is good for you. I believe God created me to be the wife of my husband, the mother of my four children, and to write the stories and speak the words He wants people to hear. My other books include; *Skinny, Hot*, and *Angry*, as well as the other titles in the Status Updates series, *It's Complicated* and *It's Over*.

Find Laura L. Smith at

www.laurasmithauthor.com

On Facebook

On Twitter

On Instagram:

Other Books by Laura L. Smith

It's Over

It's Addicting

Skinny

Hot

Angry